The Second You're Single

The Second You're Single

CARA TANAMACHI

ST. MARTIN'S GRIFFIN
NEW YORK

For my amazing husband, PJ,
who makes every day Valentine's Day

This is a work of fiction. All of the characters, organizations, and events portrayed in this novel are either products of the author's imagination or are used fictitiously.

First published in the United States by St. Martin's Griffin, an imprint of St. Martin's Publishing Group

www.stmartins.com

The Library of Congress Cataloging-in-Publication Data is available upon request.

ISBN 978-1-250-84226-8 (trade paperback)

ISBN 978-1-250-84227-5 (ebook)

First Edition: 2023

10 9 8 7 6 5 4 3 2 1

One

SORA

> Why do we treat being single like a disease that needs a cure? #GoSolo.
>
> —SOLO FEBRUARY CHALLENGE

Valentine's Day has snuck up on me like a porch pirate.

It's not even February yet, but my inbox is filled with promotions for gourmet chocolate, personalized champagne flutes, and romantic weekend getaways for two. I'm in my warm bed, aka my "office," as I scroll through email on my phone. I'll sit here until I can work up the energy to commute to my "conference room"—the kitchen table—for my first Zoom meeting of the day. I scroll past pink hearts, feeling the usual disgust rise in me, as my brown-and-white-spotted rescue pit, Larry, lays at my feet in my modest Lakeview condo. There's no end to the absurdity of the Valentine's emails. Hot stone massage for two? Matching heart-print underwear? Romantic getaway in a tree pod? Just what the hell is a tree pod? I click on the promotion. Oh, a lighted tent hanging from a tree, with two pairs of adorable bare feet hanging out of it. Why is this a thing? Who wants to vacation in a piñata for bears?

I hate Valentine's Day and the giant commercial love machine that fuels it. Of course this may—or may not—have something to do with the fact that Dan left me.

Or, technically, I left Dan.

Dan wanted to keep on having weeknight sex with me, as long as I didn't mind he had a wife. And kids. And a house in the suburbs. I kind of did, though. I guess I'm just too hung up on the details. Can't see the forest for the serial cheater.

I had no idea he was married, for the record. Call me naïve, but I hadn't thought it was weird I'd never been to his place in three months of dating. I thought he might be a hoarder. Or worse, he had ten roommates. Either way, I failed to press for answers, and we just ended up hanging out at my place. We never went out on weekends, but that was because he worked Friday and Saturday, or so he told me, pursuing his dream of being a DJ by playing faded pop hits at suburban bar mitzvahs. Of course, that changed one Saturday when I decided to surprise him by showing up at Dynasty Forever Banquet Hall in the far northwestern burbs. Except there was no bar mitzvah there. No DJ. And definitely no Dan.

He'd been forced to admit his double life, and that the reason we didn't hang on the weekends was because he coached youth league basketball.

"Are you even a DJ?" I had asked, appalled. Turns out his DJ career was a lie, too. I'd been dating a man who wasn't only married, but whose "dream" job was to be a has-been forty-one-year-old DJ. It's like his lies didn't even have ambition.

I kick my feet off the edge of my bed and slip into fuzzy purple slippers, noting that the arctic tundra that is Chicago in January has already begun to freeze the condensation on the *inside* of my windows. I don't want to leave the apartment. Maybe ever. I've already trudged down the stairs with Larry at the crack of early to let him out, so he should be good for a little while. I shuffle to the kitchen, past the jungle of houseplants perched on milk crates, telling myself that one of these days I'll actually get real plant stands. Or hang pictures on my blank walls. Or rescue Grandma Mitsuye's antique Japanese kimono-clad dolls from their multiple layers of tissue paper in a U-Haul box, one of a half dozen stacked in a corner and collecting dust in the guest bedroom. A room which, technically, I've been meaning to convert to an office, but I can't because it's a de facto storage closet. When Dan first saw my place, he'd asked if I just moved in. I've actually lived here seven years. I hate my drafty, vintage condo, but also despise putting on shoes and leaving it, which I think pretty much sums up my life's angst.

Larry, realizing I'm heading to the kitchen, otherwise known as the Place Where His Treats Are Stored, jumps off the bed and follows me, wagging his brown and white tail. As I brew my K-Cup coffee, he leans into the back of my knee.

"Good boy," I reassure him, bending down to give him a good scratch behind the ears, which makes him tap his left foot uncontrollably against my wooden kitchen floor. I hand him a bit of dog jerky, but it takes him a couple of tries to grab it. Larry, bless him, only has one working eye, thanks to a terrible run-in with a raccoon. The people at the shelter I adopted him from told me he would eventually adapt to the loss of the eye, but it's been three years and he hasn't managed to yet. The big brown circle around his forever-closed eye seems like a natural eye patch. I watch him now as he dips his head just to the left of his water bowl near the refrigerator. Kind of adorably pitiful. I nudge it toward him with my foot, and he laps up the tap water with gusto.

I carry my steaming cup of coffee to my kitchen table, where I sit and boot up my ailing laptop. "Come on, Bessie. Let's go, girl," I tell it as if I'm talking to an ox pulling my Conestoga wagon across the plains. I get up and wander around the kitchen while my laptop wheezes and flickers to life. I sip at the sweet vanilla goodness of K-Cup coffee as I sink into my kitchen table chair. The floor is uneven, so I have to move the chair around until it doesn't wobble too much. There's also a draft coming in from the kitchen window to my left, a cold ribbon of air across my ankles. I hate my "conference room" and long for the plush comfort of my "office" duvet. My laptop blinks on, and more Valentine's ads assault me. Framed heart maps of the stars in the sky on your first date! Zodiac love signs engraved in matching bangle bracelets! Chocolate-covered strawberries during your intimate massage for two!

I groan, bitter. I want to boycott Valentine's Day. Hell, I want to boycott love in general.

I start typing.

Does Valentine's Day make you want to vomit? Do you wonder why you don't have someone to share matching underwear with? Or who will hang from a tree pod with you so that you both become a perfectly pre-packaged dinner for grizzly bears? You're not alone.

I'm done with the commercial love machine. For me, I'm tired of dating. Of being disappointed. So, this year, I'm vowing to stay single for the entire month of February. That's right. No amount of chocolate can convince me being in a relationship that will only end up disappointing me is worth it. This year, we should all go on a dating cleanse. Goodbye, Dry January.

Hello, Solo February.

No dates. No dating apps. No sex.

But how will we live without romance, you ask? Frankly, the real question is how do we all live WITH romance? The stress of it? The anxiety? The inevitable soul-crushing disappointment?

Answer me this: If love's so great, then how come I've got so many exes?

So, I'm going to focus on the things I love: watching dumb reality TV. Drinking sweet, fruity cocktails. Eating all the bacon I want without judgment—and without having to share! Hell, this year, I'm going to ask bacon to be my valentine.

Think of all the things I can do with my life if I don't care what a potential date might think. I can wear my comfy, stained sweatpants to the bar because I won't care about ruining my one chance of finding love during happy hour! I won't have to get waxed. Or manicured. Or buy new date outfits. Or new shapewear to wear under said new date outfits. Or go on a diet to fit INTO said shapewear.

Think of all the hours I'll save not swiping on anyone. Or not thinking about which dating app photos make me look too thirsty.

And, best of all, if an ex pops up with a "u up?" request, I have a built-in answer:

"Sorry! I'm not up. For the entire month. It's Solo February."

If my mom, or grandparents, or sibling, or coworker asks if I'm dating anyone, I can say, "Nope! Solo February!"

The thing is, I don't want to give up on love and sex for my whole life. But I just need a break.

So, won't you all join me?

#GoSolo

As I type, I feel energized. My video invite dings then, announcing the beginning of the meeting with my editor, Arial (yes, she was named after a font). She works out of a glassy downtown Chicago high-rise, and I can see the amazing view of Lake Michigan behind her. She runs the online version of *Slick,* a women's fashion magazine that dabbles in advice on perfecting blowjob techniques and what you should be wearing to the clubs if you want to snag a "better than average" one-night stand. You know, just doing my part for feminism.

Arial looks amazing as usual, in an expensive-looking blazer from the designer freebie closet and her cinnamon-brown hair slicked back in the latest twisted fashion. Meanwhile, I'm wearing gray jersey-knit pajamas that can almost pass for street clothes, but not quite, zero makeup, and I realize I've got a cowlick sticking up at the back of my head. I try to smooth it down as I notice that my screen partially shows the dirty dishes piling up in my sink. I gently tilt the laptop so Arial doesn't see I'm a total slob.

"Sora? Good morning?" Arial speaks in questions, and ends her sentences in a lilt. She claims it's because she lived in Scotland for a year after graduation. I think it's just because she hates being a boss and telling people what to do. The question at the end makes it sound like she's politely asking me to do something instead of telling me I have to do it. "So? I was thinking we might shelve 'Don't Be Basic with Your Gym Bag'? And instead focus on 'Top Five Mascaras that Will Make Your Ex Beg to Have You Back'? Editorial just thought it will fit better? Since we're doing that 'All My Exes' theme?"

"Yeah. No problem," I say, even though I've already almost finished the story. That's a good five hours of work down the drain. But my Japanese American mom always taught me to be agreeable. Instead of "Squeaky wheel gets the grease," she always says, "The nail that sticks out gets hammered down."

And writing for *Slick* isn't quite the glamorous and important life of writing I had imagined when I won that short-story contest in eighth grade. That's the year I discovered I actually have a knack for putting words together. My eighth-grade English teacher—astonished at my skill—first accused me of plagiarism. After my sharp-tempered Scottish American dad came to the school with copies of early drafts to convince him that I was no cheat, he apologized. Then he overcompensated and started calling me a prodigy. After that, I spun dreams of winning Pulitzer Prizes. I fell a little short of that, sure, but hey, I'm living the Supporting Myself with Writing dream, so there's that. Just because I'm not exactly doing the freelance work I once imagined doesn't mean that I won't write serious stories that help the world. One day.

Still, the whole mascara article bothers me. I imagine myself slathering on expensive makeup in the desperate hope of making Dan jealous.

"You don't seem excited?" Arial questions, cocking her head to one side on my screen.

Crap. I hate video calls. And these days, it's almost all we ever do. And I have the worst poker face. Somehow, she always knows when I'm lying.

"Uh. No. I am." Lie. "It's a great story. Fantastic story. It's so relevant. I'm so glad you pitched it to me." I take a deep breath. I glance at the open document on my screen. "Solo February." It has a nice ring to it. But I hesitate. Do I really want to pitch this story? Shouldn't I just take Arial's assignment and be nice and noncontroversial because the last thing I want to do is live the Working Three Barista Shifts and Driving Rideshares dream instead of the Supporting Myself with My Writing dream?

"I do have another idea," I begin anyway, steeling myself for complete rejection. Even as I hear Mom's voice in my head, *Don't be the nail!*

"Oh, yes?"

"Well . . ." My heart thumps. I hate putting myself out there. That's why I'd rather stay here in my perpetually half-unpacked condo than pack up my laptop and go do my work at the cute coffee shop at the end of my block. Why did I even suggest this story? I haven't even fleshed it out. Not at all. She's going to tell me it's dumb. "Uh . . . you know how there's a Dry January?"

"Yeah? Of course?"

"Well, what if we tried to push Solo February?"

Arial wrinkles her brow. "What do you mean 'solo'?"

"As in, Stay-Single February or Abstinence February or Love-Free February. Think of it like a dating cleanse. Here, I wrote a rough draft about it." I cut and paste what I've written in the chat. Arial reads it lightning fast. Her face lights up.

"I *love* it, Sora? Yes, yes, yes, *yes*? You *must* do this story? #GoSolo literally sells itself?"

"Really?" I'm shocked she likes it so much.

"Why not make it a diary? One entry every day of February? You'll be the focus? And going solo for February will be a challenge *you* do, and you'll share with us what happens on your personal journey? We could make it a 'secret confessions' series?"

At the mention of the secret confessional series, I suddenly feel uneasy. Past confessions have included "Why I Can't Stop Having Sex on the Subway" and "I'm Addicted to Facials—for My Butt!"

Do I want to have my story among them? I realize too late, after I've already pitched this damn thing, that I've never written about my personal life before. I've only ever ranked cosmetics and interviewed influencers. Do I really want to write about my personal life for the readers of *Slick*? Part of me worries that they're like the cool girls in school—just making fun of me behind my back.

"This could be really great, though. Like a big break? You have to do it? Have to?" Arial's still gushing, and my concerns fade away. *Slick* pays well and pays on time, a freelancer's dream. Sure, writing about dating isn't the serious journalism

I want to do, but daily articles would triple my word count for the month, and ergo triple my pay. That would mean extra cash to get Larry the good organic, grain-free kibble, the kind that special dog-food farmers grow and cook and then freeze in hand-molded bricks and ship direct to your door. That shit is expensive.

As if reading my mind, Larry nudges my leg with his white snout. Well, I can't tell that cutie pie no.

"I'll do it!" I tell Arial, hoping I haven't made a giant mistake. That I'm not the nail sticking out, waiting to be hammered down.

Two

SORA

This year, I want bacon to be my valentine. I'd rather have a heart attack than a broken heart.

—SOLO FEBRUARY CHALLENGE

The first day of Solo February dawns dreary and frigid, with six inches of new wet snow on our already salt-laden streets, a typical welcome to February for Chicago. After a bone-dry, extra-mild, above-freezing Christmas, we get a weather-outside-is-frightful delight on February first. Mother Nature loves to procrastinate more than I do.

I snuggle deeper into the warmth of my "office" duvet, as I sneak a look at the first published article of *Solo February*. The article already has a few likes, so I let out a sigh of relief. The trolls haven't yet crucified me, so that's a good sign.

I finish the second article of the series, and even take a stab at the third. I'm going for self-empowerment, but I have niggling doubts I might be coming off as bitter and sad.

The whole point of Solo February is to find fulfillment in your life unconnected to sex, love, or another person. And I'll be frank, I have no idea what this looks like. While I never consciously meant to, my whole adult life, I've measured my own personal success by who's in my bed.

And if you look at my exes, you can see my bar was very low.

Actually, my bar was on the ground.

No, strike that. I actually had to dig into the ground, then put my bar in the hole. We're talking below-sea-level low. Someone would have to build a subway tunnel to get under my bar, so is it no wonder that any jerk who wandered into my life just stepped right on over my buried bar?

I can't trust myself to date anymore. I can't trust that I know who's good for me or who's bad. It's about time I stretched my wings. Hell, it's about time I used them at all.

I finish typing and read over the last line. At the foot of my bed, Larry lifts his head and whines. I realize he needs to go out. I pull myself out of bed to fetch Larry's leash and stuff my feet into the stained shearling-lined boots I've had for more than a decade. Together, we head out to face the brutal Chicago February. Larry bumps against the doorframe. Not once, but twice, before I gently steer him away from it, and down the winding staircase to the first floor of my four-story walk-up.

Outside, winter slaps me in the face, hard, and I feel the wind instantly sucked out of my lungs. It's literally too cold to breathe properly, as my lungs work to process the frigid February air. Thankfully, Larry's tree is all but ten feet from my front door, which really is Larry's genius. It's not his first Chicago winter, either. As he pads around the small square of gray, icy sludge at the base of the leafless tree, I burrow myself deeper into my down-lined coat, glancing up and down Montrose Avenue.

I live in one of those vintage condo buildings, complete with gargoyles hanging off the roof and a single gray stone castle turret on the east corner, sealing the building's medieval vibe. It was built in 1890, though, by a Chicago meatpacking baron, whose dream included living in a replica castle. It's since been gutted and remodeled and converted to condos. It's close to the Lincoln Square brown line stop, and a dozen bars and restaurants. In one direction lies some of the best Italian or Thai food in town, and in the other, there's tapas, upscale American, and so many other options there's no reason ever to turn my own oven on.

As I'm turning to go back inside, I see a brown delivery truck pull up and double park. The logo on the truck is obscured by a three-inch layer of salt from the icy roads. Poor guy, I think as he hops out of the truck so bundled that he can hardly move. He carries a big box that seems unwieldy and heads to my condo building.

"Uh . . . is that for 3-E?" I ask.

The delivery guy swings around and almost swats me in the face with the giant box. "No. 2-E."

Shit. That's my downstairs neighbor, Pam. She hates me, fine, but it's the fact she's picked a beef with my dog that I really can't stand. She claims his breed is "vicious" and has been leading a campaign to have him ousted from the building. Actually, she really wants to ban all dogs from the building. As president of the condo board, she brings it to a vote every meeting. So far, she's only really gotten everyone to agree no *new* dogs will be allowed. Larry, the only remaining dog in the building, is grandfathered in.

As a sidenote about Pam, she's obsessed with marathons and triathlons and all the other *lons,* at least since she broke up with her longtime live-in boyfriend, Thom, in the spring. We should've bonded over being two newly single ladies, but see: her hating my dog. And, let's get real, the only triathlon I'm ever doing will be eat-nap-watch TV, or snack-chill-laze around. I should've known the package was hers, because now I see that health-food logo on it, one of those super pricey, super healthy, super gross-tasting smoothie services called Green Gleam, except that it probably should more aptly be named Colon Blast. I mean, good for her for putting the work in and all that, but there's no way I'm going to use a blender to make my dinner, unless it's frozen margarita night.

"I can bring it inside," I offer.

He eyes me suspiciously, as if I'm trying to steal the box from him. Why would I commit porch piracy in front of my dog? That's just bad parenting. A frigid blast of arctic air blows across the sidewalk, freezing us in our tracks, and the delivery man decides possible theft is better than frostbite.

"Here," he says hastily and gives me the heavier-than-it-looks box.

I take it, considering whether or not to leave it outside on the stairs, but then reconsider because, while my neighborhood is pretty safe, there probably is a black market for Green Poop boxes. And Pam might hate me and my dog, but I'm still going to try to be a good neighbor. If I paid out the nose for special organic kale smoothie ingredients, I wouldn't want them stolen. It's just common courtesy. I head inside, fingers tingling because carrying the box to the stoop meant that I could not shove my bare hands deep in my pockets, and the thirty seconds of exposure turned my fingertips numb. I haul the box up the two flights and leave it at Pam's door. I'd knock, but my knuckles are frozen, and besides, Larry does freak her out. She explicitly told me to avoid direct contact with her when Larry is with me.

And anyway, Larry is dragging me up the stairs because he knows it's treat time when we get back to the condo. Once inside our warm apartment, Larry waits expectantly in the kitchen near his cabinet, big pink tongue lolling out. I reach into the cupboard with my numb fingers, but soon discover we're out of Larry's favorite treats. Ack! I'm a bad dog mom.

I glance at Larry's expectant face. There are only a couple of reasons I'd leave my condo again on a day like this: for Larry or a fire.

A frigid two-block walk later, I'm wheeling my shopping cart through my local upscale grocery, Margo's. The commercial love machine has thrown up on everything. Valentine's decorations jump out at me from everywhere. I see one store employee busy stocking up the aisle in front of me with oversized pink teddy bears, sappy cards, bottles of warm champagne, and chocolate truffles. Seems like just yesterday this same seasonal aisle was filled with broken Christmas ornaments at 75 percent off.

Please bring those back, I pray to the holiday marketing gods. I promise I'll buy the Minions-as-reindeer driving a sleigh full of the Avengers. Anything but all these stupid hearts.

Then I remember I don't need to care about Valentine's Day this year. Since I've taken the #GoSolo vow, I won't be expecting chocolates. Or flowers. Or having to lie to anyone who asks about having plans. Wow, there is really something empowering about that. I decide because this is the Month of Me, I might as well focus on something more uplifting: the refrigerated breakfast foods aisle. Sausage, eggs, and, of course, the true love of my life—bacon. I glance at the bright yellow sign at the shelf's edge beneath the maple-flavored, extra-thick strips: *buy one, get one.* My heart soars and ticks up a notch. Who says I'm not lovable? Bacon loves me. Bacon never lies to me. I don't have to guess whether or not he's bad for me. I know he is. Do I buy one or two packages? Hmmmm. I hedge. Six it is. I mean, it's non-GMO, organic bacon, after all. It would be unhealthy *not* to consume a pack a day. Bonus: it's *carb-free.*

I dump all the packages from the row into my cart, ignoring the judgmental stare from the size-zero strawberry blonde wearing head-to-toe Lululemon as she side-eyes my outfit. I'm wearing a faded Turkey Trot sweatshirt that's probably older than she is and has most of the lettering rubbed off, so it simply says *k . . . r . . . ot 5k.* The woman's nose wrinkles in disgust as she takes in my appearance. Ah, Lululemon, I was once bright-eyed and naïve just like you. Merely a few months ago, I, too, wore makeup to the supermarket, and lingered near the organic produce. I had hoped I could be one of those rare stories among my friends of someone who actually found their mate in the wild. *Oh no, I didn't meet the love of my life on some dating app at all. We met when we both reached for the very last ripened mango.* So quaint.

I glance down and see she's piled nonfat, plain Greek yogurt, kale, chia seeds, granola, and non-GMO frozen quinoa in her mini cart. Lululemon eyes my cart. The bacon has joined my bottle of tequila and six pints of salted caramel ice cream and, of course, treats for Larry. Her carefully lined lip turns downward in a disapproving frown. She reminds me a little too much of my downstairs neighbor Pam, who often wears the same look when she's eyeing my overstretched yoga pants. I realize she is not Pam, and it's not fair to lump her in the same dog-hater category, but she's the one doing the aggressive staring, not me.

I meet her gaze, and in that instant, a silent conversation passes between us.

You're single because you don't try hard enough, her eyes tell me.

You're trying too hard and your future boyfriend will still sext an Instagram model, my eyes clap back.

Then we look away, catfight over, because she knows damn well my size-fourteen midriff could belly bounce her into the next aisle, if I wasn't so afraid of prison food. So, she saunters off, flicking her high ponytail, to find organic, unsweetened kefir, and I focus on figuring out where they've stashed the pizza rolls in this joint. Because . . . to hell with my diet. I'd been starving myself hoping to impress Dan, and look what happened. I went hungry only to find out that the whole time I thought I'd been playing the lead role in his heart, I had been the understudy.

I turn the corner, hoping to head down the frozen food aisle (pizza rolls await!), but stop in my tracks when I see Lululemon lingering near the frozen spinach. Damn! I do not want to face the stiff breeze from Lululemon's thigh gap again. No pizza rolls then, I decide, as I turn my cart. Before I'm finished, I hear a clatter and turn to see an elderly Latinx woman desperately trying to reach the top shelf for butter, but her stooped back and curled arthritic fingers mean she swipes at the brick of butter, but it slips from her stiff grip and bounces to the floor. Lululemon shoots her a frown, her disapproval of anyone over the age of forty existing clear on her face.

I abandon my cart and head to the elderly woman's side. She looks flustered. "Dios mio," she laments.

"Puedo ayudar," I say, brushing off my ninth-grade Spanish. It comes in handy when elderly Latinx confuse me for one of their own. It's a common mistake. My dad's straight Scottish nose, paired with my mom's tawny skin, straight black hair, and dark brown eyes mean that people see in me what they want to see. If I don't at least try some Spanish, they shake their heads, grumbling bitter disappointments about the new generation. If I try to tell them I'm half Japanese, they look even sadder, as if I'm resorting to bald-faced lies.

I stoop to get the butter and she sends me a look of flat-out relief. I'm sure neither her knees nor her back were looking forward to the sacrifice demanded to bend to the floor.

See? I'm a freakin' nice person. To everyone except Lululemon. She maneuvers her cart quickly away from us as if aging is contagious.

"Oooh, look!" my adopted abuela says. "Muestras."

I don't know that word as it's beyond what I remember from my two years of Spanish, and my brief study-abroad stint in

Barcelona. But I see the woman nod toward a small table near the bakery. She must mean "samples." Leave it to the senior on a fixed income to find the free food. They're better than a metal detector on Daytona Beach after spring break. I glance over, and see it's manned by a sexy lumberjack in an apron over a red plaid flannel shirt. His sleeves are rolled up his thickly muscled forearms. He's sporting an impressive beardstache, surrounded by a week's worth of stubble, which somehow suits him. He looks like a rough-around-the-edges-but-with-a-heart-of-gold gigolo. His ethnicity seems hard to place, but I'd love to play eight rounds of "Who do you think my grandma is?" with him. He looks like he ought to be a butcher, elbow deep in spareribs, but instead, he's piping frosting on delicate little raspberry tortes. The way he's gentle with the buttercream blooms images of how soft those big, strong hands might be on delicate parts of my own anatomy. There's nothing that gets me in the mood faster than sugar and a gentle touch.

Solo February, I remind myself, and then I almost burst out laughing, because there's no way this stunning example of perfect manhood would ever in a million years be interested in *k-r-ot* sweatshirt–wearing me. Not to mention, he might not even be interested in women at all.

"After you," I say, and follow her over.

As I'm walking up to the big-shouldered man who seems equal parts sexy former professional athlete and Cake Boss, I notice his brown wavy hair is stuffed beneath a white baker's cap, and it still doesn't in any way make him look ridiculous. He looks like he's burst life-size from a package of Brawny paper towels—manly, strong, and a good listener, eager to counsel a 1960s housewife on her marital troubles. In fact, he's surrounded by a decent crowd of people, all eager to taste his wares. He carefully doles out small desserts, one by one, and I take my place in line.

He hands the elderly woman a mini torte and she thanks him with a nod and then moves on. He glances up at me and I see the biggest, brownest, most puppy doggiest eyes of all time. Damn, he has nice eyes. Playful. Smart. Sexy. Eyes always get me. Forget butts and chests and six-pack abs—give me a good set of irises, and I'm done for. And then it comes, the crooked half smile and dimple, the way a male model might smile at himself in the mirror in a razor commercial. Hell, yes. You smile, honey. You *are* the best a man can get.

When I pull up my cart next to his table, he says, "Oh, *hi,*" in a tone that seems to imply what he really means: *Oh,* hi, *you've got a fine ass even in those stained sweatpants. Why don't you bring that unwashed body over here and we can really get dirty?* But I'm probably imagining it.

"Want to try a raspberry delight?" he asks, and picks up a tiny little torte on a small white lace paper doily. I glance at the tiny cake, no bigger than a quarter.

"Can I have three?" I joke, but he glances once to the right and then to the left, and sneaks me four. I fall in love with him a little then, as I pop the first one in my mouth whole, and experience an instant burst of raspberry vanilla-cream goodness that feels like a hug from inside my mouth. I moan a little, unable to help myself. This is the best damn thing I've had in my mouth in months, and that includes bacon and Dan's overly aggressive tongue. "Oh my God, I just came a little," I exclaim, which I realize too late sounds completely inappropriate. The beefy baker just throws his head back and laughs, big and hearty, from his gut.

"Well, then, you *must* have another." Sexy Beardstache Baker nudges one more toward me. He watches me as I devour it. He's studying my mouth intently, and I get the decided vibe that he's straight. "You might need another one even."

"Careful. I'll eat them all if you let me." I sure am bold with my flirting when I've sworn off men for a month. Also, I'm pretty sure he's out of my league anyway, and I have no shot at getting those beefy shoulders into my bed and giving him the reverse cowgirl of a lifetime. I crane my neck to glance up at his face and his beardstache, which makes him look just a little bit dangerous. Even through the flannel and apron, I can tell he's got big, thick, muscular arms, and the tiniest hint of a beer belly. Not gross big, just a slight, comforting pudge. I don't date men who won't eat carbs. I don't trust them.

"I knew there was a reason I liked you." He grins, and I wonder how he knew: from the *k-r-ot* sweatshirt? From my shameless flirting? From the fact that I'm eating mini tortes like a whale chomping down fish in a 1998 SeaWorld show? "It was nice that you helped that lady."

I'd already forgotten my Good Samaritan works in the butter aisle. "Oh, that? It's nothing." If you like that, I'll carry her on my shoulders through the store. Then she can reach anything she wants, and she won't have to worry about her bad knees.

"And you're an animal person." He nods at the tons of dog treats in my cart.

"They're for my adopted pit-mix, Larry."

"Rescue dog mom, too? That earns you another sample." He

hands me one. I swallow it nearly whole. He pretends to be impressed. "You're not worried about choking?" he asks me.

"I don't have a gag reflex." I realize, after I say this, I sound like I'm promoting new content on an amateur porn app.

"That's quite a skill set." He raises his eyebrows, impressed.

I shrug. "It's my superpower," I say. "That and making bacon disappear."

He glances at my cart and laughs a little. We both share extended eye contact. Then it suddenly hits me. Is this my . . . meet-cute? Have I fallen into an adorable rom-com? Even though I'm wearing stained yoga pants with a hole at the knee and my all-natural, aluminum-free deodorant gave out hours ago? Could it possibly be?

But then someone approaches my left flank.

"Sora?" I hear my name and I freeze, no doubt my eyes communicating sheer panic to Possible Soul Mate, because his eyebrows raise in surprise. I turn, slowly, because I don't want to see the man attached to the voice. Please don't be who I think it is. Please, if there's a God at all, *please,* don't let it be . . .

It is.

My ex-husband, Marley.

Three

SORA

If love is so great, why do I have so many exes?

—SOLO FEBRUARY CHALLENGE

My ex-husband looks surprisingly fit and well put together, which means he's got to be dating someone, because he doesn't bother to match his socks otherwise. He's got new glasses—oversized wire ones—and he's grown in bushy side-burns. Ugh. That combined with the vest (seriously, a vest?) he's wearing makes him look a little bit like a doctor on the set of an old western gunslinger movie who will be shot in the first five minutes. He's actually wearing a shirt with a collar, an un-usual choice, and it seems like he's lost twenty pounds at least since the last time I saw him.

Asshole.

"Uh . . ." What do I tell the man I was married to for four brief years after college? Nice to see you? It isn't. You look good? Even if true by Marley standards, I'm not going to dignify Marley

Douchet with a compliment. He pronounces his name *Doushay,* but since our divorce, I think *Douche-it* is more apropos.

"What . . ." I was about to ask what he was doing in the city, since last I heard he was living with his parents in the western burbs. But then, out of nowhere, Lululemon comes bounding up to us in all her matching yoga, kale-eating glory, and seems to be heading straight for . . . Marley.

"Baby? Did you get the kombucha?" she asks in a childlike voice, which she absolutely, one thousand percent, is faking.

Marley and I both turn to Lululemon at the same time, and I tighten my grip on my grocery cart. Lululemon is dating Marley? I feel like I've fallen into an alternate dimension designed to torture me. Or maybe I suffered a massive widow-maker back in the bacon aisle without realizing it, and this is hell. Lululemon cannot be sleeping with Marley. It would prove that he can do better than me, much better, but I am hoping he'll die cold and lonely. I want him to understand once and for all that I am the very best he's ever going to get, and he made the worst mistake of his life when he sent an unsolicited dick pic to Pam.

Right. I forgot to mention that's the other reason Downstairs Pam and I don't get along. She hates my dog for no reason, and she hates my ex-husband for good reason. Great, now everyone's all caught up.

Lululemon eyes me with distaste. "Babe, who's . . . ?" The never-met-a-vegetable-she-trusted person with a cart full of salted meat and ice cream?

"This is Sora." Marley says it while wiggling his eyebrows like he's having a seizure or, more likely, that he's trying to convey a secret message. Marley was never any good at subtlety.

"Sora? *This* is Sora?" Lululemon seems to be trying to hold in a laugh, but doesn't bother to hide the sneer that curls her mouth into a mean, thin line. "Your ex-wife?" She seems to be unable to believe her eyes. Go on, believe it, sister. Now you know the truth: you're dating far, far below your station.

Near me, Sexy Beardstache Baker has gone stock-still, eyes darting from me to Marley and then to Lululemon. This is not my meet-cute. I am not in a rom-com. I am in a horror movie. Some angry, stringy-haired ghost child is going to crab-crawl out of the deli counter and eat my soul.

This now ranks as my most humiliating moment of the week, and that includes having to convince Dan that my self-esteem actually isn't so low that I'd be okay with him spending the night after I confronted him about being married.

So, I stand corrected: there *is* a God after all. And He/She/They most definitely hates me.

If God truly loved me, I'd be endowed with the ability to teleport to another dimension. It doesn't even have to be a *nice* dimension. I'll take a postapocalyptic hellscape. As long as Marley and Lululemon aren't there.

"Uh . . . how are you?" Marley starts.

"Good. Good. Good." Why did I say that three times?

Then the three of us stare at one another. If there's one thing I know, from that management seminar I took once in the lobby of a Hampton Inn, it's that if you cede territory to your rival, you might as well run home with your tail between your legs. And I wasn't going to do that. For one, I don't have a thigh gap. I have a thigh *squish.* If I put two pieces of kindling in there, I'd have a fire before I finished walking a full block. No tail was fitting in there, imaginary or otherwise. The second thing I learned in that seminar is that saying nothing can force the other people in a conversation to be uncomfortable, thereby giving you the upper hand. So, I just stare.

"You still living at the old condo?" Marley asks.

And I just stare. Marley, why would I admit that? Because I spent every last dime I had to buy you out and can't really afford to move? Because you might want to send Pam another backlit pic of your hot dog from an angle designed to make it look larger than it is? She wasn't impressed the first time, Marley. But I don't say any of that. I just stare at him. Power is all mine.

"Uh . . . so, you're not then? Sora?" Marley is starting to get uncomfortable. Good.

Lululemon looks confused, her feelings of superiority temporarily fading. That's right. You, too, will feel the power of awkwardness. The three of us stew in it. Yes, okay, now, you're right where I want you.

"Maybe she had a stroke," Lululemon stage-whispers loud enough for everyone to hear. "Her left side is drooping a little."

Sexy Beardstache Baker coughs, hard.

"I'm not having a stroke." The fact that I need to say this out loud makes this moment even more humiliating now that I know that my intimidation face looks like I'm having a serious health problem. God, why can't I just tell Marley "Douche-it" to go love himself? Why did I have to pretend I'm happy to see him *and his new girlfriend*? Why won't those words roll off my tongue? Because they sure as hell are banging around in my head.

Marley glances at my cart. "Having a party?" he asks me, eyeing the bacon and tequila.

"No," I say. And screw you, Marley.

"Oh, my *gawd*, are you going to . . . like . . . eat *all of that*? Yourself?" Lululemon's hand flies to her mouth as if she's just seen the murder of a kitten with a dull, number-two pencil.

"No. Of course not. I have a dog."

Lululemon freezes, not sure if I'm joking or not.

"Of course she's not going to eat all that by herself," Sexy Beardstache Baker pipes in for the first time. All three of us stare at him now. "So? You going to introduce me?"

What is that sexy hunk of a man doing?

"Uh . . . this is . . ."

Oh, God. I don't know his name.

"Jack," Sexy Beardstache Baker says easily, rescuing me as he sticks out a beefy paw and shakes Marley's comparably small, limp hand with enthusiasm. "Sora has told me so much about you." I have? "Honestly, I have to thank you, man. If you two hadn't gotten divorced, then Sora and I wouldn't have gotten together. I owe you one."

I don't know who's more stunned: me, Lululemon, or Marley.

Jack the Sexy Baker has saved me. In that moment, I want to propose to him and have his babies. As many as he wants.

Now, it's Marley and Lululemon's turn to gape. They glance at Jack the Sexy Baker and back to me. I step a smidgen closer to Jack.

"Want a raspberry torte?" Jack offers with a bright, beaming smile. "They have *extra* GMOs, non-organic saturated fat, *and* gluten."

Lululemon looks as if he's offered her a cyanide capsule. "Oh no. No, thank you."

Marley reaches for one, but Lululemon slaps his hand. "Marley! We're gluten-*free,* remember?"

Marley looks crestfallen. It becomes clear that his trade-off for screwing Lululemon is eating food that tastes like trash. I'm suddenly feeling much, much better about my life.

"Come on, Marley," Lululemon scolds, tugging him off by his sleeve. "We've got to go." She glances at me and Jack one last time. "And nice to meet you," she cries, high-pitched and fake. The subtext in her eyes tells me she hopes I choke on bacon fat and die. I want to tell her that at least I'll die happy. More than I can say for her if she ends up snorting kale into her sinuses.

When they're gone, I turn to Jack, my new hero, and we both break out laughing.

"Thank you for that."

"Oh, it's not a problem. I hate bullies." Jack's eyes narrow a bit, as he watches Marley and Lululemon scamper away like roaches across a dirty linoleum floor. He glances back at me and grins. "It was my duty to even the odds. Those guys were assholes. Did you see all that kale in her cart?"

"Kale: the taste of sadness," I say.

"Because every great story begins with 'after I downed a few rounds of kale . . .'" he snaps back.

We share a conspiratorial grin.

"Another torte?"

"Definitely." He offers the tray up and I grab one more. "If you're going to be my fake boyfriend, why not just go the whole mile and be my fake fiancé and husband, too?" I ask, after I swallow. "I mean, are you really going to commit here? Or is this just a casual fake relationship for you?"

Playfulness lights up Jack's puppy-dog eyes. "Fictional

wedding. I like it. If it's fake and we don't have to pay for it, I want like, five hundred guests, and I want to wear cowboy boots and a blue tuxedo."

"Why stop there? Llamas can be our flower girls, and the whole affair can be blessed by the Pope."

We both chuckle some more. It feels like somehow, in another life, we were best friends who caused a helluva lot of trouble in the back of some algebra class.

"All of this is getting ahead of ourselves," I add. "We just met."

Jack cocks an eyebrow, surprised. "No, we didn't."

Now I'm confused. "What do you mean?" Is this a prank?

"You don't remember me, do you?" Jack asks with a sly smile.

"Wait. Am I supposed to?" Since when? I rack my brain trying to figure out how I might know him. A drunken one-night stand years ago? A swipe-right date gone wrong? A neighbor in one of my old apartment buildings? No, no, and no. "We met before?"

"Yes." He pauses dramatically. "You always carried a Polly Pocket every day of kindergarten and I think first grade, too. You'd bust it out when the teacher wasn't looking."

"I did do that!" He *knows* me. He really *knows* me. *Jack.* I realize there is something familiar about his brown eyes. Wait. Yes . . . I imagine Jack much younger, kid-sized, same eyes, *not* the same muscles. "Jack . . . Mann? From Dewey Elementary?" I'm so unsure my voice sounds like a wobbly whisper, like I'm afraid I'm going to accidentally set off a landmine.

Instead, a big smile spreads across Jack's face. "Bingo," he says.

Four

JACK

Flying solo just means you'll have stronger wings.

—SOLO FEBRUARY CHALLENGE

I can't believe I'm talking to Sora freakin' Reid. We were in the same classroom almost every year in elementary school from kindergarten to fifth grade. I might have had a serious crush on her some, or, okay, okay—most of those years. And anytime Sora was around me then, I usually had an anxious swarm of bees in my stomach. For most of my childhood, I actually thought pretty girls caused stomachaches.

Of course, I know most kids weren't even interested in romance then. But I couldn't help but notice Sora—half Japanese, half Scottish, all gorgeous. I felt like we were meant to be together. I'm a quarter Chinese, a quarter Portuguese, a quarter Irish, and a quarter your guess is as good as mine.

She's seriously prettier than she was in elementary school. I didn't think it possible, but it's true: pink, perfect lips, doe-brown eyes, dark, luscious, jet-black hair. And she's just as sweet and caring as I remember. I can tell she wanted to tell her ex to go to hell, but she took the high road. She always did that, even in kindergarten.

"I can't believe this!" she squeals. "Like, how have you been?" She's *glad* to see me. I am stupidly elated about this. "I mean . . . you're like . . . so tall. When did this even happen?"

"Puberty?" I joke, and she laughs.

We spend a few more seconds grinning goofily at each other. She eyes me up and down.

"You've just . . ." She seems dumbfounded. "Changed so much."

"Yeah, I know, I used to be different back then." Short. Pudgy. On the heavy side of stocky. I grew about three feet in high school. Learned to work out more and eat healthier, but still never really lost my taste for sweets. Thus . . . baking. "But look at you . . ." I wave my arms like a maniac. That perfect dimpled and gorgeous smile. "You look amazing."

"I basically just rolled out of bed."

"You still look great." She makes that faded sweatshirt she's wearing with the loose neck hole showing off quite a bit of shoulder look sexy AF, like it should be on the cover of a lingerie catalog.

A blush rises on her cheeks. "Whatever happened to you? You like, disappeared after fifth grade?"

"Family moved," I said. "We ended up a few suburbs over."

"So that's what happened! I wondered."

She did? Sora Reid thought about me for even a millisecond? The thought makes my heart thump a bit harder.

A few people wander by behind her at the samples table,

hoping to get some tortes, but I'm in a happy nostalgia bubble and I don't want to leave. I refuse to make eye contact with the man in a trucker's hat who's back for a third time for tortes.

"Excuse me?" Trucker Hat says, trying to reach a big paw in and grab another sample torte. "Can I get one of those?"

"You've already had one," I say, shooing him away like a fly. Get out of here, man. I'm trying to talk to my grade-school crush.

"But she had more . . ."

I glare at him, and he backs off, wheeling his cart away.

"Wait!" she exclaims. "You had a nickname back then. I remember . . . what was it?"

No. Please no.

She snaps her fingers. "Piggy Jack!"

Oh.

Jesus.

"I hate that name." I sigh.

Hated it ever since Boyan Debnar labeled me with it in kindergarten after he dared me to stuff my whole sandwich in my mouth at lunch. He thought it was so clever. Piggy *Back*. Piggy *Jack*. One of those perfect damn insults I couldn't shake until I grew big enough to intimidate people.

She looks instantly contrite. "Oh my God. I am so sorry. That's a terrible name," she says, her face growing pink. Oh, great. Now *she* feels bad. "I just remembered and blurted it out. I didn't mean anything by it. I just . . ." She glances down as if wishing the floor would open up and swallow her whole.

"No big deal. We were kids." I shrug. The past has no control over me. *I* control how I feel about my past. Push through it,

Jack. This isn't the first time your past has reared its fat head. Punch it in the face. I take a deep breath.

"But, I mean . . ." She gives me a slow once-over, starting at my feet and working her way up my body. "You've changed *so* much. I mean *so* much." She shakes her head in disbelief. "I mean . . . wow."

Please don't say I've lost weight. Every time someone reminds me I was a chubby kid, it makes me think I'm walking around in a meat suit. That I'm an imposter. I mean, sure, I've long since banished those fat rolls with bland, tasteless lean chicken and vegetable meals for days, but I hate it when people act so *shocked,* like it's a magic trick I should be perfecting for live television.

"I mean, your legs are so freakin' long. You would totally win every single race to the swings at recess."

"You remember our race to the swings?" I'm honestly surprised.

"Of course. It was always you and me, racing for the last one!"

"You always won," I say. I know this because I always, without fail, let her.

"Yeah. I did."

She laughs. I laugh. This feels warm and comfy and perfect. Like hot chocolate and flannel pajamas on a snow day.

"Oh my gosh. Remember Mrs. Perez's fifth-grade class? All the holiday parties?"

"She'd always bring a tray of those holiday cookies from Jewel," I say, remembering the *ooh*s and *aah*s that rippled through the class when she set the giant tray of colorful, fun-shaped cookies on the reading table. "I loved Valentine's Day the best. She always brought extra lollipops!"

"That woman was so brave. Loading up all us ten-year-olds with sugar! Can you imagine?"

I laugh. "She was brave to be in there with us to begin with!"

"Yeah." Sora pauses. Stares at me in a dramatic way, long, dark lashes framing her big brown eyes, alight with . . . mischief, and something more. My heart lightens a bit. Is this when she remembers that I put a special card in her glitter-glue-decorated shoebox? I'd debated for an hour which *Rugrats* valentine to give her: *I like you* or *Will you be mine?* A whole hour. "Remember the shoeboxes we decorated for Valentine's?"

"Oh. Yeah."

This is going really well. Like, better than I could've expected. Like, surprisingly good.

"And *you* stole the candy from my box!" she declares, and laughs.

Somewhere, I hear a record scratch—*errrrrrrck*—and then someone takes that vinyl, throws it on the ground, pours lighter fluid on it, and sets it on fire.

"That's right." She wags a finger at me. "You stole all of my valentines and my candy—even the lollipop from Mrs. Perez! The only thing in my box was *your* card. With *your* name on it." She cackles. "Now, I can totally give you shit for it!"

She slaps me playfully on the arm, but I'm still in shock. She's smiling now, as if we can share an inside joke, but . . . I didn't *steal* her candy! Never took her valentines. What kind of jerk kid would that make me?

"I didn't do that." I sound offended. I don't mean to sound offended. I just absolutely, positively, did not steal her candy. Her smile instantly fades.

"You didn't?" She frowns, looking temporarily confused. The conversation suddenly turns awkward. The easy banter hits a brick wall. Sora tucks an errant strand of hair behind her ear. "Oh. Maybe . . . I'm wrong? I just thought . . . someone said . . ." She freezes then. We both freeze, staring at each other, the same realization dawning. Someone probably told her Piggy Jack stole the candy. Because why not blame the chubby kid? I'd be the perfect scapegoat.

Okay, this isn't going well. It's going terribly. Horribly. It can't get worse.

Then it does.

Because somewhere behind Sora, I see my worst nightmare—Mal, my ex-fiancée, approaching, looking like some kind of Nordic goddess. The kind that likes to disembowel men and send them to Valhalla, screaming.

"Mal," I blurt, horrified. What the hell is this, buy one, get one ex day at Margo's? First Sora's ex, and now mine. Is Mercury in retrograde? Has someone read aloud from the Book of the Dead? None of this is okay.

"Hey, Jack-a-boo," she says, using the nickname she gave me that I hate. "You ready for lunch?"

Lunch? Then it hits me: she's been texting. Promising—or threatening, more like—to drop by. I'd ignored her, as I always do. She clearly failed to take the hint.

I'm staring at Sora, who glances from Mal to me and draws all the wrong conclusions.

"Mal, I—"

"I made reservations at your favorite place!" She turns and looks at Sora. "Oh, *hello*. Did I interrupt something?"

Yes, you did.

"Uh . . ." Sora's eyes widen.

"I'm Mal," she says, extending a black-gloved hand.

Sora looks like she wishes she could teleport out of here. "I'm Sora," she says, and reaches out her own hand. Mal pinches Sora's knuckle between her finger and thumb as if it's toxic.

"Sara?"

"*Sora,*" I emphasize.

"Nice to meet you, Sadie." Now I know she's doing this on purpose. That wasn't even close. Mal releases Sora's hand.

"Uh, yeah. Well, I was just going." Sora begins to slowly back away from my table. Wait. No. Don't go. "Great to see you, Jack!" Sora cries, as she squeezes the handle of her cart so tightly her knuckles turn white.

"Sora, wait . . ." I want to explain. This isn't . . . Mal isn't . . . You've got the wrong idea. Completely. Utterly. Wrong. Come back. Please.

"Thanks for the tortes!" Sora calls over her shoulder with a little too much forced cheer. And just like the last day of fifth grade, she's gone.

"Look what you've done," I growl at Mal.

"What? Saved you from your sad little fangirl Sonar?"

"It's Sora. S-O-R-A."

"Whatever." Mal fans her face with a black leather glove. She's carrying a bag that cost more than my rent, and her coat is lined with real baby chinchilla, which says all you need to know about Mal. Her green eyes sparkle with mischief. She actually likes making me suffer. "Please, you've always got these desperate, pathetic little *grocery store* fans around you all the time." She sniffs as she glances around the supermarket, making her disdain known.

"Well, I think we both know I wouldn't be working here if it weren't for you." If it weren't for Mal, I would be a pastry chef at a Michelin-star restaurant. Which I was, a year ago.

"Well, if you'd stayed engaged to me, you wouldn't have to work *at all*." She's referring to her hotel heiress money and her offer of making me a kept man. Why—oh why—did I ever let her into my life? God, I regret that decision. Today and every day.

"Why are you here?"

"Lunch. I texted you."

"And I didn't respond."

"And . . . ?"

"And that means I didn't agree to lunch." I sigh.

"Does it?" Mal fakes innocence.

"And I can't take a lunch break now. There's no one else to run the bakery." And even if there was, no way would I go to lunch with Mal. Never.

"Oh? Well, I just wanted to talk, anyway. I made some calls. About that bakery site you're interested in." She arches a perfectly penciled brow.

"How do you know about that?" Every alarm bell in my brain sounds. The bakery is my dream. It's my ticket out of the grocery store. I've clawed some savings from my meager checks all year just to have enough for a down payment.

"I have friends. In your real estate agent's office." The alert in my gut moves from orange to full code red.

"That's stalking." And probably a hundred other offenses, all of which any of her army of on-retainer attorneys could get her out of with one phone call.

"It's *professional courtesy,*" she says. "And it's not stalking. You're just playing hard to get."

"I'm sure that's what Glenn Close said to Michael Douglas." I am 100 percent sure Mal isn't above boiling a rabbit if it'll get my attention.

"Who?" She frowns.

"*Fatal Attraction*?" I add.

She just slow blinks. Mal doesn't watch movies—old classics or any other kind. Also, she only listens to music that's in commercials. I should've run for the hills when she admitted that. I didn't. My fault.

"It's a movie." I sigh, irritated. "And, anyway, I didn't ask you to help me with the bakery."

"I know. I *want* to." She reaches out and clutches my hand. Her palms are cold, fingers frigid. It reminds me of the time she dug her frozen feet between my legs in bed. I should've known then that her heart was ice. Couldn't pump blood to her extremities.

I snatch my hand away.

"I can get them to sell," she offers, overly glossed lips parting. "Then I'd own the building and you could stay there *rent free.*"

"Mal, I don't want your help. I don't need your help."

She pouts, jutting out her lower lip, which looks like it got an extra boost of collagen recently. She can afford a whole team of medical professionals to keep her looking perfect. It's all a facade. "Of course you need my help."

"Mal." The word's a warning.

"Okay, okay, hands off the bakery." She grins at me, and I can only pray she means it. "If . . ."

I knew there's a catch. There's always a catch.

"If what?" I squint.

"If you invite me to the Golden Chef Awards. I know you were nominated for Best Pastry Chef this year."

Yes, and right up until this moment, I was happy about that. It's a huge honor, and the winner gets bragging rights and $100,000.

"And I know you need a plus-one."

"No." The idea of Mal being my date for anything—*ever*—makes me want to poke my eyes out with the blunt piping tip of an icing bag.

"Come on. Please? It'll be fun." She leans over the counter, showing me her cleavage. I'm not interested. Might as well be the Valley of Death.

"No."

Mal frowns. "Come on. *Please.*" She pauses. "You know I hate to say please." She toys with a strand of her platinum-blond hair. Her bloodred fingernails are filed down to points, making her look like a vampire. Because she is one. She feeds on human souls. If I could somehow rescind her invitation to my life, I would.

"No. I don't know how many times I need to say this, but we broke up. Because of what you did last Valentine's Day."

Even thinking about the debacle that was last Valentine's Day makes me want to hurl.

Her lower lip juts farther out.

"You know I didn't mean to hurt you."

"You slept with your brother-in-law," I say, exasperation making my throat feel thick. "So what did you think that would accomplish?"

"You know, I have . . . issues. My parents . . . my childhood." Her eyes go glassy. Mal had a rough childhood. Despite being very wealthy, her parents neglected her much of her life, leaving her to be raised by various different nannies, and then when she was old enough, shipped off to boarding school. Her parents, she said, never once said "I love you"—not even in the birthday cards that the butler would sign. For a long time, I felt bad for her. Hell, I wanted to fix her. But you can't fix someone else. I learned that the hard way. She sniffs, wiping a perfect, single tear off one thick eyelash. "You were the only one who ever really got me."

"Mal." I sigh, softer this time. "We can't do this."

"You sure felt differently last week."

Here we go. Last week. When I bumped into Mal at a bar and, after one too many whiskeys on the rocks, made the mistake of going home with her. I just opened the door and let her back into my life. I'd been lonely, and she'd talked about her mother forgetting her birthday, and I felt bad for her. And, also, did I mention too much whiskey?

"That was a mistake."

Mal whips out her phone and begins typing.

"What are you . . ."

Then my back pocket dings, announcing an incoming message.

"You didn't block me," Mal says, triumphant, as I pull out my phone and see she's texted me a heart. "So must not have been *that* much of a mistake."

"Mal . . ."

"Jack-a-boo," she says, and touches my nose with the tip of her red nail. "You'll always be my valentine."

"That's what's beginning to worry me."

"You sure you don't want to come to lunch with me? I have reservations at Omakase." A Michelin-starred gem where a single sushi roll can cost fifty dollars. "I'll buy."

"No." I shake my head firmly. "I'm not going to lunch with you."

She shrugs. "Your loss." She picks up one of the cooling mini lemon tortes off the baking sheet in front of me and lifts it to her lips. She licks the edge. Makes me think about a snake with a forked tongue.

"You're going to have to pay for that," I tell her.

"Oh, I hope so." She pops the torte in her mouth and swallows it, seemingly without chewing. Just like a snake gulping down a mouse. "Think about it, and get back to me."

"I don't need to—" She shushes me with a bloodred claw on my lips.

"Shhhh," she purrs. She scratches the top of my lip as she removes her finger. "Just promise me you'll think about it."

"I won't," I call after her as she slinks away, moving a little like a scorpion in wedge heels.

Five

SORA

> Going solo isn't just about saying no to dates. It's really all about saying yes to yourself.
>
> —SOLO FEBRUARY CHALLENGE

My chance meeting with Jack reminds me why I should be glad I've pledged to go solo for the month. Sure, meeting Jack felt almost like fate, somehow. But then Mal showed up. Leggy, blond, and gorgeous. They probably have piles of inside jokes, and spend all their time snort-laughing over take-out and wine, while clad in matching couples' pajama onesies. Either way, one day they'll have beautiful babies who will star in diaper commercials.

I mean, it all tracks. And now I know that Jack is into tall Scandinavian models, ergo the opposite of me. Not that—let's be honest—Jack's even remotely in my league anyway. I still can't get over Jack's transformation. I mean, wow. Like, really . . . wow. So many muscles. That chiseled chin. Those broad, beefy shoulders. And he bakes! I pop another one of the man's amazing tortes in my mouth and sigh. Does Mal even appreciate what she has? These are delicious.

Feeling nostalgic, I head to the study in my condo and dig through the piles of boxes. I find one in the corner marked "School Stuff." This is it. I tug off the lid and find my old cap from college, my diploma in a cardboard sleeve, and beneath that, a stack of old yearbooks. I grab the one marked "fifth grade" and open it up. I find Jack's picture first.

Aw, what a cute kid. Big brown eyes. Chubby cheeks. He was sweet, I remember. He would always let me borrow his pencil when mine broke. And he was sometimes hilarious. Like the time he did the actual worm on the playground on a dare. And, yeah, he was a little overweight, maybe. His eyes are the same, and his nose. Not to mention his bright smile. I feel bad for believing that he stole my candy, when probably that bully Boyan Debnar did.

I check out my picture and cringe. Why am I wearing a Teenage Mutant Ninja Turtles shirt on picture day *with* a My Little Pony choker necklace? Why am I smiling so hard it hurts? I'm hopeless.

I flip to the back of my yearbook where there are tons of squiggly signatures. Jack signed it. He wrote, "Have a fun summer. BEE cool." And he drew an actual bumblebee wearing sunglasses, except the drawing is kind of skewed and hilarious. The bee looks half smashed, and one of the sunglass lenses is way bigger than the other. I take a picture of this with the intent of somehow sending it to Jack just to relentlessly tease him about it, except that I can't. Because he has a girlfriend.

And I pledged to give up flirting for February.

Larry pads into the study, curious about what I'm doing in the Room That Shall Be Ignored, and sniffs at a dusty box. Then he promptly sneezes.

"You're right. I shouldn't be in here," I tell Larry, and give him a pat. "We can't live in the past."

I stand, put the yearbook back in the box, and return to my open laptop on the kitchen table.

I know some of you will think this Go Solo challenge is just nonsense. That the phrase "It's about time I date me!" sounds trite and ridiculous and would be accompanied by a dozen gross selfies of me grabbing fro-yo, or riding a tandem bike alone, or toasting myself with a flute of pink champagne. But that's not what I'm talking about.

We're all so focused on becoming one half of a pair, of making ourselves fit another person, that we don't spend nearly enough time figuring out who we are, what we want, or what we even like before we jump headfirst into a relationship. I'll be honest, I spend so much time feeling desperate just to BE *with someone that I'm willing to overlook anything that seems bad. I'm even willing to convince myself that something I didn't want is what I wanted all along. (A man who never lets me see him on the weekend? That's totally fine, Dan. I'll adjust. Really. It's what I want, too!)*

Or I'll even be okay with being with someone who doesn't even really want to be with me. (Hey, Marley, I know you only married me for a pregnancy scare, and are staying with me for convenience and because I paid all the grocery and utility bills, and that's completely fine. Because we had a real, practical marriage and that's totally better than one that's about head-over-heels love, because who wants a soul mate when you can have the practical choice?)

Solo February is really about giving us the time and space to really think about who we are all on our own. How do I even know who I should be with, if I don't even know who I am by myself? And, really, aren't I better off alone than settling for something I don't want? Rather than settling for men who don't deserve me, I really ought to wait for the man who does.

I stop typing long enough to think about Jack. Those eyes. Those shoulders. Those baker's hands. The easy flow of conversation. The way he makes me laugh. His ridiculous and hilarious bee drawing in my yearbook. No. Stop thinking about Jack. He's just another escape hatch, another (incredibly handsome) distraction. And he has a girlfriend. A capital "G," Louis Vuitton–toting girlfriend.

Larry whines then, walking over to what he thinks is the front door, but is actually the entryway table leg. He's about six inches off. Poor guy. He needs to go out. I fetch his leash. The front door sticks a little, and I tell myself I should have someone in to fix that. And to fix the leaky faucet in the bathroom. And the uneven floorboards in the corner of my bedroom. Then I have a flashback to when Marley lived here. He would've taken care of those things. Marley didn't pay his share of condo expenses, but he did putz around and fix things. Not always perfectly (he once accidently superglued the light fixture to the "on" position when he was trying to fix a broken light plate), but still.

Marley and I bought this condo the second year we were married, sometime after the pregnancy scare, but before the sexting scandal. The condo was just a flimsy excuse to stay together. If we weren't going to be parents, then we could at least be property owners, because we could qualify for a mortgage together that we never could have qualified for alone. I've never really loved the condo. It's a seven-hundred-square-foot, two-bedroom walk-up, with no central AC, no bathtub (sad because I so, so miss bubble baths), no washer/dryer, and no parking, but it had "a cool vintage vibe" and exposed brick, which Marley was all about. In the fury of the divorce, keeping the condo just somehow felt like winning, even though I'm pretty sure Marley didn't even want it in the end.

I'm on the first landing, when a door pops open and I see the orange face of Pam. She's addicted to spray tan, which makes her look like a walking clementine. Marley sent her a lewd photo after a condo meeting where everyone had too much wine and not enough cheese. His excuse was that he actually meant to send it to someone else. Pam informed me of said picture, and I stupidly apologized, even though I had nothing at all to do with it. The Pam Incident set off a spiral of discoveries about just how Marley had been using his phone, including several active profiles I found on dating apps, which eventually led to our split. Pam and I should've bonded and been lifelong friends, except then I adopted Larry to fend off the loneliness draining my will to live, and Pam hated him on sight. It's been war ever since.

"Oh. Pam." I keep forgetting Pam works from home now. Has since the first shutdown during the pandemic. It's the worst.

"I'm glad I ran into you," she says. That's a lie. "Did you leave the Green Gleam at my door?" Pam notices Larry for the first time and ducks behind her door a little, uneasy. I make sure I stand between Larry and Pam, a protective shield.

"Yes," I say, thinking it was kind of a nice olive branch, me bringing it inside, instead of tossing it into the dumpster in the alley around back. "Just trying to be a good neighbor." I say this brightly, without sarcasm, and I'm proud of myself for that.

"The produce almost spoiled," she snaps. "You need to tell me it's here, so I can put everything in the fridge."

"Oh. Sorry?" I was just trying to be nice.

"I mean, this box is expensive." She is actually, seriously, annoyed with me. I can tell, because her clementine face is turning a deeper shade of orange.

"I was just trying to help, making sure it wasn't left outside." I guess no good deed really goes unpunished.

"It would've been *better* outside."

O-kay then.

"Also, while I have you, I wanted to talk to you about *your dog*." She spits out the words as if they're poison. She glares at Larry, who hides behind my legs. "He makes a lot of noise."

"He barely barks."

"When he walks in your condo." Pam rolls her eyes. "I have a lot of meetings, and it's unprofessional to hear him galloping all over the place like an elephant."

Behind my knees, Larry whines, worried. I tighten my grip on his leash.

"He really doesn't walk around that much," I say, defensive. Larry sleeps twenty-three of twenty-four hours a day.

"I just need quiet during the workday. That's all." Pam narrows her eyes at me. I narrow mine at her.

"I'll do what I can," I say, and by that, I mean absolutely nothing.

"See that you do," she adds, meaning that she doesn't really even care if I keep Larry quiet, because she'd rather have something to lord over me, fuel for our feud.

We glare at each other for a beat. Then Pam slowly withdraws into her condo and shuts her door, without a goodbye. Because, I think, it's her way of saying she's keeping an eye on me. It's never really goodbye with her.

Nice to see you, too, Pam.

Seeing Pam reminds me that I should sell my condo and move. I could roll the equity from this one into a new one. One with a bathtub. And no Pam. Yes, yes, I'll get to it. I will. Some day. Just like looking for freelance jobs that are a bit more serious. With a bit more . . . integrity. I'll do it. Just not right this second. Because like finding new writing gigs, selling my condo seems like . . . a giant ask. I'd have to spring-clean. I'd have to stage it (I doubt anyone would buy it with all my boxes in the study). I'd have to find a real estate agent, I'd have to find a new place. So many steps. And it's easier . . . not to do all the steps. But I will. Someday.

Outside, Larry finds his tree, does his business, and I tie up the evidence in a plastic doggie bag, even though if I were a worse person (like the ones down the street), I would just kick some snow over it and call it a day. When the snow melts in the spring, sometimes it feels like a slow reveal of this mountain of literal shit around the base of every tree down the block. I buzz open the locked entry door of my apartment building and head up the stairs, Larry in tow.

I get inside and unbundle myself as Larry shakes off a bit of snow from his fur just as my phone rings. I see Mom's picture pop up on the screen.

"Mom? Hey. What's up?" I answer.

"Have you gone keto?" For a second, I have no idea what she's talking about. Mom speaks quickly—as if worried she'll get cut off mid-sentence. Mom, born in Hawaii to Japanese American parents, moved to the mainland for college in Iowa, where she met my Scottish American dad. In case you didn't know, I'm literally a walking mini melting pot. Think of me as human fondue.

"Have I . . . gone what?"

"I'm keto, too! We can do it together!" I realize, belatedly, she means the carb-free diet. I sigh and roll my eyes. Mom never asks me to do anything for fun unless it's dieting or exercise related. I'm a size fourteen. Mom is somewhere above an eighteen, though relentlessly yearns to be a size two, and talks about it endlessly. In all honesty, I'm fine with being a size fourteen. I've long since made peace with the fact that I'll never be a two, but Mom somehow thinks we're both on the same page. Yo-yo dieters forever. No matter how often I try to tell her to stop roping me into her fad diets, she does it anyway.

"Mom, I'm not on the keto diet."

"But you are all about bacon. Instead of men?" Oh no. She's been reading my articles.

"Yes. I'm giving up on men. I'm eating bacon. Donuts. Whatever I want. I am *not* dieting. That's kind of the point."

"No!" Mom gasps like I just confessed I'm a cannibal. "But your sister's wedding is coming up? The pictures?"

"Yes, I know. I'll just have to be a fat whale in them, Mom."

Mom sucks in a breath on the other end of the phone and

then barks a laugh. I can always make Mom laugh. It's a superpower. "Sora!" She chuckles. "You know that's not what I mean. You are not a fat whale."

"More like a porky porpoise, then?"

"No, no, no." She laughs some more and backtracks. "*I* need to lose weight." Mom and I have always shared the exact same body type. So, when she tells me she needs to lose weight, she might as well be telling me the same thing. "I just thought it'd be something fun to do together. We big-boned girls have to stay together!"

I hate it when she tries to lump us together as two hopeless fatties. And here, I've already called myself a fat whale to distract and divert. But Mom won't be waylaid. Years of resentment bubbles to the surface. I remember the Christmas that she got us both matching Fitbits, even though I didn't ask for one. Then there was the time she signed us up for a joint gym membership for my birthday. When I was fourteen.

"How about we just go see a movie instead?"

Mom laughs as if I'm joking, but I'm not joking. "But the popcorn! So many calories." She clicks her tongue in disapproval.

"Mom—" Here's where I need to tell her that I'm done with her fad diets, that if she feels the need to do it, great, but—then I hear my dad's voice in my head.

Sora! Be nice! This was Dad's constant refrain. He usually yelled it, because he was the only man in a house full of women, and all he desperately wanted was peace and quiet and no drama. Which he never got. And this made him short-tempered, or maybe he was just short-tempered to begin with, or maybe it was his on-call, all-hours-of-the-day-or-night job running his small plumbing business that kept him perpetually grumpy. I don't know, but from the time I was little all I remember was that he ended every argument, even if he never started them.

Dad died last year of a heart attack, but I still feel like he's right here with me, ready to shut down any disagreement with a barked command. I learned early that dissent wasn't worth enduring Dad's stormy looks and gritted teeth. Don't be the nail, indeed.

"You've got a responsibility, Sora. You're the maid of honor." She says it as if the title is actually an honor. "You can't give up, sweetie. Your sister's wedding is less than a month away."

"I know, Mom." I pace in the kitchen next to my open laptop. I accidentally hit the squeaky board. I know that will make Pam, below me, fume.

"Have you found a date yet?"

I sigh. "No, and I probably won't, either." Now I suddenly see the genius of Solo February. I kill two birds with one stone. Nami is getting married the first weekend in March. If I've sworn off men for *work*, then I don't have to worry about scrounging up some awful date, either! Genius!

"Oh, don't talk about yourself like that. Of course you will. Besides, there's always one of the groomsmen. I think one or even two of them are single."

I wrinkle my nose. "Mitch's friends are . . ." I struggle to say something that's not too critical but also honest. I don't need to set Mom off. I try not to criticize Nami to Mom. Mom never tolerates me critiquing anything Nami does. But Mitch and his friends . . . ugh. I remember meeting a couple of them at one of Nami and Mitch's Super Bowl parties last year. They talked entirely in memes. Mitch is definitely the only tolerable one in the bunch. And that's only because he doesn't talk much.

I suspect his mind works in the same way as his friends' in that he's motivated solely by beer, ass, or football. Not necessarily in that order. Mitch just has the good sense to keep his mouth shut. In that way, he's only slightly better than the rest of his friends.

"Mom, you don't understand." Time to play the trump card. "I'm not going to be looking for one. I've vowed to go solo for February. It's my assignment. For work. That means no dates. No men. For February."

Mom falls silent. All I hear are my own squeaky floorboards beneath my feet as I pace. Distantly, below me, I hear Pam retaliate by blaring her favorite *Jock Jams Volume 4* mix. The warbled sounds of Chumbawamba drift up through my uninsulated floor. This makes me want to get Larry's ball out and play fetch in the hallway, but I refrain.

"But you need a date for the wedding. And it's technically the first weekend of March."

"Yes, true. But I'd rather not try to scramble to find one in a week, and I'm not even looking for one in February. Besides, Mom, I'm tired of roller-coaster relationships."

"You don't need a relationship. You just need a date. Nami will want you to have one."

"Nami won't care!" At least, I hope she won't.

"Why don't you tell her yourself Saturday?"

Now I'm on high alert. "What's Saturday?"

"FlyFit class, remember? Nami is coming."

"Uh . . ." I don't remember agreeing to any kind of fitness class, but that's probably my fault for tuning out things I don't want to hear.

"I'll text you the address. See you at eleven!" she sings, and then hangs up before I can back out.

Six

SORA

Did you know that single people are often happier than married people? And single people are often healthier, too. What if #GoingSolo helps us live longer?

—SOLO FEBRUARY CHALLENGE

By Friday, I still haven't come up with a good excuse to get out of FlyFit, but I'm hoping, like all of the problems in my life, if I just aggressively ignore it, it will go away. In the meantime, I focus on the next installment of *Solo February*.

When did we decide as a society that paired up is the best thing to be? Why do we ALWAYS celebrate couples, but we never celebrate singles? It's like we're all afraid of being alone, like we all dislike ourselves so much that no one can imagine a single life making us happy. I think we need to work on celebrating being single. Imagine if society as a whole spent more time telling you that you are fine all on your own. What if staying single, and living a fulfilling life, was held up as just as meaningful a path as getting married and having kids?

There's actual scientific evidence that some people are happier single than they are in relationships.

I say we start with a new holiday celebrating being single. We can buy ourselves our own boxes of chocolate. I'd actually prefer bacon boxes. Bacon-wrapped bacon. Bacon-shaped hearts! Yes!

My stomach rumbles. I pause, staring at my blinking cursor. I need a break.

Preferably, one that involves food.

I fire off a quick text to Stella Rosenstein, one of my closest friends who also works from home and lives two doors down.

She texts back, *It's 10 AM.*

Brunch then? I offer.

It's one of the perks of working from home. I can eat whenever I want. This is also one of the downsides of working from home: I eat whenever I want. I've not been hungry in many months. I'm not even sure what "peckish" feels like anymore. I just constantly stuff my face with milky white coffee, cheese sticks, and pita chips all day long.

I'm in, Stella writes. *We need bagels. Little known fact: our desk jobs require carb-loading.*

I love Stella. She was born in Nigeria, but was adopted and raised by a rabbi and his wife, and grew up in the northern suburbs of Chicago. The fact that she's a licensed therapist who sees patients in virtual sessions from her home office has nothing to do with the fact that we're best friends.

Is that your therapeutic opinion? I ask her.

Everything is my therapeutic opinion.

Twenty-five minutes later I'm sitting across from Stella at her favorite bagel joint. They're certified kosher, so they don't serve bacon, but their bagels are the size of my face and literally to die for, so I'm okay with that.

Stella is the only one on earth I know who has a worse dating life than I do (she's forever ruined the idea that if only I was attracted to women, my romantic life would be simpler). She's told me multiple times that I need to get over myself. Turns out, relationships are just freakin' hard, no matter who you're attracted to.

"I dumped Terran," she announces as she unwraps her lox and bagel. She's wearing her typical work outfit: from the waist up, a tasteful sweater, muted makeup, and her dark curls loose down her shoulders. Waist down, however, she's wearing faded joggers and a pair of her most comfortable vintage sneakers.

"Finally," I say, relieved. "You can't date someone named *Terrain.*" I say her name with exaggerated disdain. I take a bite of my own everything bagel with extra cream cheese. It's toasty, warm, and chewy goodness.

"You know she doesn't pronounce it like that. And she didn't pick her name."

"Yeah, I know." I roll my eyes. "It's less about the name, and more about her being a terrible person who met up with women behind your back on apps after you both agreed to be exclusive."

Stella blinks twice, and I see a sheen of tears across her dark brown eyes. "She's emotionally unavailable. I always fall for those types. I feel like such a schmuck."

"You don't *always* fall for those types. Just almost always." I grin. "Besides, I actually think you set good boundaries with Terran. You told her what you needed, and when she didn't give it to you, you let her go."

"Then why do I feel so lousy?" Stella laments.

"In a couple of weeks, you will feel better. Besides, you'll be the toast of all the apps the second you put your profile back up."

Stella is objectively gorgeous. She's got this mane of cascading dark curls and deep umber skin that is absolutely pore-free and breathtaking. She looks like she ought to be a model rather than a therapist, and whenever we go out together, all the men flirt with her and ignore me, but then, I get the joy of telling them she'll never be interested in them, no matter what they do. "I'm not going to set unrealistic expectations. I tell my patients this all the time, but look at me."

"Hey, you know it's always harder to follow your own advice! Plus, you can't be objective about yourself. That's why no one can be their own therapist."

"Thanks." She smiles at me, wiping her nose with a napkin. "Hey, by the way, I've been reading *Solo February.* The articles are good. Really good."

"They are?" I blink.

"Yes! I'm really proud of you—usually you just run headfirst into a new relationship, but I'm so glad you're taking some time for you, and really evaluating what you need before you start crushing on some new guy."

I think about meeting Jack at Margo's and wonder if I should tell Stella about him. Then again, why bother? Jack has a girlfriend. Ergo, I can't be crushing on him. Even if I am. A little.

"I don't always jump into a new crush," I protest.

"That's your MO," Stella scoffs. "Remember how you met Dan? That was right after you just broke up with Chris."

"Ugh. Chris," I groan. After we had our "let's be exclusive" talk and agreed not to date anyone else, he went to Cancún with his ex-girlfriend.

"And Chris came right after Nathan."

"Don't remind me." Nathan, who told me, flat-out, there were too many options out there for men over thirty, and that the older he got, the more options he had, whereas my dating pool as a straight woman sharply dwindles every year. The numbers, he said, didn't lie, and it made no sense for him to ever settle down, until he reached his fifties. I spent a few months thinking I might be able to change his mind. Dumb, I know.

"And Nathan was right after Marley. So, you've kind of got a pattern. A little bit." Stella takes a big bite of bagel and chews thoughtfully. "I'm just glad you're taking some time, exploring what you need. The articles are authentic and real. In fact, I think it's the most authentic thing you've written."

"You're saying I'm not authentic when I write about the best toothpastes to use before a blowjob?"

"Uh, ew?" Stella wrinkles her nose in distaste. "I'm just saying, you've always talked about wanting to write something more meaningful. I think this could be it." Stella takes a sip of her coffee. "I think I'll do the challenge, too, actually. Solo February sounds pretty good to me."

"Seriously?" I can't believe Stella is joining me.

"Why not? It's healthy to take stock of one's life. And lots of people are doing it."

"They are?"

Stella pulls up my first article, which I haven't looked at in a while. It's gotten fifteen thousand likes. That's more likes than any one of my articles before. By about 14,850.

> *You go, girl! Thank you for saying what we've all been thinking. We need a relationship detox.*

> *You write it, sister!*

> *To hell with love. #GoSoloYolo*

The door near our table dings and a sharp blast of February air rips across the back of my neck. I glance up in time to see none other than Jack Mann, wearing a navy wool peacoat, cargo pants, and sturdy, winter-proof lug boots, saunter in. I feel pure happiness, followed by existential dread. Stella, meanwhile, doesn't notice him.

"See? Your words are really resonating with people."

"Uh . . . yeah." Jack hasn't seen me yet. He's more gorgeous than I remember, and in my memory, he's the love child of Keanu Reeves and Jason Momoa.

He's alone. Is his girlfriend meeting him here? I watch as he heads to the cashier, who turns behind her to pour him a cup of coffee—to go. He must be on break. Margo's is just down the street.

"I'm serious, Sora," Stella continues. "You might really be onto something here. Something good."

"Yeah. I probably am . . . " When Jack turns around, there's no way he won't see me. We're sitting right by the door. The cashier hands Jack a receipt and his to-go cup. Should I hide? I don't know what to do! Jack turns. We make eye contact. Jack's gorgeous face breaks into a smile so perfect and sexy and stunning that I can't actually breathe for two whole seconds. He closes the distance between the cashier and our table in two long strides.

"Sora?" he says in his stupidly deep voice.

"J-Jack!" I sputter, just as Stella swivels to eye Jack, who's standing over our table. The to-go coffee cup looks like a tiny toddler sippy cup in his massive paw. "Uh. How are you?"

"Good. Better now that I've run into you." He grins at me. Stella clears her throat.

"Uh . . . Jack, meet my friend Stella."

Jack grins. "Oh, nice to meet you," he says, offering up his strong hand. Stella takes it cautiously, a gleam of "who the hell is this man" in her eyes as she glances at me, eyebrow raised.

"How do you know Sora?" she asks, the question laced with about a dozen different meanings.

"We went to elementary school together."

"Oh. Really?" Stella can't contain her surprise, likely because I never mentioned that I shared a classroom with a Greek god.

"In fact, I know all of Sora's secrets," Jack teases. "She made a paper fortune-teller in third grade that predicted she'd own a

Volkswagen, have four children, and be president of the United States. All by age thirty-three."

"Cootie catchers are notoriously accurate," I agree, loving the way I fall into easy banter with this man like a pair of comfortable slippers. "It's why I'm getting my presidential exploration committee together now."

"Oh, good, and I assume you've already got the Volkswagen."

"Plan to purchase one next month. And the quintuplets will be on the way. Any day now." I pat my stomach. We grin at each other. Stella coughs. Right. Solo February. And the fact that Jack has a girlfriend.

"Listen," Jack begins. "I just wanted you to know that Mal—"

Ugh, the girlfriend. "You don't have to explain," I jump in, quickly. Please don't. I already have terrible nightmares of them wearing matching heart underwear as they tickle each other in their swinging bear piñata.

"I feel like I have to. I mean, we're not dating. We used to date, but, uh . . ." This is becoming awkward. "I mean, we're not. Dating, that is . . ."

"What?"

"We're not dating. We used to. But we're not now. I know she made it look like we are, but we're not."

Stella makes a snorting sound. Probably because that's exactly what Terran would say.

"You're not dating." I still can't believe it. Mal seemed so cozy and territorial when she called him "Jack-a-boo." Which . . . gross.

"No. Absolutely not. We broke up a year ago." Jack rubs his neck in discomfort. "She's just not over it."

Given how his bicep is so large when flexed that I can see

the impression of the muscle through his wool peacoat, then, yeah, I get why she's not over Jack.

"So, listen, before she interrupted us yesterday, I was going to see if . . ." He starts talking a little bit faster. "If maybe you wanted to go out sometime? Grab a drink? Coffee?"

Stella's eyes widen as she looks at me. She's as surprised as I am. Neither one of us has probably been asked on a date in person in years. Usually, the ask comes in the form of a vague text message, hinting about a possible, theoretical date, like *Been meaning to check out that new bar in River North.*

"Or, you know," he says, a gleam in his eye, "we could just find a playground and race to the swings like old times."

"Yes!" I cry, but just as I'm about to jump up and down like I've won *The Price Is Right* showcase showdown, I see Stella's disapproving face. Crap. Solo February. "I mean, yes, I'd love to do that, but . . ."

Stella raises both brows.

"I kind of . . . sort of . . . pledged to give up men for the month of February."

Jack looks like I've just handed him a calculus problem. "You don't like men?" he asks.

"No. I mean, I like men too much. I love them. Can't get enough of them," I say. Okay, not what I mean, exactly. "I've just sworn off dating for February."

He squints, still not sure what the hell I mean. I don't even know what I mean anymore. Not with Jack's big brown eyes in front of me, pools of warm chocolate.

"So, it's not me, it's *all men*?" he asks, trying to wrap his big sexy arms around this rejection. Real disappointment flashes in his eyes. I hate that. I want to immediately reverse course.

"Just for February," I say, hoping that tinge of sadness in his eyes goes away. It doesn't. Crap. He thinks I'm rejecting him permanently. He covers up his dejection with a flat smile.

"Oh. Okay. I get it." He flips up his wool coat collar, not meeting my gaze. "Well, uh, then I'll be going. Stella, nice to meet you."

She nods at him. "You, too, Jack."

I watch him as he exits the restaurant, my stomach twisting painfully in knots. Why do I feel like I've blown it?

"Who the hell *was* that?" Stella hisses when he's gone. "You, my friend, have a lot of explaining to do."

Seven

JACK

> Valentine's Day began as the Roman festival Lupercalia. The festival included fertility rites and the pairing off of women with men, usually by lottery. By lottery! Tell me how that's at all romantic? Also, I believe the sacrificing of goats was involved.
>
> —SOLO FEBRUARY CHALLENGE

Okay, so that went well. No, it's not me. It's all men on planet Earth. I just can't believe I read the room so wrong. I kind of thought . . . we had a connection. Clearly, I'm wrong.

I slide the tray of unbaked raspberry tortes into the oven at Margo's. It's a relatively slow Friday. It's been a few days since Sora blew me off. I hate to admit this, but I still look for her to walk in the sliding automatic doors of the store. Stupid, really. I should give up. I'm like Charlie Brown and that damn football. Every single time Lucy holds it, he runs full speed toward it. Only to have it swiped away at the last second. Again.

My phone dings and I pull it out of my pocket.

The Spark dating app tells me I have more than a dozen new matches. I aimlessly look through them. There's a woman on her patio with a fish face. "Kissy face" might be the technical term, but they all look like fish faces to me: lips puckered, cheeks sucked in. Fish face with sunglasses. Fish face without. Woman in a bikini staring off into the distance. Fish face and cleavage shot. Cleavage shot and fish face. Another bikini. More cleavage. More fish faces. And a long list of new messages from interested parties, all consisting of one-word openers.

Hey.

Hi.

'Sup?

Hey.

Hi.

All gorgeous enough to pique my inner Neanderthal's interest. But my inner Homo sapiens craves a conversation. A connection that goes beyond one-syllable answers. Because I've had enough of the casual swipe-right circuit. I want more. I want something real. Someone who makes me laugh. Someone with substance. Someone who understands the concept of an inside joke. Or, hell: humor, period. Someone who doesn't spend hours trying to get the perfect fish face and semi-tasteful cleavage shot for their social. Someone who eats food on dates, instead of nibbling on the edge of a piece of lettuce like a guinea pig.

Someone like Sora.

Confession time.

I might have noticed her at Margo's in the produce section, maybe back near Christmas, looking pretty damn crisp herself. I'd recognized her instantly. Those sweet brown eyes and perfect pink bow lips are impossible to forget. Plus, she has that little beauty mark, to the left of her mouth, and the dimple on the right when she smiles. She'd been wearing a plaid scarf, knee-high black shiny boots, and a red wool thigh-length coat with lipstick to match. Like the perfect Christmas present I wanted to see under my tree. Red—the color of good luck, the color Po Po, my Chinese American grandma, said scared away bad spirits. But then, I realize, she's not alone. Some guy is tagging behind her, an ugly version of Lance Bass, that she called Dan.

I guess if she really has vowed to go solo this month, then that means no Dan, either. I guess that's a consolation prize. Still, Solo February could've just been an excuse to let me down easy. Sora's nice like that. Of course, the rejection still stings. More than I'd like to admit.

The timer of the oven at Margo's goes off, letting me know the raspberry mini tortes are ready. I shove my phone in my pocket, grab a couple of oven mitts that are too small for my hands, and open the oven. Heat blasts my face as I grab hold of the tray of desserts and slide them out. They look perfect, if I do say so myself. I glance around, but I'm alone in the grocery kitchen that looks out to the glass cases of the bakery section. I sigh. It's no Alestra, the fancy Michelin-star restaurant where I worked last year, making dessert delicacies that got five-star reviews in the *Chicago Tribune*. Ah, how far I've fallen.

I shake my head. No need to dredge up bad memories now. What's done is done. Can't remix a cake that's already baked. I glance up from the counter and see a woman debating whether or not to come up and order something. Two others stand behind her, whispering. I sigh. I know I've become the local single ladies' (and some men's) obsession. It's just all kinds of embarrassing, really. I don't want that kind of attention.

It doesn't matter, though. Soon, I'll open my own bakery. At my shop, they can flirt with me all they want. I've got half the cash I need to open it. Plus, now I'm nominated for Best Pastry Chef, and if I win the award this year, and the $100,000 prize, I'll be set.

My luck has to be changing. After the disaster that was last year, I've got to get a break.

My phone rings in my pocket. My older brother, Marc, is calling.

"Hey." Marc sounds echo-y, so I know he's calling me from his fancy new car, probably stuck in traffic on the way to his law office. He never has time to call anyone unless he's stuck in traffic. "You remember Allie's birthday tomorrow?"

I roll my eyes. "Of *course* I remember our niece's birthday." The fact that Marc feels the need to remind me is slightly annoying. "I'm baking the cake, remember?"

"Okay, just checking. You know this party is . . . important."

"I know." A year ago, the poor four-year-old was stuck in the cancer ward at Chicago Hospital, fighting off leukemia. That spunky, adorable, fearless girl gave us the scare of our lives. But she fought through it like a champ and kicked cancer's ass with her light-up sparkling unicorn sneakers. That soon-to-be-five-year-old is my damn hero. "I'm making her favorite cake—chocolate chocolate. And I *might* have picked up a few things. Pink and glittery."

"Ian isn't going to like that. You know how he feels about glitter." Ian's our other brother and Allie's dad, and has lamented a million times how glitter gets all over every surface of the house, no matter how much they try to contain it.

"Ian can bite me," I joke. "The girl loves glitter? She's getting glitter. After all that she's been through? Least I can do."

"Yeah, and she's got a doctor's checkup later this month . . ." Marc trails off, because he doesn't want to say what we're both thinking: the cancer could come back anytime. It's a sneaky, cowardly son of a bitch.

"That's why Allie gets all the glitter and chocolate she can handle right now."

Because the truth is, we don't know how many birthdays Allie will get. Whether she stays well is up to the big guy upstairs. All the doctors tell us the odds are good. Still, it's the Big C. And it's scary as hell.

"Okay, well, don't be late. It's eleven at Ian's place."

"I know, Marc. I *know*." Marc feels the need to police us all, being the oldest. Even when we were little, he promoted himself to Mann Family boss.

I hang up with Marc, heart a little bit heavy. But Allie won, I tell myself. She beat it. No use in letting doubts about her future creep in. She's going to live long and well. Allie reminds me that we only get one shot on planet Earth. You never know when your time is up. Might as well make the most of it.

I think about Sora again and sigh. I just wish I could be making the most of it with her.

Eight

SORA

> Only you can make yourself happy. No one else can do that. Stop trying to delegate the duty to someone else.
>
> —SOLO FEBRUARY CHALLENGE

Saturday morning, I still feel a nagging worry that blowing off Jack might have been a mistake. I'm consumed by all the what ifs. Could he have been The One? Or am I just using him as an excuse not to work on myself? I'll admit, I'm more than a little haunted by the look of disappointment on his face. I hate that I'm responsible for that. I am working through my guilt by eating my feelings. Stella would tell me this is decidedly unhealthy, but bacon just makes everything better, okay?

My short-tempered dad was impatient with everyone and everything, *except* when he made breakfast Saturday mornings when I was a kid. His specialties were pancakes and bacon. He'd always fry up a full package at a time, and because Nami and Mom weren't huge fans of the crunchy breakfast meat, Dad and I had more to ourselves. It's one of the few really, truly good memories I have of Dad.

Larry whines, winking at me with his forever-shut eye, pink tongue out. I put a couple of pieces in his bowl, and he gobbles them up.

"What should we do today?" I ask Larry. He looks up, hopeful for another piece of bacon.

My phone pings. *Solo February is becoming a thing, seriously,* Arial texts me. *Check your inbox.*

I glance at my phone and realize I've got hundreds of new emails. The last article I posted has four hundred thousand likes! What the . . . !

> *I've been feeling like you do for a long time,* one woman wrote. *Thank you for writing what we've all been thinking. I've been looking for happiness through a man for too long. Thank you for giving me the courage to be on my own.*

Wow. I browse through dozens of other messages, and the theme is the same. What I'm writing is resonating with people. Really hitting home. Stella was right!

My phone buzzes with another text. This one from Nami.

> *You coming to FlyFit today, right? It's in a half hour.*

I glance down at my bacon-grease-laden fingers. The very last thing on earth I want to do is go *work out.* The whole point of eating my feelings is to *not* burn off the calories that are coating my interior fat, which is like a hug on the inside. But I also know that Mom and Nami will keep on bugging me until

I show up, and then I'll have the avalanche of texts afterward if I don't, the guilt trip in stereo.

Do I have to come?

I type. Maybe, this one time in our lives, Nami will show me a little pity.

Mom says you have to talk to me about the wedding. What's up?

I don't actually think Nami will care about me going solo, one way or another, but part of me is worried she will care. She's become obsessed with little details since she started planning her nuptials and she's wound tighter than a violin these days. She broke out in tears in the pots and pans section of Crate & Barrel last week because she couldn't find the nonstick saucepan she wanted for her registry. So, probably best if I break the news in person.

Will tell you when I get there. I'm on my way.

I grab the newly nuked bacon off the table and wrap it in a napkin. No sense in wasting good farm-to-table thick-sliced goodness. I can eat it in the car.

I walk into the sleek FlyFit studio and everything has the FlyFit logo on it, a loopy double "F" that, if you squint, kind of looks like a double infinity sign. This is terrifying because if there's one thing I don't need an infinite amount of, it's exercise. People wait for the studio door to open, about six so far, and every person is clad in expensive, coordinated athleisure wear. I glance down at my (washed!) *k-r-ot* sweatshirt and faded, ultra-stretchy yoga pants, so worn the brand name has long since worn off the lower back. I'm pretty sure the fabric might even be sheer in places, but who cares? I'm at the *gym*. I don't need to impress anyone. Not that there are any men here to impress. It's all women of various ages, all fully matching, from their colored hair ties to the logos on their designer cross-trainers.

"You made it!" calls Nami, emerging from the crowd. She's outfitted in something bright and shiny, black and pink. She's normally a size two on a bloated day, but since her stressful wedding planning, she's plummeted to a size double zero. She hugs me, and she feels like all sharp edges. I'll need to talk to her about eating something. She pulls back from me, frowning. "Why do you smell like bacon?" she asks me, perplexed.

"No reason," I lie.

Then she looks at my outfit and frowns. "Uh, what are you wearing?" she asks, uncertain, as if she's never seen my once-white, now grungy yellow sneakers, with the rubber on the toe half peeling off. She glances uneasily around at the well-coifed crowd. Two more ladies push through the revolving door, wearing matching mauve spandex.

"Clothes?" I offer.

She frowns, disappointed. Okay, so I'm sorry I can't afford stylish workout gear. I'm not a corporate attorney at a start-up tech firm that I helped to get off the ground, which will probably, one day, net her millions. Plus, I remind myself, Solo February gives me the license to dress how I want, not how I think other people want me to dress. I can just, for once, be comfortable.

"Glad you made it," Mom says, and thankfully doesn't comment on my shirt or shoes. She's cut her jet-black hair into a layered bob. She's wearing new lipstick, too, a coral that suits her. She's in her early sixties, but her age seems undefinable. She could be thirty-five. She could be sixty-five. Mom likes to joke often that her Japanese heritage means that she'll look young until one day, suddenly, she'll just look very, very old. Her Japanese ancestors have two speeds: ageless and old as hell. Right now, she's ageless: no wrinkles, still mostly flawless skin except for a sunspot or two. I'm just thirty-two, but I hope those are the genes she's passed along to me.

"You can use this!" she adds, ruining her opening by patting my shoulder sympathetically. She sniffs loudly. "Do I smell *bacon*?" She clucks her tongue in disapproval. "You *know* you and I can't eat like Nami does."

"Mom, Nami doesn't eat."

"I eat," Nami protests.

"Right." I glance at her sharp collarbone.

I wish I'd saved some bacon in my pocket. I could use it now. Then, when they ask why I have bacon in class, I can just tell them it's my comfort animal.

"So? What do you want to tell me about the wedding?" Nami asks me, eyes bright. She's clearly somehow under the impression this is good news. Did Mom make her think I'd landed a famous DJ for the reception or something?

"Uh . . . I . . ." Why is this so hard? "I don't have a date for the wedding."

Nami blinks fast. This is not what she's expecting. "Oh." She shrugs. "Well, you'll get one. You still have plenty of time." She waves a dismissive, perfectly manicured hand.

"She's not going to even *look* for one," Mom chimes in. "She's giving up on men."

"Mom, I'm not giving up on them. I'm taking a break. For the month of February."

Nami now looks a little more concerned. That wrinkle in the middle of her forehead appears, the one when she's backed into a corner, like pretty much any time we played Connect Four. She hates to lose. She also hates, more than anything, to have one of her meticulous plans derailed. I love Nami to death. She's smart and fiercely loyal, but wedding planning has brought out her worst qualities. I should've seen this coming. More women pour in from outside, and the three of us move closer to the studio door with the giant gold infinity sign.

"I can't believe you're doing this to me." Her voice is getting higher pitched and squeaky. I realize I have completely underestimated the ripple effect of me not having a date. Who knew it was this important? "I'm already so stressed right now, and you throw this on me? Now I've got to find you a date?"

"I was actually thinking I'd just go without one."

Nami presses her lips in a thin line. This isn't what she wants to hear. "I've already made the seating arrangements."

"I know. I'm sorry. But, I mean, can't we just take away a chair?"

"Take away a chair!" Nami huffs, as if I've asked her to sever her pinkie to prove her loyalty. "No, we can't."

"Oh." I guess I wasn't aware we couldn't take away a chair. More would-be fly-fitters crowd into the lobby. Now, we're nearly elbow to elbow. I glance at the giant door leading into the studio, willing it to open. "Nami, I don't want to mess anything up, but it's just that I'm doing this thing for work and—"

"Work is more important than my wedding?" Nami's fuming.

"No, that's not what I mean." Ugh. I'm just digging myself in deeper.

"What about the couples' dance?" Nami demands. "The second dance? The wedding party is supposed to dance—as couples." Nami's brow wrinkles further.

"I didn't know about the couples' dance."

"How can you not know about the couples' dance?" Nami says, exasperated. I don't point out that this is the first time I've even heard of a planned couples' dance. That would only make Nami angrier. "And all the groomsmen already have dates. Now, I have to find you someone to dance with?"

"What about Uncle Bob?"

"*Great*-Uncle Bob is eighty-five years old," Nami huffs. "He'll ruin the pictures."

Ouch. Poor Uncle Bob. He's an adorable old man who likes to wear plaid ties and talks in a faint Scottish lilt.

"He'll be fine in pictures."

"He has a walker. How can he even dance?"

"I'll help him," I offer. "It'll be cute. Or I can dance with Grandma Mitsuye. She loves to do the jitterbug."

Nami lets out an exasperated sigh. "You don't get it." Nami glares at the ceiling of FlyFit. "Why do you always do this to me, Sora? Seriously?" There's a lifetime of closely kept grudges in that one word. Just like Dad, Nami neither forgets nor forgives.

"I can just sit out the dance. It's okay."

"You have to dance. It's my day and you have to dance." I see Dad's old temper in the flare of her nostrils.

"Okay, okay!" I raise my hands in surrender.

The studio door slips open then. And the instructor, I presume, steps out.

"All right, ladies!" cries the instructor, a petite blue-headed pixie clad head to toe in a leopard-print full-body leotard. "Are we ready to go in?"

Everyone gives a loud shout of approval, so loud that I jump. Are we in the marines?

The instructor, bouncing with exaggerated enthusiasm, swings open the birch door to the studio and we all file in. That's when I notice the harnesses hanging from the higher-than-normal ceiling and the long, colored drapes knotted at the bottom and dragging on the wooden floor. Worse, a few of the ladies jump right into the swinging drapes and begin warm-up stretches, hanging in them like pros from Cirque du Soleil.

"What the hell is this?" I whisper to Mom.

"Aerial aerobics," she says. "Haven't you heard of FlyFit? And what did you think it was?"

"My idea of hell. Since when is this a thing?" I ask Nami, but she's gone mute. She's pissed at me now and I'm getting the Nami cold shoulder. Great. I feel a pang of guilt, even though, objectively, I know I'm not ruining her wedding. She's overreacting because she's stressed and Mitch has been zero help in planning any of this. It's hard to help when he spends eight hours a day online shooting aliens. She'll calm down. I hope.

Nami follows Mom as they both head to the *front* of the class, closest to the mirrors, and I suddenly forget any wedding tension as Mom climbs into a turquoise knotted drape and Nami hangs on to a pink one, grabbing it with both hands and bending forward in a stretch. Why are they so close to the front and the mirrors where everyone can see? It's at that moment I realize Mom and Nami have been doing this every Saturday for likely months now. I've been politely (and not so politely) refusing to come for ages. I try to inch back to a red drape at the very back, but Mom spots me. She gestures wildly for me to come to them. She's holding a kelly green drape just for me. Great. I'll look like the Jolly Green Giant stuck on Jack's beanstalk.

Reluctantly, I move forward and stand beside the silky fabric, all the while trying not to stare at the other, far more fit women, sitting in their knotted cradles, contorting themselves into pointed-toe warm-ups. Why is there no padding on this floor? Even for yoga we get mats, and the worst I can do is fall six inches when doing Downward Dog. I'm not suspended five feet in the air.

"Ladies!" cries the leopard-print-clad instructor. "For those of you who don't know me, my name is Amethyst. But you can call me Amee—two e's!"

Really? Did she really need to tell us her name was *Amethyst*? Or that she spells Amee with two e's? I feel like it's an unnecessary flex.

"Okay, first off, we're going to do some stretches. Everyone, I want you to reach high, high up in the sky, both hands!" Everyone stands facing the mirrors, the drape swings to their left, and they lift their arms in the air, fingers spread. Mom positions herself to my left and Nami is to my right. "Come on now, high enough to touch those dreams!"

Dreams? My dream right now is to escape to my car and see if I can find any bacon crumbs in the crevice of a floor mat. I'm sure I dropped some on the way. I frown, and Mom makes eye contact with me in the mirror. Her eyes say, *you'd better really be trying.*

"All right-y, ladies. Now we're going to make our bodies into a half moon. Reach up and take hold of your wings . . ."

Wings? I glance around and then notice that everyone is grabbing the drapes next to them. They're wings?

"And stretch forward . . ." Amee bends forward, still holding on to the drapes, curling her body into a C shape. "And walk around and stretch backward . . ." Now, Amee bends backward.

I feel like a fool, but at least I can kind of keep up.

"And now, it's time to be airborne, ladies! Step up into your cradle . . ." Amee puts one bare pointed toe onto the knot of the drape and steps up in one easy, fluid movement, as do almost all the other ladies in class. I stick my foot onto my green silk knot, which hangs at least three feet off the ground—more, even—and try to heave myself up. I realize instantly the folly of having had bacon right before this damn exercise: my hands might as well have a thick coating of Crisco. I can't hold on to the damn fabric to save my life. It's silky, my hands are greasy, and the combination is going to land me in an ambulance, on the hook for a $950 co-pay. It takes me four tries, but I finally get enough leverage to hoist myself up.

"Kick out that leg, ladies, point that toe!" Amee barks at us. "Hook your arms into your silk lines!" The instructor wraps her arms into each drape, so that the fabric is beneath her armpits, and then she does a scissor kick, her legs in near splits. "Fly, ladies! Fly!"

I can't get enough leverage to hoist myself up by my armpits, and instead, my arm just gets tangled in the fabric and I start twisting around in a circle. I am holding on for dear life, though the entire silky drape has become lubed with bacon fat. Meanwhile, Mom and Nami are flipping and twisting around like some kind of mother–daughter circus act. I, however, am just a circus. This continues on for half an hour, and for every move I'm three steps behind and look like a fool.

Then Amee does a twist and a roll, and we're all hanging backward, heads dipping low, feet supposed to be working as anchors, except that I'm too tangled to quite make the maneuver, and so I end up flopping backward off the knot, missing the hard wooden floor by mere inches, as I'm now tangled at the knees, arms dragging the floor. The blood rushes to my head. I reach up to try to save myself, but my hands are too slick, or the drape is too slippery—whatever the case, I can't get a handhold and I'm stuck. It's just a matter of time before I flop out of this headfirst on the floor below. All I can think is: I'm going to die right here. *Sora Reid loved bacon and tequila. Pork distributors across the nation mourn her loss. Her estate is suing aerial aerobics for being the most ridiculous exercise trend since pole-dancing.*

Amee sees me and frowns, hopping down off her drape to come and save me. It takes a lot of grunting and groaning before she's able to get me back into a sitting position in the knotted drapes, and so now I'm sitting there like a kid on a swing.

"There," Amee grunts. "Now, we're going to open our hearts and head into our cocoon. Let the silk line expand and envelope you into its silk bosom."

Silk bosom? I look over and see every woman in the class spreading one half of the drape and easing into it, wrapping it around their entire body and disappearing inside as if it's a kind of upright hammock. This might not be so bad. I might be able to take a nap. I spread open the drape and lean in, wondering if the thin, silky fabric can actually hold me and disappear into it, but kind of side-flop into it, so my face is pressed against the hammock. Not my best angle. I scramble up and manage to get into the fetal position, but the fabric is squeezing me into a ball.

"Now, deep breath in, and then . . . let it out . . . relax. You deserve this peace. Think of it like you're back in your mother's womb . . ."

I realize my actual mother is swinging in a slow circle in her drape cocoon next to me. This is just weird. That's all I'm saying.

I'm squished in like a fetus two weeks after its due date, and my arm *and* leg are falling asleep. I just want to get out of here and go home.

"Now, ladies, we're all done! Go ahead and hop down from your silks."

Hallelujah. I make a move to exit, but with my right side essentially numb, I struggle and fail to extricate myself from the Curtains from Hell. Through the little slit in my cocoon, I can see the other ladies have had no trouble freeing themselves. I'm just a big green blob slowly circling.

"What are you doing?" I hear my sister, but don't see her. She's somewhere behind me.

"Get out of there," Mom adds. "I know you're pouting. If you would just do the keto diet with me, you wouldn't have this problem."

"I'm not pouting. I'm stuck." Also, this has nothing to do with dieting. I reach out with my working hand and wave. It's palm up, so I can't grab anything. I'm facedown in the cocoon. "My leg is asleep. So is my arm."

"Get *out* of there. You're embarrassing us." Mom again, voice low. Mom reaches in and tries to grab me, but it just causes me to spin faster. "This is ridiculous," she says. "Come on out!"

I flounder some more. “I can’t!”

“What’s the problem here?” Amee asks, voice a tad concerned. That’s right, sister. Better check on the status of that liability insurance.

“I’m stuck.” I wave my hand again. Amee grabs it, and tugs. Nothing. I’m caught in a slow, humiliating death spiral. Nami helps her, and before I know it I’ve fallen out, awkwardly, on my left leg. My ankle twists at a weird angle. “Ow.” It doesn’t feel good.

“Are you all right?” Amee asks, face pinched.

“I’m not sure,” I manage, as I try to stand, but pain shoots up my leg and I can’t put any pressure on my foot.

“You might need to go see a doctor. Get that X-rayed.” Nami looks worried. She’s not pissed at me anymore, so that’s good? Still, all I can think of is my crappy insurance with the $12,000 deductible. And who knows how much an X-ray costs, $5,000?

“Chicago Med is right next door,” Mom suggests, referring to one of Chicago’s smaller hospitals. It’s not a big trauma center, but then again, it’s going to cost way more than just urgent care. “Why don’t we stop in there?”

“An ER?” I gasp. “Are you trying to bankrupt me? Isn’t there a pharmacy quick clinic around here?” I’m hopeful. Even though I know they’re really just a glorified school nurse. “I’m feeling better,” I say, but I still can’t put any weight on my ankle. I’m hopping on one foot.

“I’ll take you over. Now,” Mom says. Nami loops her arm under mine to help me walk.

“So, you’re not mad at me about not bringing a date to your wedding?” I finally ask, as we walk together out the door.

“Oh, don’t worry. I’m still pissed about that,” she says.

Nine

JACK

> I'm sure there are still good potential partners out there. But I just haven't met any yet.
>
> —SOLO FEBRUARY CHALLENGE

My older brother, Marc, greets me at Allie's front door. I hand him three big glittery pink gift bags with balloons attached, while I juggle the two huge cake boxes.

"Did you buy the entire party store?" Marc asks me, frowning, even as I free a single hand to give his a shake. I grip it hard, reminding him I'm not Piggy Jack anymore. He grips back harder, reminding me that in a pinch, he might still be able to strong-arm me into a closet. "Also, what the hell is on your face?" Marc frowns.

"I'm growing a beard," I tell him.

"You look ridiculous." Marc shakes his head. He helps me with the two cake boxes, taking them from my hands.

"Uncle Jack!" Allie cries in sheer delight. She jogs up to me wearing head-to-toe pink and purple, her brand-new bejeweled flashing sneakers lighting up the tile floor in a blaze of seizure-inducing light. I let the balloons hit the ceiling, and I give her a huge hug. She pulls away and squeals, "Are these for me?"

She grabs the pink gift bags in a flash. They're almost as big as she is. "Thank you, thank you, Uncle Jack!" She looks at the cake boxes. "Is that *my cake*?" she asks innocently, batting those thick, dark eyelashes.

"You better believe it is," I say with a grin. "Chocolate-chocolate!"

"*Yes!*" she cries, and pumps a fist in victory. "I love birthdays!"

Kylie, my sister-in-law, comes into the foyer then. She flashes her bright white smile, her dark hair long past her shoulders. Her mother was a nurse, born in Manila, and she met and married Kylie's father, an army sergeant from Illinois, when he was stationed in the Philippines in the early 1980s.

"Did you say thank you to Uncle Jack?" she asks Allie, who nods vigorously. "Go on and put those presents with the others." She gives me a hug. "Hi, Jack. Thanks for coming."

"Wouldn't miss it," I say.

"You did too much," she cries, shaking her head.

"Never too much for Allie." I want that cancer-fighting superhero to get everything she wants for her birthday. And I'm grateful to be here, since seeing Allie means I can't mope around about Sora. It's hard to feel bad for myself when I realize life is precious, and why spend my time moaning about setbacks when I've got my health and my family, and things aren't really, actually so bad?

"Well, your parents brought gifts, too." She nods to the other bags lining the hallway leading to the kitchen. "They just flew in this morning."

Mom finds me as I'm shrugging out of my jacket. "Jack! You look so handsome!"

"Mom." She gives me a hug so tight that I can't breathe for a minute. For a small thing, she's mighty.

We see them a little less now she and Dad retired and moved to Flagstaff. She's wearing her trademark red cardigan, sensible flats, and her bobbed salt-and-pepper hair is perfectly combed. She's half Chinese, via my grandmother, and part Portuguese, via my grandfather.

"Is that Jack? Hey! Hey!" Dad stashes his reading glasses on top of his full head of white hair. He's Irish, German, Dutch, and a little Portuguese. He gives me a handshake strong enough to crush a weaker man. "Looking fit as ever, Jack! Been hitting the weights?"

"You know I have." I grin. Dad smacks my biceps and then pretends he's hurt his hand. Classic dad move.

A pack of wild glitter-bow-wearing girls flies by.

"Look out, they bite," Dad jokes and he and Mom follow the partygoers to Allie's room. Marc and I head to the kitchen with the cakes, where every available surface is covered in pink and purple.

"Looks like a glitter bomb exploded in here." I shake my head.

"Ian's not going to like it. He's such a neat freak," Marc adds. "Beer?" he asks me, grabbing one from the fridge. I nod.

"Where is he, anyway?"

Marc frowns. "Took a shift in the ER."

"You're kidding me. He's missing Allie's birthday party?" This I can't believe.

Marc gives a one-shoulder shrug. "Yeah, the thing is, I don't even know that he was called in. I think he took the shift on purpose."

"Why? That doesn't make any sense."

"I don't know what's going on with Ian these days. But Kylie's not happy." Marc glances around, making sure our sister-in-law isn't in earshot. "I think they're having trouble."

"Why do you say that?" I ask.

"Been a tough year for them."

"That's an understatement." The pandemic patients that flooded Ian's hospital, and then Allie's cancer.

"Not sure it brought them together. That's all. Ian's working more hours, not less. I think he's avoiding being home. I think he's—"

Kylie bustles into the kitchen then and Marc clams up. We both look at her with concern.

"What?" she says, hands flying to her dark hair. "Do I have glitter in my hair?"

"No, you're good," I say, then swallow. "I was wondering where Ian was. Is he avoiding us?"

A strained look passes across Kylie's face. "He's working. Saving lives." She smiles brightly. Too brightly. Definitely something going on there. But now is not the time to press.

"Shall I get Allie's cake ready?" I ask Kylie.

She brightens, grateful for the distraction. "Yes! Please. I'll wrangle the kids."

In a few minutes, everybody's sitting around the kitchen table, the party guests with their eyes on the cake boxes. I brought two: one for Allie, and one for everyone else. Because this time last year, she could barely eat the cake we brought to the hospital. Chemo and radiation knocked out her appetite. She got two bites before she couldn't eat anymore. Not this year. Not on my watch.

I pull out the chocolate-on-chocolate cake—the round one *just* for her. Her eyes grow big as she sees that I've scrawled "Happy 5th Birthday, Allie!" in loopy pink icing—her favorite color.

I stick a candle in the top, and Mom helps light it. We all gather in the room for a rendition of the birthday song. Allie glances at each one of us, face beaming with pure joy. When we finish, I nod at her.

"Make a wish," I say.

She squeezes her eyes shut, taking the wish completely seriously, and it kills me. She opens her eyes.

"What did you wish for?" I ask.

"You know I can't tell you that!" she cries, and giggles.

"Good girl." I grin. Then I grab a fork from the table. "Go ahead," I tell her.

"Really?" She blinks.

"This is *your* cake. You don't have to share it with *anyone.* Especially Uncle Marc."

"Hey," Marc cries in protest.

"Now, who's your favorite uncle?" I ask Allie.

"Uncle Jack!" she cries.

Marc, frowning, shakes his head slowly in defeat. She hugs me and I stick out my tongue over her shoulder. Take that, Marc. Uncle Jack: 1, Uncle Marc: 0.

"Careful you don't eat all of that at once! You'll get a stomach-ache!" Kylie chides, but she doesn't really mean it. She sends me a grateful smile as she cuts pieces of the other chocolate sheet cake I brought for the guests.

Allie rips into her cake and soon it's all over her face, a big chocolate clown smile. That's a 180-degree turn from last year, when she'd been pale and bald, barely able to hold her little head up in that oversize hospital bed. I love seeing her so happy, and I'm glad she's enjoying the cake I made. Kylie hands me a piece and I stand with Mom, Dad, Marc, and Kylie as we dig in. Not bad, if I do say so myself.

"How's the bakery coming?" Dad asks me. He and Mom have been champions of the whole idea of me going out on my own.

"Good, but . . . Mal's trying to interfere."

"Sh—" Marc swallows his curse mid-sentence when he realizes Allie sits in earshot. "Mal has more issues than *Sports Illustrated*," Marc finishes and shakes his head in disapproval.

"Mal? She isn't my favorite," Mom says, because Mom never says anything truly bad about anyone.

"She's been snooping around the bakery sites. She's threatening to buy the one I'm interested in."

"She can't do that!" Kylie exclaims. "Can she?"

"Well, she is richer than God," Dad points out. Her full name, after all, is Mal Starr—yes, as in the international Starr Hotels. That's her family. Her father died years ago, and now it's just her and her mother. One day, she'll own it all. So many hotels, and so many zeroes in her bank account that the sum would bring up an error message on your average calculator.

"Is there any way to stop her from buying your bakery?" Mom asks.

We all look at Marc.

"No way to stop her from buying a property. And I'm sure she can pay cash."

"She says she'll leave the bakery alone . . . *if* I ask her out to the Golden Chef Awards," I say.

"Isn't that blackmail?" Mom asks, worried.

"Technically, extortion," Marc corrects. He shakes his head. "Well, you could just bite the bullet. Ask her."

"He can't do that!" Mom exclaims. "Not after what she's done."

There's a moment of silence as my family ponders Mal's sins.

"She's probably bluffing," I venture.

Kylie frowns. Mom wrinkles her nose. Dad stays silent.

"What would it take to get a restraining order?" Mom asks Marc, who doesn't bother to hide the smirk rolling across his face.

Marc rubs his chin, considering this. "The problem is state law says she's got to make a threat or be threatening in her behavior. Just following you around and annoying you isn't enough. And I'll be honest, Jack. Without any domestic abuse charges, it would be an uphill slog."

"So she just gets to mentally torture him? That's not fair," Kylie pipes in.

"Anyone else you can ask to the Golden Chef Awards?" Mom asks me.

Oh, sure. There are plenty of fish faces on my dating apps. Or there's . . . Sora. "Well, I ran into Sora Reid the other day."

"Oh! *Sora Reid!*" Mom claps her hands in glee. "*The* Sora Reid?"

"Sora who?" Dad asks, squinting and trying to remember.

"That girl he mooned over forever." Marc rolls his eyes. He thinks crushes are disgusting signs of human weakness.

"Oh, you were so sweet about that girl. You'd spend *hours* picking out her Valentine's card in grade school." Mom smiles softly, nostalgic at the memory. "How is she?"

"Good."

"You should ask her out!" Mom cries. "It's like . . . it's like destiny." Mom's always been the romantic one.

"I did ask her out, but she's taken a go-solo vow."

"She's flying a plane around the world by herself?" Dad asks, confused.

"No. She—"

"Just doesn't want to hang around with you?" Marc teases.

I'm beginning to regret ever bringing up Sora. Why did I, anyway?

"Give up on this girl, man," Marc says. "She's not into you. Never was." Ah, family. Can't live with them . . . and can't live with them.

Kylie clears her throat. "Jack, this cake is amazing," she says, blissfully changing the subject. She's pure gold, my sister-in-law.

"Aw, thanks, Kylie," I say. "Hey. You think I should take a piece to Ian at the ER? I could drop one by on my way home."

"I'm sure he'd like that." That strained look comes across Kylie's face again. I don't like it. Not one bit.

A few snowflakes fall on the sidewalk as I walk toward the hospital entrance from the parking garage. I've got Ian's slice of cake and also a few questions for him, like: Did he really need to miss Allie's birthday? Given last year? Look, I mean, I know the man saves lives for a living. I know he's pretty much always on call but . . . Allie's birthday? Really?

I plan to give him the cake and the third degree. I'm almost to the entrance of the ER when I see . . . Sora? She's sitting on a bench outside the ER. Her red coat is buttoned to the top and she's got a soft, fluffy white scarf wrapped cutely around her neck. Her long, wavy hair sits tucked beneath her white ski cap. She's staring intently at her phone.

What is she doing here?

Anxious bees buzz in my stomach.

I almost want to bolt. To hell with Ian and his cake. Then again, maybe I should go talk to her. My feet make the decision for me, moving me toward her.

"Sora?" She glances up at me, surprised, blinking fast.

"Oh, uh . . . Jack. Hi." She smiles at me, a smile that reaches her brown eyes and for just a second, I'm convinced she's happy to see me. But then something else comes over her face. Discomfort? Angst? Ugh. She thinks I'm going to ask her out again. She's already working out ways to tell me no.

"Look, I'm not going to bug you. Don't worry. I know you're not interested. Just wanted to say hi. That's all. I . . . uh . . . hope we can be friends." Because I think we could make about a million inside jokes. Because . . . being a friend is better than being nothing. "I'm not some weirdo stalker who doesn't respect a woman's right to tell me to get lost. Which, I realize, is exactly what a weirdo stalker would say." Nice one, Jack. "Okay. Uh. Bye!"

I'm so damn smooth.

I walk away from her bench, my ears burning.

"Wait . . . Jack . . ." Sora stands and I turn just in time to see her lose her balance. Oh no. She's flailing. She's . . . going down.

One big step and I've caught her awkwardly under one armpit, but still, I've got her, *and* I didn't even drop the chocolate cake. Bonus.

"Jack! Uh . . ." Sora tries to scramble to her feet, except one isn't working. She falls against my chest. I don't mind. Not at all. She's warm and soft and amazing. She looks up at me with those amazing doe-brown eyes. How did her eyelashes get so long?

"Sora? Are you okay?" I glance down and for the first time realize she's just wearing one shoe. And her ankle is the size of a grapefruit. She is definitely not okay.

"Uh . . . kind of." She struggles a little as I help her to her feet. Sora grins up at me after she's found her one-foot footing. She balances there precariously. I keep an arm under her just to make sure she doesn't topple.

"Thank you."

"For what? For saving this poor sidewalk from you falling on it? Just defending this frozen concrete from assault." We grin at each other. I frown at her swollen ankle. "What happened to your ankle?"

"Oh . . . uh . . . long story." Sora glances anxiously at the entrance to the ER, as if she's planning a speedy getaway. "Nami—er, my sister—thinks I should get my ankle checked out. But I've got crappy insurance and . . ."

"I've been there. And an ER visit will cost a bajillion dollars?"

Sora nods quickly. "I mean . . . who needs an ankle? Probably just sprained. Probably." She puts some weight on it and flinches, shifts her weight to me. "Ow. Still . . . a little rest, some ibuprofen . . ."

"My brother's an ER doc." I nod to the automatic glass doors. "I can ask him to check you out, off the books. If you want."

"You think he'd do that?" Sora's face brightens. I raise the piece of chocolate cake I've managed to keep hold of.

"I can bribe him with cake."

Sora raises a hopeful eyebrow. "Really?"

"Really."

A woman flies out of the ER then, shouting Sora's name. "There you are! You're on the wait list, but they say it'll be a couple of hours."

Must be Sora's younger sister, Nami. She rushes over and then skids to a stop in front of me. She glances at me, shocked, craning her neck upward like she's trying to see the top of a hundred-year-old oak. Nami is striking, too, just like her sister, but if they stood up in a beauty pageant, I'd crown Sora every time. "Uh, who's your friend?"

"This is Jack. Jack Mann. We were in grade school together. Nami was two years behind us," she tells me. Thankfully, she doesn't mention Piggy Jack.

We shake hands. Nami's the thinner, frailer version of Sora with longer, straighter hair and much more eye makeup. I vaguely remember her from grade school, waiting at the bus stop with her sister. But two years might as well have been ten back then. Fifth-graders and third-graders did not hang out.

“Jack, *nice* to meet you.” Nami glances at Sora. “And *you* told me you were swearing off men.”

“I seem to have that effect on women,” I joke.

Nami’s smart watch pings and she glances at it and gasps. “Oh my God! The cake tasting! I forgot all about it! It’s in ten minutes!”

“You don’t have to stay,” Sora says.

“I should, though.” Nami glances at me.

I realize I can actually help. Maybe. “I can stay with her.” I glance at Sora. “But only if that’s okay with Sora.”

Sora nods.

“Would you? That would be great! I don’t really want to let Mitch pick out the cake. He’s hopeless without me.”

“Are you sure you don’t mind?” Sora asks me.

“I can’t leave you alone,” I joke. “Who will protect Chicago’s sidewalks from you? Someone has to think of the taxpayers.” I offer Sora my arm.

“You’re right. We have to think of the poor sidewalks,” Sora says, as she loops her arm through mine.

Ten

SORA

> We've been programmed to believe that someday Prince Charming will just waltz into our life. Slay the dragon or whatever. But what if Prince Charming never arrives? We need to be able to save ourselves.
>
> —SOLO FEBRUARY CHALLENGE

Jack steers me into the ER waiting room and gently helps me into the only open spot, an old maroon chair covered in geometric shapes and one mystery stain, which I desperately hope isn't blood. Not too far from me, a man holds a frozen bag of peas to his eye. He flashes a grin at me, and I feel light-headed. I don't think it has anything to do with my throbbing ankle.

"Wait here and I'll go see if I can find my brother."

"Hey." I glance up at Jack. Wow, the stubble. The angled chin. Those amazing chocolate fondue eyes. Warm. Kind. For a second, I forget what I was going to say.

"Yeah?" he asks.

"Uh . . . thanks. Really."

"Not a problem," Jack says, flashing me that toothpaste-commercial grin. "I'll talk to the nurse." He leaves me to saunter up to the nursing station, his shoulders so broad they take up all the air in the room. He's really going to do it . . . save me from my exorbitant co-pay. What next? He does my taxes? Negotiates my next car loan? Makes sure I orgasm first?

Men like him don't exist.

They're like flying unicorns. Or diets that work. Or Thanksgiving dinners where no one talks politics.

They're figments of an optimist's imagination.

I glance at his back as he walks away. His jeans hug his perfect butt.

Okay. Stop looking at the man's butt. I glance up at the white-tiled ceiling. A man this perfect has to have skeletons in his closet. It's the only explanation. Otherwise, I'll need to start believing in knights slaying dragons and being able to pay off a credit card for good. Fairy tales. I glance back at Jack, who looks like he's starring in his own rom-com. Perfectly cast as the muscle-bound, baby-faced lumberjack with a heart of gold.

Then I remember the next installment of *Solo February.* A flash of the article runs through my brain.

> *I realize I spent a good part of my life waiting for a man to take care of things for me. I'm not proud of it, but it's true. For example, I've had a leaky faucet for a while. Until last year, I always counted on my dad to come over and fix things like this. I couldn't afford a plumber, so I thought I just had to live with it, until the Solo February Challenge. I looked up how to fix it*

online, and went to the local hardware store, where I bought a washer and a wrench. Fifteen minutes after I'd gotten home, I'd fixed the darn thing. All by myself.

Lesson learned a bit late, but still learned: I don't need someone to fix things for me. I can do it myself.

Yet here I am, letting Jack help me.

But I also kind of *like* Jack helping me.

Argh.

I play a game of Twenty Questions with myself. Could I be at this ER by myself? Yes, of course. Do I want to be at this ER by myself? I glance at a red-headed man two seats down from me who's periodically retching into a McDonald's bag with some unknown illness. No, I definitely don't want to be here alone.

And I remind myself, it's not my fault that my sister bailed on me, and Jack just happened to be here. I didn't ask for his help. He just . . . volunteered it. And I didn't say no.

I watch as Jack talks with the nurse for a bit. He points to the back of the room, and she glances at me, and nods.

"Asha has a room for us," Jack says when he returns to me. "She's letting us skip the line."

"How did you manage that?" I ask him, amazed.

"You'd be surprised what dropping off freshly baked scones in the ER once a month will get you." He offers his hand. I put my hand in his and his big palm dwarfs mine. I wobble on one foot.

"I think it would be easier if I carried you."

"Not easier for your back!"

Jack raises an eyebrow in challenge. "You can't weigh much."

Oh, I can. And I do. "Would you mind . . . ?"

"Wait, is this where you spike me on the ground like a football in revenge for turning you down for a date?"

Jack throws back his head and laughs. "No, I'm not going to spike you like a football."

"No hard feelings for the other day?"

"Would I be here helping you if there were?" Could it be that Jack's an . . . adult, too? Most men I've ever met were man-boys. Second-stage larvae who hold grudges.

"Okay, then." He hands me the piece of cake to hold and sweeps me up in his arms, like I weigh nothing. I cling to his big brawny neck and notice he's not even straining. Like not even a little bit. Veins in his forehead are not protruding. It's unbelievably hot. I wish he was carrying me into his bedroom and not into an ER exam room.

"See? Isn't this easier than limping around the waiting room? Asha says we can take exam room four. And Ian will be in to see us soon."

Several people turn to watch Jack carry me across the ER. I feel like a princess, and Jack, my prince. And I have to remind myself that I don't need a prince. I really don't. Even if it does feel nice.

"Are you okay? Ankle okay?" Jack dotes on me as he swings me gently through the automatic doors to the large, bustling treatment center beyond the waiting room.

"How's your back?" I ask him, worried.

"Back's fine. You're not heavy, Sora."

"Liar." With the amount of bacon I've consumed since the first of February, I know I have gained weight. But it's a Solo and Scale-Free February for me.

We find exam room four, and he takes me through the curtain. He lays me like Snow White down on the exam bed. For a second, our noses are so close that they're almost touching. His big brown eyes find mine, concerned, sweet, and gentle. Damn, those fine eyes. Those fine, fine eyes. They're big and beautiful, just like his triceps. His lips part, and for a second, I wonder what it would feel like to have that beardstache rubbing up against my face. Razor burn would be a thousand percent worth it. Could he kiss me, right here? Would I transform from a bacon-loving, bitter singleton to a pretty, pretty princess? His eyes flick down to my lips. That's it. That's it. Right there . . .

Then he meets my gaze again. He laughs a little, sheepish. "I kind of need my neck back."

And that's when I realize that I've got one hand around the back of his neck in a death grip. For all practical purposes, I'm still holding him hostage, inches from my face. Damn. I've only been without men for a little while, and already I've turned into a sex-starved maniac. I balance the plastic-wrapped plate of chocolate cake on my thighs.

"Oh, right, sorry." Not sorry. I release his thick neck and he straightens, grinning. He shrugs out of his peacoat and hangs it on the hook behind him. He straightens to his full height, before he sinks into a nearby chair.

An incoming text lights up my phone. Good. Something to do other than to worry about Jack Mann studying me like I'm a modern piece of art that defies logic and explanation.

Can't wait for the new installment! Arial texts. *We're doing so well. What's next?*

Then I'm reminded that I am supposed to be single. Solo. Independent.

I try to imagine writing this ER scene and can't. I'll have to focus on FlyFit, but I'd have to leave out Jack's gallantry.

Exercise classes are next. How we're killing ourselves to look good for dates!

Arial gives the message a thumbs-up.

"Do you run a lot? Five k's?" Jack asks me, nodding to my *k-r-ot* sweatshirt that I forgot I'm wearing, tearing my attention away from the possibility of full-time, steady employment. "That's cool you help fund the children's hospital."

I glance down at the charity patch on my sleeve. "I walk more than I jog, but I give the parents with strollers a run for their money."

Jack laughs. "Phew. I hate running. If you see me running down the street, call nine one one because someone is chasing me."

We grin at each other again.

"How's the ankle?" Jack nods at my ever-swelling appendage.

"Hurts. I blame Valentine's Day." I nod at a stupid heart-shaped cardboard decoration on the back of the door.

"Why?"

"I blame everything on Valentine's Day. It's just convenient that way."

"You don't like Valentine's Day?" He leans forward, puzzled. "Does this have to do with the fifth-grade candy incident?"

"No. Yes. Maybe." I have flashbacks to the Valentine's Day aisle. "I just hate Valentine's Day. Actually, hate is an understatement. If I could disembowel a holiday and wear its entrails as a trophy necklace I would."

"Wow." Jack whistles. "But what about all the chocolates?"

"I've never had those on Valentine's Day."

"Romantic walks? Candlelit dinners? Fresh-cut roses?" he prompts.

"My wallet was stolen on Valentine's Day last year by a date I met on Spark. That's about it in terms of excitement."

"That's terrible. Just *who* have you spent Valentine's Day with?" Jack snaps his fingers. "Oh, wait. I remember. Marley." He shifts a bit in his seat. "That explains so much."

"Yeah. He refused to celebrate Valentine's Day. He said it was against his belief system."

Jack looks astonished. "Wow. That's sad."

Oh no. Now I sound like a pathetic girl who never got a valentine. I shift on the exam table, and a twinge of pain runs up my ankle to my leg. Ugh. Stupid ankle.

"Well, the Romans decapitated Saint Valentine for marrying couples," I point out, trying to keep my ankle still. "How does it follow that we need to give each other boxes of cream-stuffed chocolates?"

"I suppose I hadn't thought about it that way before," he concedes. He stuffs his big hands in his pockets and rocks back, taking his chair onto two legs. The back of his head touches the wall.

"And did you know that Saint Valentine isn't the patron saint of love? He's the patron saint of epilepsy." I'm on a roll.

"Because love gives you seizures?" he ventures, eyeing me as he sets his chair down again on four legs.

"Exactly! I mean, do you know that Hallmark and other arms of the commercial love machine—"

"Wait . . . commercial love machine?" Jack asks, confused.

"Yes. Jewelry companies. Chocolate manufacturers. All the people trying to make money by pressuring us all to be in love."

I make a face. "They grew this hardly noticed holiday into a billion-dollar industry. Last year, one hundred and forty-five million cards were exchanged. The average person spent nearly two hundred dollars on Valentine's Day! Can you believe that?"

"So . . . this Solo February thing. It's real."

"Yes! Why?" I blink at him, confused.

"Oh, I just kind of thought you made it up. To blow me off."

"Oh . . . oh, geez. No. It is real." I pull up the entries on my phone and show him.

His eyes bulge. "Oh, it *is* real. Wow." He leans forward in his chair, intent on the screen as he scrolls through for a second, before whistling low and handing me back my phone. "You've got a following. That's cool. I mean, *really* cool." Admiration shines in his eyes.

"Yeah." I suddenly feel sheepish.

"I definitely think this should be a movie. We could call it *The Sex Cleanse*. Better than juice."

"Or . . . *Relationships: We Never Really Needed Them Anyway*."

"Or . . . *Solo February: Now You Don't Have to Share Your Chocolates Anymore*."

"Or . . . *Bacon: The Other Man Meat*."

"No, no, no . . . *Man-Dependence Day*!"

We're both cackling and I laugh so hard, I snort. Which makes Jack snort. My stomach hurts, and somehow, I've already felt like I've found my new best friend, or actually, the old one I've always had.

"You're sure you're not free the entire month of February?" he asks me. He raises his eyebrow in a challenge. How can I say no to those puppy-dog brown eyes? I mean . . . come on. But. I have to. I think about Arial. About Larry's fancy kibble. "Yeah. I'm afraid so."

Jack stares at the ceiling, as if sending up a prayer. He lets out a long sigh, his left knee bouncing. "What about March?"

"March is absolutely available." We gaze at each other, a long, meaningful look, and about a million possibilities pass between us. But before we can talk about any of them, the door to the exam room swings open, and a younger, almost-as-gorgeous-but-not-quite version of Jack walks into exam room four. Okay, so clearly Jack's genome just screams sex. It's not an accident he turned out to be so damn fine. His parents did this at least twice on purpose.

"Ian!" Jack hops to his feet and gives his brother a hug and a couple of hearty back slaps.

"Jack." Ian grins. "Who's your . . ." He pauses a bit too long. "Uh, friend?"

"Sora," Jack says quickly.

"Wait! Sora. Why is that name so familiar?" Ian asks.

"We went to school together." Jack almost mumbles the answer.

"Sora! Yes. I remember! *Sora*." He says the name with weird emphasis. Ian grins. "I was a year behind you in school. Good to see you again." He sends Jack a look. Then he glances at my swollen ankle. "Though, I wish we'd met under different circumstances. Mind if I examine you?"

I shake my head, and Ian tentatively explores the ankle with his fingers. "Ow!" I cry, and pull back.

Ian frowns. "Well, it could be broken. Or just sprained. We'll need an X-ray to be sure. How did this happen?"

"FlyFit," I mumble.

"Fly what?" Jack echoes.

Ian just shakes his head. "That gym brings us twenty percent of our business. Whoever thought hanging from silk curtains is a good idea?"

"I know, right?" I shake my head. "The whole thing is ridiculous. My mom and sister wanted me to go."

"Well, no more FlyFit. That's doctor's orders."

"No problem. I plan on never exercising again. You know, just to be safe."

Both Ian and Jack laugh, and it's like baritone chuckling in stereo. "Okay, then. How about that X-ray?"

"Oh . . . no, I can't afford that." I shake my head. I don't care how much extra I'm getting paid for *Solo February*.

Jack takes the chocolate cake from me and holds it up. "Okay, Ian, what deals can you cut us?"

Thankfully, I broke no bones. I just need rest and Advil, and Jack escorts me home in his car, a newish SUV, which he keeps pristine. The dashboard actually seems to gleam. There's no trash anywhere, and even the cupholders are swiped and *empty*. Impressive. I sit sideways a bit, the seat pressed all the way back to allow for my ankle brace. My crutches lie in the back. The brace and crutches I got for free. Guess it really does pay to know the right people. Ian told me to ice and elevate the ankle and take a dose of ibuprofen. Even though we cut in line, the afternoon has slipped away, and now dusk quickly descends on the city. Jack parks the car, rushes around back to get my crutches, and then meets me on the passenger side, offering an arm to help me out.

"Are you seriously always this nice?" I ask as he helps me up the stoop of my vintage apartment building.

Jack laughs. "What do you mean?"

"I mean . . . you give out free tortes *and* free medical care?"

"Well, why not be generous." He grins.

"Even after I accused you of grand theft candy."

He laughs. "Hey, looks like we were *both* victims of that Valentine's Day kindergarten party. I was framed."

I snort. "Indeed. But now you're driving me home? I mean, you're too nice."

"You think I was going to let you brave the icy sidewalks alone with crutches? After we've already established that I'm on the Save Chicago Sidewalks task force?"

I've never been more grateful for Jack's strong arms. For one, the management company failed to shovel the new snow off the sidewalk, so there's a three-inch layer of snow over the already-frozen two inches of ice. I plant one crutch and it instantly loses traction.

"Here, hang on to me." Jack offers his neck and I throw an arm around it. He takes the crutches and holds them while steering me to the stoop. I lean against him, digging out my front keys. I slide the key in the lock and turn. As I push the door open, my boot catches on the mat.

"Whoa," Jack cries, and steadies me with his big strong hands. "We don't need another trip to the ER today."

"No," I say, and laugh.

"Can I?" Jack asks, holding out his arms.

"I'm on the third floor. I can't let you carry me up there."

"I can't let you hop up there, either. It'll take days. I've got other things to do today," he teases. "Come on."

I nod, and Jack whisks me into his arms again. Well, damn, I could get used to this. I've got my arms wrapped around the man's neck and all I can think is: Mama like.

Also, he smells like Mexican hot chocolate. Spicy, sweet goodness. He doesn't break a sweat as he hauls me up my apartment stairs. He even easily avoids the ornately carved oak staircase banister, somehow making sure my feet don't clip the square baluster at each landing.

Just as I'm soaking up all this chivalry, a door bursts open, and Pam sticks her nosy tangerine-orange self out. "Sora? What the hell?" she asks.

Jack whirls, me in his arms.

"I sprained my ankle," I tell her. "He's just helping me up to my condo. That's all."

"Oh." She eyes Jack with suspicion, as if trying to match his face to the FBI's most-wanted list, which I am sure she regularly memorizes.

"This is Jack." I nod to him.

"I'd shake, but I have my hands full."

"I see that." Pam purses her lips in disapproval. "Well, just so you know, if there will be strangers in the building *regularly,* you'll need to let the condo board know."

Since when? "Really? Why?"

"We're cracking down on vacation rentals because I'm a single woman now that Thom isn't here anymore. And *my* safety comes first."

Nice how I'm not included in that.

"I guess you can't be too careful these days," Jack pipes in cheerfully, undeterred.

"Hey . . . one more thing," Pam adds, almost as an afterthought. "I, uh . . ." She backtracks. "You started that #GoSolo thing?"

"Yeah?" I ask, almost fearing what she'll say.

"A few of my friends are doing it." Pam hesitates. "I think they're being extreme or whatever, but . . . they seem to like it. They rave about it."

"Really?" This might be the closest thing to a compliment Pam's ever given me.

Jack clears his throat, and then I realize he's still holding me, patiently, in his arms. Right. There's this little bit of a problem about me doing #GoSolo and being cradled by the sexiest, sweetest man I've ever met.

"But isn't he . . . against the rules?" Pam glances at Jack, a frown bending her mouth. "I don't know much about it. *I* haven't read any of it, or anything. Not my cup of tea."

No, of course not. She makes it sound like dating problems are for lesser people.

"But . . ." She stares at him suspiciously. Annoyance flares in me. Pam does not get to tell me how I should do Solo February.

"Good to see you, Pam," I cut her off. "We've got to go."

She stares at us a beat, and then eventually ducks back into her condo as we continue up to my floor. Soon enough, I've forgotten about Pam. It's hard to worry about my downstairs neighbor when Jack is cradling me gently to his chest. When we reach my door, he eases me gingerly down on my feet. I unlock my door and slide it open. I hesitate, hand on the knob. I glance up at Jack.

He stares at me as if he's considering adding me to his

dessert menu. Just slather some whipped cream on me, and I'll happily hop on your plate, mister.

"Sorry about my neighbor. She's just . . . a lot."

"It's fine." He shrugs.

"And thanks again. For the ER visit. For the door-to-door service."

"It's not a problem." And looking at him, right in his warm brown eyes, I believe him. That he really doesn't mind helping me.

"I—"

"Hey—"

We both speak at the same time. Then we both giggle awkwardly. I want to climb him like a tree and ride him like a tire swing.

"Go ahead," Jack says, a blush creeping on his high cheekbones.

"I just want to say thank you. I mean, really," I say. "And . . . uh . . ." In the heat of my moment of gratitude, I reach up on the tiptoe of my good foot and kiss him.

Brazenly.

Before I can even think about it. Because this man has carried me up three flights of stairs. Because he's the sexiest man I might have ever met, and because he's *nice,* like, deep, *good person* nice, and because damn it, I want to. I've wanted to kiss this man since I first saw him frosting baked goods at Margo's.

It's brief. It's closed-mouthed, but I still feel a bolt of lust run straight through me. Or maybe that's static electricity. In any case, I kiss him, and then I withdraw. He blinks at me, surprised, but I duck into my apartment like a coward, and leave him standing there on my doormat.

Eleven

JACK

Going solo might not always be easy, but it will always be worth it.

—SOLO FEBRUARY CHALLENGE

Sora Reid kissed me.

On the lips.

Sora freakin' Reid *kissed* me.

I think I might have stood there on her door mat for a good five minutes, trying to process what happened. Wondering if I just imagined it happened at all.

My little inner five-year-old does an awkward celebratory somersault. My inner Neanderthal gives that adorable, pudgy kindergartener a high five.

Yes.

So, I was right. We do have a connection. Something. Still, I try not to read anything into it. I shouldn't get my hopes up. She's still doing that Solo February thing. Right? Isn't she?

Then again, she did smash her face against mine. How can I *not* read something into it?

"Maybe it was just a pity kiss," says Ian, on his lunch break later that week. It's the day before Valentine's Day and I'm trying to convince Ian to spend tomorrow doing something romantic with his wife. But he seems too intent on trying to distract me.

"Thanks, man. That does not help me." We're eating sandwiches at the place across the street from the hospital. We're sitting at a four-top near the front windows.

"I'm just saying that you basically got her out of at least a grand's worth of ER expenses. Could've just been a pity kiss."

"Didn't feel like a pity kiss," I grumble. Felt more like a *real* kiss. I know the difference. Besides, I've been wondering what that woman's lips tasted like ever since I first considered that girls might *not* be gross and covered in cooties. Now I know: vanilla. The woman tastes like a vanilla crème brûlée. Don't know if it was her lip gloss or just her, but she tastes like perfection.

"I don't know, man." Ian shakes his head. He takes another big bite of his sandwich, a bit of turkey falling onto the paper wrapping he's spread across the bright yellow plastic table. "Why waste your time with a head case? I mean, she's pretty. I mean, *really* pretty, but just because you knew her way back when doesn't mean you *know* her, know her. She's doing this 'solo' thing or whatever? And it sounds a little crazy. Or bitter. Or both."

"I don't think she wants to hate men. I just think she's had bad luck." And I know a thing or two about bad luck. I nibble on a chip.

"No. It's not bad luck. She's hot. And crazy. Which, given the fact you spent so much time with Mal, I'd say is your type."

"Hey." I nudge my younger brother, but he just laughs. "She's not crazy. She loves bacon, that's all."

"Sounds like she wants to marry bacon." Ian raises an eyebrow, nodding down at the open screen on my phone. Maybe it was a mistake to show him some of those articles.

"Who doesn't?" I ask, defensive.

"Don't do that threesome," my brother warns. "You can seriously still get trichinosis."

I laugh and shake my head and take another bite of Italian beef.

My phone pings. A DM from Sora? I open it eagerly.

There is a photo of her signed fifth-grade yearbook.

And my deranged drawing of a bee.

I snort a laugh. It's perfect. "She might be the perfect woman," I say, showing Ian the picture.

"What the hell is that? A sheep with rabies?"

"It's a bee. *Bee* cool. Get it? That's my drawing. From when we were kids." I type off a quick response.

That's not even my best work. You should see some of my Pictionary masterpieces of 1999.

"You are such a nerd." Ian shakes his head.

A frazzled-looking nurse bursts through the door then, sending a blast of arctic air to our table. She sends us a look of apology and I realize she's without her coat. Probably thought she could sprint the distance from the hospital entrance to the sub shop without bothering to get her coat, but the wind chill outside is negative two degrees. Good luck with that.

We chew in silence for a bit. The nurse gets a hastily made sandwich and then sprints back out into the cold again. I watch her run back to the hospital through the window.

I'm going to have to bring up Kylie and why he skipped Allie's birthday party sometime. I hate getting into this stuff, but if Marc does it, he'll come in heavy-handed like a military dad and Ian will clam up. "So, what was up with Saturday?"

"What do you mean?" Ian glances up, dark eyes meeting mine and looking wary.

"Allie's birthday. How come the double shift?"

Ian chews and says nothing for a long while. I almost think he might not answer and just pretend I never asked the question.

"Extra hours come with the job," he says, studying his turkey sandwich. "You know that."

"Yeah." I nod, deliberately not mentioning that I know he volunteered for the shift. That would just make him defensive. "I bet someone would've covered for Allie's birthday." Everyone at the hospital knows Allie, knows about her struggles. They even all chipped in to buy her balloons on her birthday the year before.

Ian takes a sip of his cup of water, and drops into a moody silence. I don't want to press. If Ian wants to tell me what's on his mind, he will.

I take another bite and we munch in silence for a minute.

"Things have been hard this year, for both of us," Ian says eventually, studying the open sandwich wrapper on the table as if it's a picture roll of all the memories of the last year. "And sometimes . . . I mean . . . it feels like we're just waiting for the other shoe to drop."

"What do you mean?" I take a sip of my Coke and wait.

"You know there's a twenty percent chance that cancer comes back. A one-in-five chance."

"Yeah? So there's an *eighty* percent chance it doesn't. I'll take those odds."

Ian shakes his head, looking grim. "Yeah, but I just don't know if I can do it again. Allie was it, you know that. First time I saw that kid, I was gone, hook, line, and sinker. And last year . . . when we almost lost her . . ." Ian swallows the rest of his sentence and drops his sandwich down on the wrapper.

"But you didn't lose her."

"Yeah, but this will hang over her for the rest of her life. And then who knows what the hell that chemo will do to her development." Ian grits his teeth together and meets my gaze, eyes full of pain. "You know they don't have good medicine for children. We use adult drugs on them and just hope for the best. We need more research."

"Yeah." Ian often went down this rabbit hole, and I get it. Frustrated the hell out of all of us about how much we ought to be doing to help find better treatments for kids with cancer. Hell, maybe even one day cure the damn thing. "So you're worried about Allie. That's why you're spending more time at the hospital? I'm just trying to understand."

"I guess. I don't know." He gazes out at the street as cars rush by, a few of them pulling into the parking garage of the hospital across the street. "I think part of me is just scared."

"Man, you're the bravest guy I know. You take care of *gunshot* victims. Remember that time you said you were elbow-deep in that guy's chest? And don't even get me started on the pandemic. You went in to work every day, without complaint, even though it meant you slept in an RV away from your family so Kylie and Allie wouldn't get sick. You are brave as hell."

But I know what he means. He means he's scared of losing Allie, scared the cancer will come back, and scared to let his family get too close because that means the possibility of losing them all over again. We both stare out the window, watching the people bustle in and out of the hospital. Workers but patients, too. You can identify the relatives of the patients. They look worried, anxious.

"I'm not that brave." He glances at me. "Just braver than you, and that's not hard."

"Hey!" I shove his shoulder.

"Just saying—didn't you keep the closet light on to sleep until high school?"

"Middle school."

"Same difference," Ian says, and laughs. He stares out the window and watches a bus rumble by, a big puff of black smoke coming out of the back.

"Look, why don't you take my sweet sister-in-law out for dinner tomorrow night. I'll babysit," I offer. "Try to reconnect or something? You know?"

"You'd babysit Allie." He studies me, not quite sure the offer is real.

"Of course! She can even paint my nails like last time." That was one helluva mess. But I can't say no to that kid.

"Okay. Maybe. I'll ask Kylie if she wants to go out."

"She'll want to go out." I remember her strained smile at Allie's birthday party. She wants help. Wants a lifeline. I can feel it.

I finish the last of my sandwich and wad up the empty wrapper. "What's that quote from *Shawshank Redemption* you used to always say?"

"Better get busy living, or get busy dying," he says.

"That's the one." I grin. The high-pitched ambulance siren blaring down the street draws our attention then, and the big white box arrives with flashing red and blue lights, pulling up to the emergency entrance of the hospital. Ian tosses his trash in a nearby can.

"Well, that's my cue," he says. "Work calls. Thanks for lunch, man." He shrugs into his jacket. "What are you up to this afternoon?"

"I'm going to drop by Sora's place. See if she needs anything." The bee text made me hopeful she might be up for company.

Ian clucks his tongue in disapproval. "You sure that's a good idea?"

"No. But she did sprain her ankle. She might need soup or something."

"Soup is for colds." Ian rolls his eyes.

"You know what I mean."

"What I think you mean is you're hoping for another pity kiss."

I DM Sora to let her know I'm in her neighborhood. Just your friendly *Hey, let me know if you need anything* DM. *Or, if you want an impromptu game of Pictionary that you will definitely win, I'm ready and able.*

She pings me back instantly.

> *Pictionary is a yes, but only if alcohol is involved, because I only think I can draw when I'm drunk. And . . . maybe ibuprofen? I'm out! I'll pay you back.*

I type *The first bottle of ibuprofen is free. Second will cost you.*

I head to a drugstore near her condo, grab an industrial-sized bottle of ibuprofen, and as I do, I see the Valentine's aisle. I glance around at the fancy cream-filled chocolates in big red heart-shaped boxes and wonder if they have an "I Hate Valentine's Day" assortment. Flavors? Bitter Lemon. Dark Chocolate of Despair. Forever Single Strawberry. Never Getting In My Bed Buttercream?

Maybe chocolates aren't such a bad idea. Besides, thanks to Valentine's Day being this week, they're on sale. Buy one, get one 50 percent off. I think she needs at least two. Plus, okay, didn't she have a dog? I could get her that dog toy, the one at the end of the aisle that has the big plush heart with the white hands and feet. Maybe watching her pit-mix tear into it will amuse her?

I grab the chocolates and dog toy along with an impulse-buy purchase of a bottle of red wine.

Outside, the sun has slunk beyond the horizon, even though it's not yet 4 P.M. Welcome to winter in Chicago. In less than a block, I'm standing at the buzzer of her vintage apartment building. The outer door has a full-length window, showing the silver mailboxes, and it's big enough for someone to have left their bike.

I hit the buzzer next to *Reid*.

I wait. A cold February chill whips up, swirling the patch of snow by my feet. I shiver as I hear Sora's voice crackling through the speaker.

"Hello?"

"Hey. Uh. It's me. Jack. I've got that ibuprofen!"

"Oh! Yes!"

The buzzer sounds. A bleating-goat call from heaven. I shake off the shock and grab the front door and swing it open.

I kick snow from my black boots on the rug then head up the stairs to her place. I get to her door and knock gently.

I hear frantic scurrying around inside, and a dog's unmistakable bark, and then what sounds like the opening and shutting of a cabinet or door and mumbled curses. Then she swings open the door looking flushed and slightly sweaty, wearing her long, dark hair up in a high ponytail, her faded blue T-shirt not doing much of a job covering her black leggings. She's got fuzzy socks on, and it looks like her ankles are almost the same size. She grins and her brown eyes meet mine, bright and happy. Right then, I am very, very glad I came. She eyes the bags in my hands with surprise.

"I . . . got more than just ibuprofen. Figured you might need some chocolate. Or wine. Especially if we're busting out the Pictionary."

She hesitates a moment, glancing at the bags. Crap. Did I overstep? But the texts were flirty. Or so I thought. Am I misreading everything again? Then I realize she's laser-focused on the heart-shaped boxes of chocolate. "You brought Valentine's chocolate."

"You said no one has bought chocolates for you before and that's a crime. I mean, you can burn it if you want. But it's the good kind." I nod at the brand. "Or we could also just have wine instead." I offer up the bottle. She blinks fast, still confused.

"You brought all this. For me."

"And this—" I grab the plush dog toy from the bottom of the bag. "For your rescue dog."

Sora bites her bottom lip, and for a second, I think she might cry. Then she moves in and lets her big pit-mix hedge his way out. Woah, he's huge. Stout. Intimidating looking. He could take a bite out of me without really trying.

"Larry's a softie, really," Sora reassures me.

"Oh, hey, boy." I offer my hand, but he reaches up to sniff and misses me by at least two inches. It's then I realize that his perpetual wink is because he's missing an eye.

"He's not good spatially. He never adjusted to losing an eye—raccoon, the shelter said," Sora explains, and so I move my hand so he can sniff it. Then I hold up the round plush toy and figure I'll toss it to him, and maybe he'll catch it.

"Here, boy. Here! Catch it!" I toss it in the air, and he jumps up to get it, but he misses by a good six inches.

"He can't catch things very well. Or fetch," she adds, as Larry scrambles to pick up the plush, but misses it time and again. Poor dude.

Taking pity on him, I lean in and pick it up, then manage to put it right in his giant, open mouth. "Here you go." Larry happily trots off to a back corner of the apartment. "I don't want to intrude. I just wanted to see if you're okay."

Sora studies me. "Want to come in?"

"Can I? Or does that violate Solo February?"

"Get in here before I change my mind," Sora teases, and I hop to it, following her into her modest vintage condo. "Shall we have wine?" she asks.

"I think it's a must."

The kitchen looks newish, but rarely used, as the stove and oven seem pristine. She limps over to the gray cabinets and retrieves a couple of wineglasses and then a bottle opener from a drawer.

"Let me do that. You rest your ankle."

She laughs a little. "I'm fine."

"You may not have broken anything, but you need to rest." I move closer to reach for the corkscrew, and as I do, I brush her arm. She flails a little, and I worry her weak ankle will bring her down. I steady her with one hand, and she glances up at me, eyes grateful. And sexy as hell. Damn, but . . . those lips. Big, plump, kissable. And now I know they taste like crème brûlée. And for a second, everything stops, and we just stare at each other, the pure desire taut between us like a guitar string.

She's got to feel that. She can't help but feel it. Right?

Then I remember she's standing on a hurt ankle.

"How about I help you to the couch?" I offer.

"I can manage," she says, limping a little. But I follow her, acting as her crutch, just in case. She sinks into the blue-gray cushions and smiles up at me. "Thank you." Her voice is barely a whisper. I reluctantly leave her to uncork the wine.

"I like your place," I say, glancing around her small but neat living room. It works as living room/dining room and part of the open kitchen. A compact blue sectional and small matching armchair sit in the middle of the room, and a jungle of plants lines the small hallway to the kitchen. She doesn't have much on her walls, and there's an unpacked box or two making the place feel a little like she just arrived, but not in a bad way, I think. Her flat-screen TV stands on a glass console table to the left. Windows line the back of the room, and a door to the right leads to what seems like a bedroom, as I can just see the white corner of an unmade bed. The exposed red brick on the wall behind the couch makes the room feel warmer and brighter, as does the pine floor. I see a small silver laptop open on her kitchen table.

"You writing another *Solo February* post?" I ask.

"Yeah," she says, and nods. "This one's about the joy of spending time with friends instead of . . . on dates."

"Oh. That's good." I guess it's good. Are we friends? I was hoping for more than friends, but I'll take friends.

I fill her oversized wineglasses with two generous pours and head to the sofa. Since it's an L-shaped sectional, I take the shorter end of the L.

"To healing quickly," I say, offering up my glass for a toast.

"Amen," she says, and leans forward to clink my glass. I take a sip of the drugstore wine, relieved to discover it's drinkable. She doesn't seem to mind it either as she takes a big gulp. We stare at each other for a small beat of awkward silence.

"Want a chocolate?" I offer up the first giant red heart full of delicacies.

She opens the lid of the giant heart, tapping her finger on her plump, pink lips. "Which one?" she debates, as she scans all the options—light, dark, and white truffles, all with mystery fillings.

"Well, you should eat them all," I say. "If this is your first true box of Valentine's chocolates, then I think, by law, you have to try them all."

"Well, I have bought some myself. On February fifteenth, when they're seventy-five percent off."

"Full-price chocolates taste better. And gifted chocolate? That's always the best. I mean, it's just basic science."

Sora laughs, her head tilted back, face a perfect heart shape. She takes one and bites into it. "Mmmm. Salted caramel. I think you're right." She glances at me through her thick, pretty lashes. "Want to try it?" she offers up the half-bitten chocolate.

"Hell, yes."

And then she feeds it to me.

I taste the burst of salty sweetness.

"Delicious." I wash it down with wine and she does the same, and before I know it, we've eaten more than half the damn box, all while debating the merits of nougat versus caramel. We've also drained our wineglasses and refilled them again. A warm buzz sinks into my brain. I'm feeling more relaxed. That's probably a dangerous thing.

"Can I ask you a question?" I say, after we've both shared a new milk chocolate almond truffle. We've settled into the couch, Sora laying on the long part of the L, her feet toward me, swollen ankle elevated on a pillow, ice pack on it (my idea), and me, back against the short end of the L. My left arm sits inches from her socked feet. It feels comfortable. Cozy. Like we could relax together forever.

"Sure," she says, licking the chocolate off her finger.

The bees are back in my brain, buzzing, making me feel light-headed. It's because Sora might have short-circuited all the neurons in my frontal lobe.

"I know you vowed to go solo this month."

She tenses a little. "Yeah?"

"So does that mean you're not dating . . . that other guy?"

"What other guy?" She straightens a little, putting the chocolates on her distressed driftwood coffee table.

I think about Lance Bass and how his hand was cupped possessively on her ass in the produce section.

"Soul patch/shell necklace guy?" I know I shouldn't bring him up, but I can't help it. I need to know.

Sora's eyes grow as round as dishes. "Dan? How did you know about him?"

"I saw you two together. At Margo's."

Now Sora sits up, back ramrod straight. "What?"

"I saw you—and Dan?—in the produce section. Back around Christmas. You two seemed friendly. I thought . . ." I drift off.

But she's leaning ever closer to me now, hunched over her legs. "Wait, you saw me *over a month ago* and you didn't say hi?"

And this is why I should just keep my mouth shut. "Well, I wasn't one hundred percent sure it was you." Lie. Terrible lie. "And . . ." I was a chickenshit who didn't have the courage to say hi. "And . . . I don't know, you were in and out. Quickly."

"I was?"

"Yeah. But that guy. I thought . . . you could do better."

"You did?" She falls back into the couch cushions, arms above her head in surrender. "You and me both. Turns out he was married. Lied to me about it. Then I thought I would just go along with it. Be his weeknight mistress or something." She covers her face with both hands and blows out an exasperated breath. I already had a low opinion of Soul Patch but now it's even lower. The snake.

"You deserve better than that. Much better. You are *no* man's side chick."

Her eyes grow wide in surprise, as if no man has told her this before.

"So the first time you saw me was with Dan? Not when you gave out free tortes?"

"Yeah." I'm already in deep, so why not take the plunge the

rest of the way down? "You were wearing a red wool coat and knee-high black boots. Red lipstick, too. Looking downright beautiful, actually."

Sora's mouth opens ever so slightly in surprise. She studies me. "So, you're stalking me?" she teases.

I shrug. "Kind of." I meet her gaze. The wine buzzing in my veins makes me feel bold.

"Sounds like you kind of have a crush on me, Jack Mann."

Now's my moment. Now's the time. I've got to tell her.

"Actually, this is going to sound dumb . . ." I take a deep breath. "I actually had a crush on you in kindergarten."

"What?" She nudges my hip with her good foot. She's grinning.

"Yeah, well . . . I kind of had a crush on you . . . all through grade school."

Her grin fades, ever so slightly. "You did?" She shifts and her ice pack falls off her ankle. She doesn't notice, so I reach over and grab it, placing it back gingerly.

"Yeah." I stare at the ceiling. This is either going to be the best thing I ever did in my life, or the worst. There's no in between. "One time, I think it was first grade, or maybe second, you told Boyan Debnar he was a jerk who shouldn't bully people."

"I did?"

"Yeah, he was singing that damn Piggy Jack song in the cafeteria line. You told him he was a jerk and to stop it."

"I don't remember that."

"I do. You were the first kid to stick up for me. Maybe the only kid." I glance at Sora, who looks as if she wants to hug me. "Ever since then, anytime I saw you, it felt like my stomach was full of bees."

"Is that why you drew one on my yearbook?"

I hadn't put that together before. "Yeah, probably."

She laughs but then grows serious. Her brown eyes focus on mine, and for a second, I feel like I can swim in them. "Does it still feel like it's full of bees?"

"Yes. Big ones. Angry." Humming loudly in my ears. Or maybe it's the wine. No, I think, looking at Sora's amazing brown eyes. It's Sora. Definitely Sora. "So imagine how I feel when my grade-school crush walks into my grocery store."

Sora laughs. "Eats all your tortes and then gets horribly embarrassed by her ex-husband and his new girlfriend. And then accuses you of theft. Yeah, I'm sure you were *very* glad to see me."

"Actually, that day, I realized . . ." I take a deep breath. Fine. "It's not just that I *used to* have a crush on you. I kind of . . . well . . . I still do."

Now things get serious. Sora stares at me, without blinking. Is she going to tell me to go to hell? Have I overstepped?

But then, she moves slowly over to my side of the couch, crawling, almost like a sleek lioness on the prowl, looking like the sexiest damn predator I've ever seen.

"Maybe I have a crush, too," she tells me, her voice low in her throat. She meets my gaze and then focuses her attention on my lips. And something in the air changes. It feels . . . more dangerous, suddenly. I can feel her breath on my face, smell her crème brûlée lip gloss.

And then she presses her lips to mine.

Twelve

SORA

I'm not saying I hate men. On the contrary, I love them too much.

—SOLO FEBRUARY CHALLENGE

So, Jack might be patient, but I am not. I've been called many things, but "reasonable" and "patient" and "mature" aren't any of them. And that's why I'm trying to eat Jack's face off because he's the sexiest man I've ever met. I may have impulse-control problems. Plus, I have just enough wine buzzing around in my brain to think it's a damn fine idea. Because . . . this super-hot, super-sexy man tells me I'm beautiful and he's had a crush on me? Since kindergarten?

And he noticed me back in December. What the hell? I'd been so busy being distracted by Mr. Wrong that I'd completely missed Mr. Right.

My tongue lashes his and all I can taste is him and wine and chocolate. It's like an orgasm in my mouth. I'm lying on top of his hard body and his hands are roving down my curves, and I'm having the teenage make-out party of my life. And this is what I've been missing since February first. It's like having that first bite of chocolate after starving oneself on a trendy diet. And now I know that the thing I've been depriving myself of is the very thing I need to *live.* The very thing that makes life worth living.

I break away, gulping in air. I shouldn't do this. I've been encouraging people all around the world to take a break from love for this month, and here I am, breaking my own rules.

"Are you sure you want to do this?" he pants, hands firmly on my hips. "What about Solo—" But I hush him with a finger to his lips. I am not going to think about Solo February anymore tonight.

"Yes, I want to do this," I say. "Hell, yes."

I dive down for another kiss, and our lips meld together as if they're two halves of the same heart-shaped chocolate box. I squirm against his body, and he groans, gripping my hips tighter, need in his fingertips. I feel that need quivering through my own body like a living, breathing thing, like a force that won't be contained. I've wanted this man since I first laid eyes on him at Margo's. Now he's beneath me on my own couch, pinned by my body, and I want to keep him prisoner there for the rest of his life.

Before I know it, I've ripped off my T-shirt and it's on my floor, and in another second, the lacy bralette comes off, too. Jack stares at my nipples with a kind of reverence usually reserved for fine art in museums, as he first kisses one and then the other. Damn, I love a man who knows his way around an areola. I shiver beneath the man's expert mouth and hands.

I fumble with his shirt buttons, and he sits up, with me tumbling back a bit on the couch. He literally *rips* his own shirt off, the buttons pinging off and scattering across the wood floor and I think I might just die of want right there. Can this man get sexier? Then I see his bare chest, strong, defined pecs, big, muscular shoulders, the kind I want to bite *right now*. Just a little nibble. That's all, I tell myself. He's got miles of muscle, and he's stout, too, his abs not the no-carbs, no-fun, ridged kind, but the not-too-skinny, not-too-fat, not-gonna-make-you-feel-unworthy kind. In short, he's 100 percent grade-A *that man*.

I feather kisses down his neck, while he cups my girls with reverence. I haven't had a man this enamored, this worshipful of my body since I don't know how long. If ever.

"You're gorgeous," he whispers in my ear. "Completely gorgeous."

The words feel like liquid molten lava straight to my core. They light me up from the inside, powering up all my buttons, sending electric sparks to every nerve ending in my body. Jack stands then, and I fight the urge to zip down his fly and show him just how much I appreciate him, but before I can, he reaches down, and puts my hands behind his neck. His gaze meets mine.

"Let's go to the bedroom," he says, and then he reaches down beneath my butt and lifts me, and I let him. I wrap my legs around him, only vaguely aware of the fact that I'm wearing only tights and a thong beneath.

"Yes," I croak. "Let's go."

I'm kissing him, our bare chests pressed together as he carries me toward my bedroom. Jack kicks open the door like a lumberjack who doesn't have the time or patience to use a doorknob. I only vaguely register Larry as he scrambles out of the way and runs into the living room. Jack kicks shut the door, and lays me down like a queen he plans to worship.

He stands at the foot of the bed and slowly unzips his fly, his jeans dropping to the floor. And I see him.

In all his bare glory. And there is lots. And lots. Of glory.

So.

Much.

Glory.

I push myself up on my elbows, and my jaw drops so hard I can hear the joint pop.

Did I mention the glory?

"Is this okay?" he asks me. And I know he means sex. In general. Because he's getting consent, but it also sounds like he's asking if his glory is okay.

"It's more than okay," I manage. Only then do I remember the condoms I keep in my bedside drawer. "Uh . . . I've got condoms . . ." I try to reach for the drawer, preparing myself for the backlash. The "I don't like condoms" or "Do we have to" or "I really don't like the feel of them" discussions that usually follow my attempts to practice safe sex. Most guys cave after small pushback, but I had one who outright refused. "I don't believe in them," he had said, as if condoms were like Santa Claus or organized religion. There's nothing to *believe* in. They're latex. They protect against a bevy of STDs. But, no, he was adamant. So I showed him the door.

Jack, however, doesn't even miss a beat. He reaches for the drawer and grabs one silently, one of only a few magnum-sized swimming around in the drawer from a gag gift I got from

Nami's bachelorette party last month. I never really thought I'd ever use them, except maybe to try my hand at making balloon animals. In seconds, he's got it unsheathed and rolled down his impressiveness.

I already knew Marley was on the small side. And Dan was about average, but this . . . this in front of me. Hell, it's a whole other category. Super-sized.

"Are you sure you want to do this?" he asks me. "I just want to be sure you're sure." He hesitates as he stands between my spread legs, his glory completely at attention.

"Yes," I say. "Oh, hell, *yes.*"

I wake up the next morning feeling wrapped in the perfect cocoon of snuggly warmth and realize that Jack has his beefy arms around me in bed, spooning me from behind, and there's literally not a better feeling in the world. I'm sore, the very best kind of sore, from a night filled with the best sex I've ever had in my life. The kind of sex that makes me realize for all my adult life, I've been doing it wrong.

With the wrong people.

Because *this* sex, this amazing, electric sex, should never, ever be boycotted.

I close my eyes and lean back into Jack's strong, muscled chest and inhale, listening to his deep, rhythmic breaths. He's still sleeping. Then my phone dings with an incoming message.

I think about ignoring it. Why break this beautiful moment? Why risk rousing Jack? But curiosity gets the best of me. I glance at the face of my phone and see Arial's name.

> *Hey, Sora. Great news. Solo February is going bananas. I've got your extra-hefty freelance check. Thought I'd stop by and give it to you in person? I can drop by your condo on my way to work?*

Wait. What?

Before I can text back that I'm indisposed, my buzzer sounds.

It sounds like a goose dying a horrible death, and also, taking my dreams of a full-time magazine writing gig with benefits down the drain with it. Larry barks, too, a reflex to hearing the buzzer. I glance behind me, at Jack's big, naked body.

I am pretty sure if Arial sees Jack in my bed . . . that check will be canceled. Immediately.

I sit up, feeling like a cold bucket of reality just fell on my head, as I scramble to reach for my clothes on the floor. Then hobble on my still-tender ankle to the door buzzer, hitting the intercom. Larry meets me in the living room, trying to get to the door, but running into the small foyer table instead, making the glass bowl where I keep my keys and mail wobble.

"Hello? Arial?"

"Yes? Can you buzz me up?" she answers.

"I'm . . . I'm not dressed." That's an understatement. I have no underwear on and only my oversize T-shirt, which, I notice, is inside out *and* backward. Plus, my condo smells like sex and wine. Larry barks once more. Even he agrees it's a bad idea. "So sweet of you to bring the check by, but you can just leave it on the mailboxes!"

"Oh?" Arial sounds disappointed. "But I've got some other news to tell you. I'll just be one second? I promise?"

Damn it. I can't tell my boss no. That would seem weird. But . . . I have a naked man in my condo, which I do *not* think she'd appreciate. I hit the buzzer, and then I notice my bedroom door is open a crack, and somehow, Jack *still* seems to be asleep because I see his big, bare man foot hanging off the corner of my bed. I rush over and close the door, and by the time I get to the front door, I hear Arial on the steps, and then there's a quick rap on my door. I swing it open, holding it like a shield in front of me.

Arial's eyes widen in surprise. "I am so sorry? I know you're getting dressed. I just have the check, but I also have super fun news that I wanted to deliver in person!"

"You really didn't have to come." Wouldn't a Zoom call and a stamped envelope have done it?

"I wanted to? Because *Solo February* is like, an amazing smash? They want you to go on *Let's Talk*!"

I blink. That's my mom's favorite morning show. I think it's every mom's favorite morning show. They offer a book club, a Steal this Deal! segment, and real-time makeovers for studio audience members at least once a month.

"They do?"

"Yes! Oh, and here's your check?" She hands a manila envelope through the cracked door. I take it.

"Oh, that's so sweet. So thoughtful. Okay, well, bye!" I swipe it out of her hands and try to close the door.

"Wait! Can I come in?"

"Uh. No!" Arial jumps. "I mean, my stomach. It's not feeling so great. I'm a little hungover."

"It won't take long?" Arial promises. "I thought maybe we could chat about what you could wear? I mean, if you need to borrow something from The Closet, I have tons of options."

She glances over my shoulder into my apartment. I look backward, too, afraid. That's when I see . . . the two empty wineglasses on my coffee table. And the overturned boxes of Valentine's Day candy . . . and even worse, Jack's very large black boots, clearly not mine, near my couch. And his peacoat. And . . . is that his shirt? And . . . my bra?

Shit. Shit. Shit.

"Did you . . . have a party last night?" Arial asks innocently, her blue eyes sweeping the room and settling on Jack's boots. How am I going to explain those?

"Yes. Party. Galentine's." I grin, anxious.

"Are those . . . your boots?" she asks. "They look . . . big?"

"Uh. Yeah. My . . . uh . . . dad's actually. I keep them around for . . . uh . . . shoveling snow." Lies. So many lies. "And I haven't had time to clean up since the . . . party."

Oh, Lord. Larry is headed over to my bra. He sniffs at it. I pray Arial hasn't noticed he's inspecting my lingerie.

"The party for two?"

"Uh . . . yeah. Just one girlfriend." Cold sweat trickles down my back. Flop sweat breaks out all over the rest of my body. Arial sees right through me. Ack.

Larry's back at the front door. He dips down and licks her shoelaces.

"Larry!" I push him back in. "Sorry about that," I apologize to Arial. "Look, sorry. My stomach! Oh, I am so hungover . . . I really need to go." I need to close this door. *Now.*

"Oh! Okay, well then, just let me know if you need anything?"

Just then, back in the bedroom, I hear Jack yawn. A monstrous, Tarzan-like, chandelier-shaking yawn.

Arial and I freeze. Larry's head whips back and he stares at the bedroom.

"What was that?" Arial asks.

"What was what?" Playing dumb is my only hope. Larry trots over to the bedroom and scratches at the door.

"That sounded like a man yawning. In your bedroom."

"Oh? That?" Think. Think. Think. "Uh . . . probably my neighbor. My walls are like . . . *paper* thin."

"Really?" The skepticism in Arial's voice could fill a Russian novel.

I try to push the door closed, but Arial is not moving her foot. Her brown boot stays wedged in there like a designer bootie of doom.

"Sorry, but I've got to go. I'm going to be sick!" I hear my bedroom door creak open, and pure adrenaline rushes into my veins. "You have to go! Sorry!" I push Arial back a step and she wobbles back over my threshold, shocked.

"Whoa?" she cries, arms pinwheeling as I slam the door shut and throw myself against it, just as my bedroom door swings open. Jack comes wandering into my kitchen, clad only in his boxer briefs, dark hair tousled, sexy beardstache rumpled, and looking like the sex god he is. I'm panting, back against my front door, and I put a finger to my lips, gesturing for him to be quiet.

"Um, Sora?" I hear Arial's voice outside. "That was . . . uh, weird? But hope you feel better soon. I'll send you info on the talk show? Okay? We can coordinate your outfit?"

“Sorry! My stomach!” I cry, hoping that excuse is good enough for strong-arming my boss.

“Oh, uh? Feel better?” Then I hear Arial’s footsteps retreat down my stairs. Thank God.

I glance at the gorgeous and mostly naked Jack Mann.

That was close. Too damn close.

“Uh . . . good morning?” he offers tentatively. “Is everything okay?”

Thirteen

SORA

> The problem with sleeping with someone is that it clouds our judgment. According to actual science, the lateral orbitofrontal cortex is less active during sex. That's the part of our minds responsible for reason, decision-making, and value judgments. In other words, our brain.
>
> —SOLO FEBRUARY CHALLENGE

Everything is not okay. I have no idea what I'm going to do. I've just had the best sex of my life, during a month when I'm supposed to have *no sex whatsoever.* Because . . . the universe hates me. Because this is rotten timing. Because how can I keep having sex with Jack Mann and give Arial the articles she wants, not to mention keep on feeding the fans? Who are, by the way, filling up every available DM with their need for more and more and more.

My ex is pressuring me to get with her. Can I take one night off? What are the rules of #SoloFeb? asks one.

My mom just tried to set me up on a blind date, but he's kind of cute. Can I really ask him to wait until March? Is that reasonable? asks another.

My best friend says casual sex is okay during #GoSolo because it's about avoiding deep emotional commitments. True or false? asks a third.

Can you #GoSolo if you're married? This reader got an equal amount of blasting and support, with people divided into two camps. So, now, it was up to me to issue an official ruling from on high.

It's almost too much. People are really trying to navigate #GoSolo, and they're treating me like the ultimate referee. I guess I did come up with it, but am I the Supreme Court on dating now? Seriously? *Me?*

This is all wrong.

Not to mention, with my own #GoSolo slipup, I'm increasingly feeling like a fraud, weighing in on arguments online, telling people they must stay strong when I didn't.

Still, I've got just a little less than two weeks left until the end of February, I remind myself. I can just suck it up. Can't I?

I say goodbye to Jack Mann, even as I worry someone might see him leave my apartment. But who? Arial? I made sure to watch her walk down the street all the way to the L stop. I don't need her circling back and catching Jack Mann in his morning walk of shame. Pam might rat on me, too. That would be terrible. I remember her side-eying Jack in the hallway, and wonder if she's planning to blow my cover.

I'm racked with guilt, and yet, I don't really regret anything, because . . . I just had the best sex of my life. Maybe there's some way to still go solo but not be Mann-free?

"Sounds like you're trying to have it both ways," says Stella. We're grabbing a quick lunch nearby at a vegan diner. It's kosher and healthy, which Stella loves, and I happen to love their sweet potato fries, so it all works out. Outside, a brutal February wind kicks down the street, knocking the snow off the tree branches, as passersby waddle by the window bundled in hearty woolen layers: ankle-length coats, thick scarves, ski caps, and striped mittens. Even the dogs on leashes have on their puffy coats today.

"Well, of *course* I'm trying to have it both ways. And Jack Mann? All ways." I stretch out my ankle, which is much better. There's still swelling and it's a tad tender to walk on, but I ditched the crutches and can hobble most places without them. Jack's tender loving care the night before must've sped up my recovery, because now I hardly even have a limp. Amazing what a half-dozen orgasms will do.

Stella pushes up the thick wool sleeves of her chunky sweater and squints at me. "You didn't tell me you *slept* with him."

"What do you mean? I didn't sleep with him." I may have only mentioned the kissing part. I didn't mention the him-buck-naked-in-my-apartment-when-Arial-arrived part. Or the part about the many, *many* orgasms achieved in the wee hours of the night. "What! Me? No." I study the menu as if it's the fine print of a winning lottery ticket.

"You're a terrible liar. Also, you have that 'I spent the night making love to a gorgeous man' vibe. You're actually giggly."

I giggle. "No, I'm not." I giggle again.

"I rest my case." She stares at me. "Also, you have stubble burn."

"Where?" I reach up to feel my face. I thought it was windburn.

"Everywhere. Even your neck. And your arms. Did he lick you from head to toe?"

"Maybe." I shiver, remembering. I'll let him exfoliate my whole body with his beardstache any damn day of the week.

She shakes her head at me. "What happened to Solo February? To solidarity? *I've* kept the pledge!"

"I know. I'm sorry."

"Your readers will be disappointed if they find out."

I sink my face into my palms. "I know," I groan, thinking of the two dozen debates on #GoSolo that I weighed in on just this morning alone. "I can't be trusted. I just can't!"

The waiter drops off two glasses of water. "I'll be right back to take your order!" he promises. There's only one waiter for the whole diner, which is surprisingly busy at 11 A.M. on a weekday. But I'm in no rush to get back into the polar vortex outside, anyway.

"This is not something out of your control, and I don't think it's lust that's driving you." She takes a thoughtful sip of her water. "I think it's a desire for approval. It's because inside, you don't feel worthy of love."

"I sound like the subject of an after-school special."

"I'm serious," Stella continues. "Your dad was short-tempered with you, and your mom is always trying to put you on a diet, so you look for men to tell you that you *are* good enough, and you seek that approval from men in bed—especially assholes."

"Jack's not an asshole." I have her there. Jack's the nicest guy I've ever met. Period. Full stop.

"Okay, okay." Stella raises her hands in surrender. "Jack's different. You're right. He does seem like a mensch." She studies me a minute. "But are you sure this is the right time for him?"

"No. It's not. I'm supposed to go solo."

"Right. Because you were going to do some soul-searching in February," she reminds me. "And not just rush into your next relationship."

"That, and because it was a catchy series title for Arial." I sigh. "Also, it gets worse. I'm supposed to be on *Let's Talk!* this week. Apparently, *Solo February* has so many followers that I've made the local news."

"Seriously?" Stella looks both impressed and alarmed.

"What if everybody finds out I'm a fraud?"

"Hey," Stella says, pushing her thick, black curls off her forehead, as she settles into what I call her therapist stance: shoulders squared, eyes locked on mine, palms flat on the table. She vibrates with sincerity. "You know you are enough. Just all on your own. You don't need anybody or anything to save you. Jack sounds great, but if he's as great as you say, he'll wait. And getting into a bind where you're lying to your boss and to the *Let's Talk!* audience, that's just not good. You're only as sick as your secrets."

"Then, if I just have one, doesn't that make me not very sick?"

Stella sighs, shoulders slumping. "I think you're missing the point."

"Am I?" I know I am. Deliberately.

Stella sucks in a breath. "I'm sure Jack is great—he's just not the answer to your problems. You are."

"You know your therapist speak doesn't work on me." Though it does, kind of, and we both know it.

"Maybe you *ought* to do some self-care, be nicer to yourself. Give yourself a break. Also, you need to parent yourself a little more. Maybe make healthier food choices, like less bacon."

"I know your feelings on bacon."

"I just think you should make more healthy choices."

"I feel . . ." I glance at the vegan menu, suddenly craving bacon with my sweet potato fries. "Like eating more bacon."

"You're ridiculous." Stella shakes her head, but she's grinning, so I know there's no hard feelings. Also, she already knows I'd make the worst patient on earth. She's already told me that.

"Hey, mind if I interview you really quick for the column? I like the idea of delving more into this self-care stuff. That's perfect for *Solo February*."

Stella shakes her head slowly. "Self-care isn't just for February. You should do it all year round!"

"And that, my friend, is going to be the headline."

When I head back to my place, I take it slow on the icy Chicago sidewalks, as I meander through my eclectic neighborhood: half new condos, half old brownstones, all Chicago. The wind dies down, and the sun peeks out from behind the clouds, and suddenly it's warmer than the usual February afternoon. Just your typical temperature swing in the Midwest: one second, it's Antarctica. The next? Florida. The sun melts a little of the snow from the sidewalk, making the street gleam wet as if it's just rained, and a few brown puddles pool at the intersections. I leap over them, thankful my ankle is nearly back to normal.

My phone pings with a message from Jack.

Hey, gorgeous.

Seeing that makes me feel all warm inside.

Hey yourself, I text back. It's been only a few hours since he's left my bed and he's already *checking in*? This seriously might be the man I marry.

Just wanted you to know I'm thinking about you.

I'm thinking about you, too. Naked in my bed.

I text it before I can stop myself.

Mmmmm. I like how you think.

Oh, boy, we're on our way to a sexting session, and that's not going to work for me here out on the sidewalk in Chicago. Abort!

Was just talking about you to my friend, Stella.

I hope good things?

ALL good things, I write and only feel slightly bad about the lie. Jack doesn't need to know about Stella's hesitations.

Maybe we could get together again?

I stop, dead still, and glare at my phone.

Also, I forgot to ask . . . today being THE holiday. Will you be my valentine?

I haven't ever, in my entire life, had a man ask me to be his valentine. I don't actually know what to say.

A car honks at me, and I jump, realizing that I've stopped in the middle of a crosswalk. I throw my hand up in an "I'm sorry" gesture and hurry across the street.

I'm not too far from Margo's, I realize. What could it hurt if I just dropped by to say hi?

Fourteen

JACK

> Every year, we buy and send 145 million Valentine's Day cards. Imagine if we sent 145 million cards every year that simply said "You, alone, are enough"?
>
> —SOLO FEBRUARY CHALLENGE

I think I might be in love.

Real love.

Not fake, bullshit, reality TV love. And not adorable kid-crush love, either.

Real.

Freakin'.

Love.

I can't stop thinking about Sora. Everything reminds me of her. Like the woman in the red coat—like Sora's—who's lingering in the produce section. Or the display near the bakery of the pre-cooked, pre-packaged bacon—her favorite. Or the small table in front of the bakery covered in pink and red heart-shaped cookies—the cookies I made just this morning, and each time I piped a heart, I thought of Sora.

Sora.

Sora.

Sora.

Everywhere, Sora.

Yeah, I got it bad.

Dude. One night of lovemaking does not a marriage make. I keep trying to tell myself to slow down.

"Uh, excuse me?" a Margo's customer in a purple coat asks. "Are you going to get those eclairs or . . . ?"

Oh, right. My job.

"Sorry," I say, contrite, grabbing her requested two chocolate, cream-filled desserts from behind the bakery glass, and bagging them. I hand them over and she shakes her head, disapproving.

I watch her walk away and then slip back into Sora world.

Sure, it's the sex. The amazing, life-changing sex. The white-hot chemistry between us that's impossible to fake.

But it's also that she's smart.

And funny.

And the most interesting woman maybe I've ever met, maybe. And the kindest. And she's only gotten more so since grade school.

But to be honest, I was already a little in love with her anyway. I was probably always going to be a goner.

And now I've gone and asked her to be my valentine.

Like we're both in second grade.

Sometimes, I want to kick my own ass. It's no wonder she hasn't responded yet. What does she say to that?

Hell, might as well have sent her a note that said: Do you like me? Check "yes" or "no."

I am an idiot.

The woman already told me she hates Valentine's Day. Plus, we haven't even talked about the Solo February stuff and the fact that her boss didn't seem all that keen on her breaking it.

Not that it's a topic of conversation to be broached in bed.

Because, I'm pretty sure . . . she wasn't doing anything solo then.

I glance at the clock in Margo's bakery, which reminds me I'm still on shift for a few more minutes. If I keep daydreaming about Sora's fine, fine body, then I'm going to burn *all* the croissants. Plus, I've only got a million other things that need my attention right now. There's the Golden Chef Awards coming up, and I really need to win that $100,000 cash award, since it will help me launch the bakery. There's also the fact that I just got the keys to the new store space, which I have to work on getting into shape in the next month. We gotta open by May 1st and at least start making money or I'm going to go broke.

I've got to clean it. Paint it. Get it stocked. Hire a front counter person—all in the next month. And here I am daydreaming about Sora.

Well, because . . . she's Sora.

My phone dings and I pull it out like I'm in a gunfight in the Old West. Did she respond?

No. I feel instant disappointment.

It's Mal.

I was expecting you to call. About the Golden Chef Awards. You're supposed to be my valentine. Come on, Jack-a-boo. I got a new dress.

A photo pops up on the feed. Yep. That's Mal all right. She's wearing a sheer red negligee, nothing underneath. She's got a good body, I'll give her that. It's too bad there's an empty chest cavity filled with cobwebs where her heart should be.

I ignore the text.

"Jack?" I glance up and see Sora standing on the other side of the glass bakery counter. I straighten, surprised, and dump my phone in my pocket, feeling guilty, even though, technically, I didn't do anything wrong. I definitely didn't ask for that text! My heart hammers in my chest.

I focus on Sora, who's wearing her formfitting red wool coat and a white cashmere cap. Her lips perfectly match her rich red lapel.

"Sora." I grin, unable to help myself. "Glad you came by. I thought I scared you off with that 'be mine,' Valentine's stuff."

She laughs—uncomfortably. "You know how I feel about Valentine's Day."

"Yeah. I was hoping to change that."

She meets my gaze, startled. "That's a long road," she says after a bit. Okay, back off, Jack. Tread carefully.

"Well, why don't we start with chocolate chip cookie samples?" I nod at the open display case in front of the glass bakery counter.

Sora grabs the tongs and digs into the cookies, picking the biggest one. She plucks it from the tongs and takes a healthy bite. Damn, the woman does *not* mind eating. Love that. Also love her lips on . . . pretty much any part of my body. Lady's choice.

"Thank you," she murmurs, mouth full.

"I'm glad you came by. I was thinking about you." Like every minute.

"You were?"

"Yeah." I grin, goofy. And she grins back.

There it is, that connection between us. There's no mistaking it. It's like a panting dog, desperate for attention.

Damn, I have it bad for this woman.

Sora lets out an exaggerated sigh. "I shouldn't even be here." She glances up at me, looking pained. "My boss, Arial, for a start. Solo February."

Oh. Right. That.

"I thought we kind of totally demolished Solo February . . . last night." I'm confused.

"We did. That's the problem." She stares at me, worried.

"But . . . you don't want to lose your job. So . . ." I'm connecting the dots.

She bites her lip.

"Yeah. So." She shifts uncomfortably from one foot to the other.

"Listen, I get it." I don't want to put Sora in a position where she has to choose between her job and me.

"You do?" She's shocked. "You're *okay* with this . . . or . . . *not* . . .this?" She gestures wildly between us.

I laugh. "There's really only two more weeks in February," I say. "And then, I assume, *after* that, your boss won't care who you date?"

She thinks about this a moment, tapping her chin with one gloved hand. "Yes, that's true."

"Okay, then. I can wait."

"You can?" She shakes her head in disbelief. "You're sure?"

"Yes. Absolutely." I'd wait months. Hell, I've already waited years, if you think about it.

"These days, guys won't wait five minutes on Spark."

"Well, I'm not most guys." I think about all the fish-faced cleavage. Nah, I'm good. I'm tired of the flatness, the sameness of all those many profiles on my dating apps.

We stare at each other, and a small smile teases the corner of Sora's lips.

I don't want her to go. She doesn't want to leave. It's like we're tethered together by an invisible cord.

"So, do you have any plans? For tonight?"

"Valentine's Day?" she scoffs, offended. "Well, I can't go out to eat, because every single restaurant will be mobbed. Can't GrubDash because, see: all restaurants being packed. And, I just checked—there's no horror movie marathon like there ought to be on cable tonight. So I'll probably just go home and rewatch *The Shining* again."

"Evil haunted hotel does scream Valentine's Day."

"I mean, it's the next best thing to a masked killer with a chain saw." She lingers at my counter. "Do . . . you have plans?" She says it haltingly, as if worried about my answer. Does she think I would just fall into bed with her and then go out with a new woman the next night? I'm not that much of a jerk. But that doesn't mean I can't have a little fun. At her expense.

"Well, I do have a date."

She stiffens. "You do?" She tries desperately to look uninterested.

"With a beautiful brunette."

"Oh." Sora glances down at her feet, not meeting my gaze. "I figured a guy like you wouldn't be staying home."

Guy like me? Wonder what she means by that?

"I am just giving you a hard time. I'm babysitting my five-year-old niece." I grab my phone from my pocket and pull up a picture of her in pink heart-shaped sunglasses and ice cream dripping from her nose. A picture taken outside last summer when she'd somehow managed to get her ice cream cone on 90 percent of her face.

Sora blinks. "Oh! Oh, *God.*" She laughs, brighter suddenly. "She's adorable. Really."

I glance up and see I'm at the end of my shift.

"Want to come over to my brother's house? Help me babysit? I'm watching her while Ian and his wife go out." I'm already taking off my apron, hope lifting in my chest.

"I don't know. Is that a date?" She hesitates, biting her red lip, and looking absolutely 100 percent fuckable.

She wants to come with me. I can see it in her eyes. All she needs is a little push.

"Hell, no. It's a *job*. Even your boss won't see anything wrong with *babysitting,* would she?"

"I guess not," she relents.

"Trust me. It's not safe for you to stay home alone tonight."

"It's not?"

"Yeah, no." I shake my head vigorously as I take off my baker's hat and stick it on the hook. "You know that, just like Thanksgiving and Christmas, Valentine's Day is a likely holiday to be hit up by some sleazy ex? Your phone will be going off all night."

"Oh no. You think?" Sora looks worried.

"Oh, I'm *sure*. Starting at ten, you'll be getting 'U up?' Maybe even . . ." I lower my voice and glance around the store as if worried one of her exes might jump out from the cereal aisle. "Dick pics."

"Ugh." Sora wrinkles her nose. "Not those."

"I know. If you want, I can respond to them. I don't mind." I would *love* to tell them what they can do with those X-rated pictures.

She laughs. "Are you going to undermine their self-esteem?"

"Absolutely." I grab my coat from a hook near the bakery and put it on, slapping a wool cap on my head.

"So you're just going to make my exes feel badly about themselves. That's your only motive?" She laughs as she follows me down the bakery aisle.

"Of course." I pretend to be affronted. "Why else would I want you with me all night?"

"I could think of one or two things. Also, they might *not* involve clothes."

Now it's my turn to laugh. "That is no way to try to keep your Solo February vow."

"I know. I've never been good with willpower."

"Well, Allie will keep us *both* in line, anyway. Also, so you know, she will insist on painting your nails. It's a rite of passage. Be prepared."

Fifteen

SORA

> The best thing you can do on Valentine's Day is stay home. Don't let the commercial love machine win.
>
> —SOLO FEBRUARY CHALLENGE

We stand on his brother's porch in front of a tiny bungalow in Evanston, the suburb just north of Chicago where Jack and I went to grade school, patiently waiting for the door to open. Our breath comes out in big puffs, and I am oddly nervous to meet more of Jack's people. Maybe he senses this, because Jack reaches out and takes my hand, squeezing it, and I feel a little ripple of goosebumps run up my arm and they have nothing to do with the chilly February night and everything to do with his big, strong hand holding mine. Instantly, I feel calmer. Icicles hang above the small porch, and someone—I'm assuming Allie—has built a little snowman in the tiny yard and dressed it in a pink hat and matching mittens on its little stick hands.

Okay, so me helping Jack Mann babysit his adorable niece surely doesn't violate Solo February, as there's technically a little girl involved. An adorable, precious little girl who flings open the door and squeals as she claps her tiny, tiny hands.

"Uncle Jack!" she cries, jumping into his arms and squeezing his neck for all she's worth. It's so damn sweet, I nearly get a cavity. She glances over at me, big doe eyes assessing, her pink sequined bows pinning her pigtails adorably in place catching the foyer light.

"I'm Allie!" she says. "My teacher says I can't shake hands because of germs, but we can do elbow bumps!" She offers up her adorable elbow and I tap it with my own.

Uncle Jack laughs. "Good call," he says. "Allie, this is Sora."

"Hey, Allie." I elbow-bump her, noticing she's wearing a stack of about fifteen glittery rubber bracelets, some glittery lip gloss, and shoes that light up pink and purple every time she moves. "I love your shoes!"

"Thank you," she says, and then blinks up at me. "So is Uncle Jack your *boyfriend*?" she says in the blunt way only young children and old people can get away with.

"Well, uh . . ." I don't know how to answer that.

"Sora pleads the fifth," Jack says easily. "Come on, Allie, where's your dad?" he says as he carries her inside. I follow.

"Hey, Sora." It's his doctor brother, Ian, who's shrugging into a blazer in the foyer, and looking less disheveled than when I last saw him in the ER, unshaven and in his scrubs. "How's that ankle?"

"Doing just fine," I say. "Thanks to your fine care."

"Is that Jack?" comes a female voice and I look up to see Allie's mom standing on the stairs, looking like she's ready for a cover shoot with perfect amber skin, tasteful makeup, and her jet-black hair worn straight to her shoulders. She's part Asian like me, and I feel instantly like she could be my long-lost sister. She has Allie's brown eyes, and is dressed in a formfitting mauve, knee-length dress and stiletto heels. When she sees me, her whole face lights up.

"Sora!" she cries. "Jack told us all about you." He did? I glance at him, but he gives me an unreadable smile. Kylie moves quickly down the stairs. "But she's even *prettier* than you said!" Kylie sends Jack a scolding look as she reaches the landing. "I'm Kylie. Ian's wife." I hold out my hand for a shake, but she bats it away and pulls me into a big hug. "We're huggers," she explains. "And I'm so, so very excited to meet you."

"Me, too!" So Jack has been talking about me? I like that.

"Sora! Sora!" cries Allie, grabbing my hand. "Do you want to see my room?"

"Of course I do," I say.

"Uncle Jack! Come, too. We'll play spa."

Jack grins at me. "Told you," he whispers as we follow Allie as she bounds up the stairs.

An hour later, Jack has his hair up in two short pigtails and he's wearing big plastic pink clip-on earrings and a matching necklace, as well as a pink feather boa that's far too small for him. Allie is meticulously painting his fingernails what she calls "princess pink" and all the while Jack patiently sits at her tiny little play table, with the heart-backed chairs, and lets her do exactly what she likes.

I stifle a laugh as he wiggles his eyebrows at me. I don't think I've ever found a man as adorable as I do now.

I'm sitting at the table, too, but Allie just put little glittery heart stickers on my already painted nails, telling me she liked my pale pink and that I have "very good taste." It's sweet seeing Allie working so hard. Her little pink tongue pokes out from between her lips as she concentrates.

"How often do you give Uncle Jack a makeover?" I ask Allie.

"*Every* time," she says. "He needs it. He doesn't wear *any* pink." She wrinkles her nose in disapproval.

"What the princess wants, she gets," Jack says. "I don't want to be fed to any dragons."

Allie just giggles. "You're silly, Uncle Jack." Then she swishes one last swipe of nail polish on his left pinkie nail. "All done!" she cries, and Jack looks down at his nails—which are only partially covered with nail polish, as most of it landed on his cuticles. I've never seen a man so patient, or so willing to play along as Jack. When I try to think about Marley or Dan getting dressed up in a feather boa, I can't even imagine it. Jack would seriously make an excellent dad. He's so patient. So kind.

"Beautiful," he says. "Am I a pretty, pretty princess now?" He keeps his voice completely serious. That's the beauty of it.

Allie stands up and studies him, serious. "Wait," she says, and runs off to the corner of her room where she digs out a sparkling silver light-up tiara. Then she gingerly places it on his head. "*Now* you're all done," she says, and does a cute little curtsy in front of him. She giggles, covering her mouth with both hands.

Allie digs out another crown from beneath her pile of stuffed animals in the corner and puts it on her own head. "I got this in the hospital when I was sick," she tells me.

"What was wrong?" I ask. I glance at Jack, who suddenly seems serious.

"I had . . ." Allie lowers her voice. "The Bad Stuff."

"She had leukemia," Jack explains.

I blink, shocked. Allie looks like any other healthy little girl. I can't imagine her sick in a hospital with . . . cancer.

"She went into remission last summer. You kicked that Bad Stuff, kiddo." Jack stretches his arms out for a hug, and she gives him a big one.

Allie giggles. "I sure did." She looks at me, green eyes wide. "You know what I call the Bad Stuff? I call it a bad word." She looks around as if the four-letter-word police will bust down the door. "I call it the S-word."

Well, cancer *sure* is shitty, that's for sure.

"What's the S-word?" Jack asks, guard up.

She glances at me, and then at Jack, and lowers her voice so we can barely hear her. "*Stupid,*" she whispers, as if she's really cursing. Makes my heart want to explode.

"Cancer really *is* stupid," I agree, and she giggles at my use of the word.

"You said a bad word!" she cries, and claps her hands in glee. When she's grown, she's going to be a very, very fun drunk.

The doorbell rings then.

"Pizza's here," Jack declares, standing up, not bothering to take off his jewelry or his tiara as he moves to the stairs.

"Pizza! Pizza! Pizza!" chants Allie, tearing down the stairs after Jack.

After he pays the pizza delivery guy, he grabs two pizza

boxes—Allie's small cheese and ours to share—and sets them down on the counter. In a few minutes he's got Allie set up in the breakfast nook, with cheese pizza and her favorite cartoons on the small flat screen on the counter. Then he motions me over to check out our order. He opens it to reveal a heart-shaped meat lovers' pizza—complete with bacon crumbles.

"I knew it wouldn't be Valentine's Day without bacon," he says.

I wrap my arm around his shoulders. He pulls me in for a quick, tender kiss, and with Allie's attention elsewhere, I kiss him back, his tiny feather boa tickling my throat. I feel a shiver of delight all the way to my toes, and all I can think about is last night, when we thoroughly explored each other's bodies. How *easy* it all was, how seamless. How I feel at home with Jack, now, naked, anytime.

"This *might* just be the most romantic thing a man has ever done for me," I say.

"You need to get out more," Jack quips as he offers me a paper plate. I grab a piece of pizza at the point of the heart. Jack opts for three square slices from the middle. His tiara falls forward a little, and he gently takes it and the feather boa off.

"So," I say, voice low so Allie can't hear me. "Leukemia?"

Jack nods, solemn. "Yeah, it was bad. And Ian is worried it might come back. But doctors say that's just a twenty percent chance."

I feel my heart tighten as I take my pizza and slide onto a nearby barstool near the kitchen island. "That would be terrible."

"I know. And Ian worries about all the chemo she had, how that will affect her . . . later on." Jack's tone is somber, his mood suddenly turning serious. I can tell he's worried, too.

He grabs his own piece of pizza and sits on the stool next to me. His leg brushes mine, and I like the contact. Warm. Steady. Nice. "But I say she beat it, and we've got to be glad she did, and enjoy every day with her." He nods at his niece, growing somber. "Only the big guy upstairs knows how much time we have. Got to make the most of it." A look of pure determination crosses his face. I love that he's not letting a setback define his family. It takes courage to choose to be optimistic.

"You're brave," I say, really seeing Jack. He is brave. He is so many things.

"I am?" He looks surprised. "Why do you say that?"

"I mean, it takes courage to face something terrible, like cancer in the family, and keep looking for the bright side . . ." I realize as I'm saying these words how perfectly they fit Jack. Dan was scared—scared his wife would find out he's a louse and has a girlfriend in the city. Marley was scared, terrified of settling down with one woman lest he miss something. "You are just about making the most of the moment. I think that's brave."

Jack meets my gaze. "In life, bad times come," he says after a beat. "I know that because of all those years of bullying. I always told myself that I can't control what other people say or do, but I can control me. What I do. How I feel. So, you have to make the most of the good times. What I'm really scared of is regret. Life is too short to sit on the sidelines. I think you should go for what you want."

He stares at me. I feel the heat, the meaning of his gaze, all the way to my toes. Can it all really be this easy? Can love just fall into place like this, like the last piece of a jigsaw puzzle?

"You always know what you want?" Because I don't. Rarely ever.

"I know some things. Like I'm going to open my own bakery."

"You are? That's . . . awesome." I think about all the risk, too, how so few new businesses make it, but, once more, Jack is not afraid. He's excited about the prospect of wrestling the odds. I can see it on his face. "Well, then, this *is* a happy Valentine's Day for you."

"It is. Because you're here." He stares at me. I stare at him. This might be one of the sweetest things anyone's said to me.

I have the sudden urge to swipe the pizza boxes off the counter and make out with him in a way that would very likely scar Allie for life. But that would be bad, so instead, I tear my gaze away from his and shove more pizza in my mouth.

"I can't imagine you ever having a bad Valentine's Day," I mumble, mouth full. Someone as sexy and warm as Jack? Someone who's both a strong lumberjack *and* an adorable uncle? Please. I'm surprised women don't rip his clothes off while he's walking down the street.

Jack snorts. "Not true. I have *the worst* Valentine's Days of all time."

"I don't believe you." I glance over at Allie, chomping on pizza absently while she watches her show about some kind of computer-animated animal family.

He sighs, looking a little defeated, as he takes another bite. A crumb of crust falls into his beardstache.

"Uh . . . you have a little . . ." I point to my chin.

He swipes at it with his napkin, grinning. "Did I get it? Or are we going to need a rescue team?"

I laugh. I love this easy feeling between us. Like I've known him all my life. Which, I guess, I almost have. "No, you got it.

Okay, so this allegedly bad Valentine's Day? I'm going to need details."

"Last year, the week of Valentine's Day, I worked as a pastry chef at Alestra."

"That five-star, one-meal-costs-your-whole-paycheck place?" I raise an eyebrow, impressed. It's the kind of place that's booked months in advance. You need to be a celebrity or a friend of the mayor's to get a table there.

He looks sheepish. "Yeah, worked directly under the Michelin-star chef, Pierre Benoit."

"Wait. I've heard of him! He's on the Foodie Network."

"You watch the Foodie Network?" he asks, surprised.

"Do you think I love bacon by accident?" I laugh.

Jack laughs, hearty and loud. We grin at each other, goofy.

"What was I even saying?" Jack asks, after a beat.

"Your worst Valentine's."

"Right." He frowns as if he tastes something rotten. "So, Valentine's Day is any restaurant's big night. Pierre naturally asked me to work. But Mal was upset about that."

I perk up at the mention of Mal. I've been wanting to ask how it ended, and I have a feeling I'm going to find out. "What? Did she think nobody wants desserts on Valentine's Day?"

Jack laughs. "I promised to take her on the most romantic date of her life on February fifteenth, but she just wouldn't have it. It was Valentine's Day or nothing. She said everyone would have already posted their pictures and it would be too late. And threatened that if I went into work, she'd do something I wouldn't like."

"Wow." Petulant much?

"So, while I'm at work, she texts me a photo of herself." Jack glances at Allie, still watching TV, and lowers his voice. "In bed with her brother-in-law."

My hand flies to my mouth. "Oh my God. No way."

"Yeah. That really happened." He nods his head, a frustration line appearing between his eyebrows. "Needless to say, I'm beside myself. I don't even finish my shift. I run home."

"What happened?" My stomach tightens.

"Well, I was too late. He's gone. I confront her. She admits they've slept together. We argue. She tells me that she had to get my attention somehow."

I must have an incredulous look on my face, because he adds, "She had a rough childhood. Her parents neglected her. Sometimes, she acts out."

"With her sister's husband?" I cry, outraged.

"Well, she has issues with her sister, too." Jack flashes me a wry smile.

"Clearly." I shake my head, dumbfounded. Nami and I might bicker about small stuff, but neither one of us would ever cross that line. "There's acting out, and then there's being a child. At some point, we're adults, and we have to take ownership of our sh—" I pause and glance at Allie, who has just at that moment tuned into our conversation. "—stuff," I finish, flashing her a smile. Allie just nods, and turns back to the TV.

"But anyway, it gets worse. Turns out, her brother-in-law is one of Pierre's major investors. He threatened to pull his support for the restaurant, so Pierre had no other option but to fire me. I don't blame Pierre. I don't. He felt terrible about it."

"That's awful, Jack." I'm grateful that he trusts me enough to share this. He's let me have my first peek behind the curtain strung across his heart, and now I see he's also been living with old scars made from deep wounds.

"Mal just never really got why it was a big deal. She always said with her money, I didn't need to work. Never mind that I love working. That I take pride in it. I couldn't trust her anymore, so I called off the wedding." Jack exhales, and his shoulders sag, his whole body seeming to fold under the weight of her dismissing his profession and, thus, dismissing him. The bitter note in his voice makes me worry he still cares a little about what she thinks.

"You called off the wedding?" I keep my voice neutral, even though I'm surprised. I actually thought Mal might have done the leaving. Because I remember Mal at the grocery store the day Jack and I reconnected. The lunch plans that were never exactly explained. After this terrible end to their relationship, how could they even be on speaking terms?

"I did," he tells me, jaw twitching. "It was the right decision."

"Definitely." I hesitate, wondering if I should ask if he still has feelings for Mal. But that question seems too direct. Too dangerous. If I poke too much, I might send him running. Men have ghosted me for far less. I've learned the hard way that men share only what they want to share. If you ask for more, you're greedy. Demanding. Difficult.

Of course, Jack seems different. The ice looks thick enough to walk on, but do I really want to risk it by trying?

"Have you thought about taking up country music?" I opt for a flippant joke, an orange life ring that I hope will float him to the surface, away from his painful past. Away from Mal. I hate to admit that I'm jealous of any time he spends with her, even if it's in his mind.

"Often."

"We could write a song about how we prefer beer to Valentine's Day," I offer. "It would be a huge hit."

Jack looks up and meets my gaze once more, and the sadness has vanished. That playful spark has returned. I feel relieved that he doesn't want to linger in that old hurt. Maybe he has put it to rest. After all, there are a million innocent reasons he could've had lunch with Mal that day, and I feel silly for second-guessing it.

"I think it definitely needs to be pickup trucks and whiskey are better than Valentine's chocolates and champagne."

"I like that even better."

Jack takes my hand in his and draws a line down the center of my palm. I shiver, glad as much for his touch as his attention, now squarely focused back on me.

"What kind of name is Mal, anyway? Short for Malorie?" I ask, even though I don't really care about the answer. I'm intently focused on Jack stroking my hand.

"Short for Malort," he says.

"She's named after the bitter liqueur people dare each other to drink on St. Paddy's?" I snort a laugh. Actual reviews of Malort call it the taste of turpentine and sadness, with a hint of grapefruit.

Jack grins, and begins to massage my palm a bit, reminding me just how well he massaged other parts of my anatomy. "Yep. Her parents are part Swedish. And Malort, as you know, is a Swedish brand. They thought it was cheeky, I guess."

"Turns out, the name really does fit."

"Yeah, well." Jack shrugs. "She kind of had terrible parents. It's why she's had so many issues." He clears his throat. "Speaking of ghosts of exes past," he says, changing the subject, "what was the deal with you and Marley?" O-kay, well, tables turned. Now it's my turn for show-and-tell. I tug my hand back to me, and Jack releases it.

"I mean . . ." Jack backtracks quickly. "You do not have to answer that question, obviously. I don't want to be nosy." He hesitates. "Okay, that's a lie. I am absolutely being nosy. I just wondered why you two got married."

"Pregnancy scare," I say, but that answer doesn't sound like enough. It's the flippant answer I give to acquaintances or co-workers who might ask. It's not the whole story. "It wasn't just a scare," I admit. "I was pregnant."

Jack's eyes widen and he sits very still.

"What happened? I mean . . . if you don't mind me asking?" Jack's face, open, warm, his eyes telegraphing to me that he really, truly wants to know. There's his heady focus again, the way he makes me feel like I'm the only thing in the world he cares about.

I feel my throat tighten. "In the middle of my second trimester, when I think everything's going to be fine, I go in for a normal doctor's appointment, but she can't find the heartbeat. They do an ultrasound and . . ." I feel the tears choke me. I still can't believe all these years later, the wound feels so fresh. "The baby had died. In utero. We never knew why." I sniff back stupid tears. My stomach feels tight. Uneasy. "Marley wanted to celebrate. He was so happy. But I was . . ." I remember being curled up on the couch, not being able to get up for two straight days. "I was devastated."

Jack squeezes my hand. His fingers feel like a lifeline.

"He was celebrating. My mom and sister thought it was good

news, too." I shake my head, disagreeing with them even now. "But even though I knew it wasn't the right time for me to have a baby, I really, really wanted that child. Even if now I can say that it's probably best Marley and I weren't parents, I'm still mourning her loss."

"The baby was a girl?"

I nod. Jack grabs both my hands now, and it's his turn to make sure I don't sink below the surface of the past. He swings his stool to the side, so we're knees-to-knees. He looks at me. Really looks at me.

"I'm sorry, Sora. So sorry. Sometimes, I don't know why things happen the way they do. Sometimes, things just aren't fair."

I nod. And I'm stupidly relieved he didn't tell me I have plenty of time to have another baby. That I'm young, like my mom told me, that I'll have other boyfriends, like Nami told me, or that this was a blessing in disguise, like all my friends told me. It sure didn't feel like a blessing. Felt like a punch in the face. Felt like the one thing I truly knew I wanted in all the world would never be mine.

"The worst part is that we stayed married nearly four more years after that." I shake my head, remembering that dark time.

"Why?" Jack asks, surprised.

"Inertia," I say. "I was in such a dark place after the miscarriage, nothing seemed worth doing. I should've left Marley, but, honestly, I just couldn't work up the energy to do it. Nothing seemed to matter, so why not stay with Marley? Marley stayed around because he liked that together we could qualify for a mortgage and that I paid more than my share of the bills. I'd come to find out later that being married hadn't really slowed down his dating life any. So. There's that."

Jack shakes his head slowly and makes a disapproving sound deep in his throat. He looks at our clasped hands. "Well, then, he's probably not going to change for his new girlfriend. Or anyone else."

"Probably not. It seems obvious now that I should've left him right after the miscarriage, but, honestly, I just went on autopilot," I say, and as the words tumble out, I realize I've never really talked at any length about this time in my life. "When Marley got it in his head we should buy a condo, I said yes. When a friend of a friend put me in touch with Arial at *Slick* for freelancing opportunities, I went ahead with it, ignoring that small warning in my gut that makeup and fashion, as awesome as they are, just weren't really what I wanted to write about. I was in a dark place where nothing seemed to matter, so why not just let the world decide things for me, you know? If I couldn't control what happened to my own body, or baby, then why even bother trying to control anything?"

Jack squeezes my hands and nods. He doesn't try to talk me out of my sadness. He just sits with me in it. Talking to Jack is *nice.* He doesn't make my problems seem little, but at the same time, doesn't let me wallow in self-pity, either. It's that delicate balance he manages to strike every time. Jack flashes me a killer smile that looks even whiter against his beard, and the sparkle in his eyes makes my stomach do cartwheels.

"He wasn't the right man for you," he presses.

"I don't know if there is one, though," I admit.

"I get it. Really. I do." He rubs the top of my knuckle with his thumb. "But I think we can live our lives afraid, or we can live our lives like we don't know what tomorrow brings. Because we don't." He grows silent. "I mean, look at her." He nods toward Allie, who's swinging her feet beneath her chair, eyes glued to her show. "She got a really rough deal, but she's not bitter. She's not afraid. She's a little pink glitter Powerpuff." He glances at me, brown eyes soulful. "So I'm not going to be afraid of broken hearts. That just comes with living. Just a risk we all take to find happiness."

"You make it sound so simple." He slips his thumb down the side of my hand, and I feel electric pulses straight up to my elbow.

"For me, it is simple." Jack leans in closer. I want to believe him, I do. "You deserve to be happy."

"I do?"

"For starters, you were so nice to me in grade school. You never made fun of me." His eyes gleamed. "It's one of the reasons I crushed on you so hard. You're always looking after the underdogs."

"Really?" Yet I feel warmed by Jack's compliments, a heat that warms me from within.

"You adopted a one-eyed pit bull from the pound! You help elderly customers in the store. You have an amazing heart."

Jack gazes at me as if I should win the Nobel Peace Prize. I hope he always looks at me like that.

I don't think I do anything all that out of the ordinary, but I guess it is true that I have a sweet spot for outsiders, maybe because I often think of myself as one.

He interlaces his fingers with mine. "I know you're doing

the Solo February thing, and I respect that. I do." He glances at our hands. "I'll wait as long as you want me to."

"You will?"

"Of course."

Our grins fade as serious emotion takes over. I'm leaning into him, and he's leaning into me. Dangerous hope flares up in my chest and I defensively tamp it down. Can't start chasing rainbows and unicorns now. What would the demanding hordes of Soloists have to say?

"Are you going to kiss her, Uncle Jack?" asks Allie, who has abandoned her show, now on commercial break, and has bounded up right to us, and is looking from Jack to me, expectantly, hugging a stuffed pink rabbit to her chest. We both chuckle, the seriousness of the moment gone.

"That's none of your beeswax, kiddo," Jack says.

"You should kiss her," she demands.

"Do you want us to kiss or do you want dessert?" Jack challenges. Allie considers this seriously, as if weighing which college application she ought to fill out first.

"Dessert," she finally answers, deadly serious.

Jack kicks open a box from Margo's that contains heart-shaped chocolate chip cookies.

"Hearts are my favorite!" she declares. "So are chocolate chips!" She pads back to her chair near the kitchen TV, commercial break done.

"She's adorable," I say.

"She's relentless," Jack corrects. "When that sugar high wears off, she'll be back, this time asking when we plan to get married."

I laugh. I love Allie. I love this moment. I suddenly want dozens of other nights just like this one, stretching out for weeks, or months, or more.

Jack offers me a cookie. I take it. "I do wonder, though, like, how strict is Solo February?"

"What do you mean?" I ask. Suddenly, I feel I'm right back to looking at all of my DMs, the logjam of questions from readers about the technicalities of #GoingSolo.

"I've got this black-tie thing. The Golden Chef Awards on February twenty-eighth. I'm up for Best Pastry Chef. It's kind of a big deal. Like an Academy Award, sort of. But for chefs." He digs in his pocket, and pulls out an ivory invitation with two golden-edged tickets.

"You're inviting me to the Oscars of baking."

He grins. "Yeah." He shrugs his shoulders as if to show it's no big deal. "I want you to go with me, but I respect the Solo February thing. And I do not want to cause problems with your boss."

"Yeah." Going on a black-tie date might just cause problems. Not just with her, but with the serious Soloists out there.

"But here, take the ticket. You're under *no* obligation to go, at all. But if I'm not going with you, I don't really want to go with anyone else."

My heart flutters as he hands me the ticket.

"No matter if you go with me or not, if you stick to Solo February or not . . . you should know that whatever it is between us right now? It's not casual. Not for me."

I meet his gaze, dark and serious.

"I think . . . I think I'm falling in love with you, Sora."

Sixteen

SORA

> Love comes when you least expect it. That's why they need to make security surveillance systems for the heart.
>
> —SOLO FEBRUARY CHALLENGE

Okay.

He said he's *falling* IN LOVE with me. Say . . . what? How can he be on the edge of L-bomb territory? It's been a nanosecond. I mean, I know we've known each other forever, but most of that was when we were kids, and not to mention a big chunk in the middle where we didn't really know each other at all. But he seems so sure. So confident.

I don't know what to do. I'm freaking out, if I'm honest, because Jack *seems* like the real deal. That's the only way to describe him: hot, selfless, genuine, wise, and he's into me.

Maybe he's . . . my one?

I fidget with the gorgeous, gold-lined invite. My ticket to the

Golden Chef Awards. I can't believe he gave it to me. Of all the women in the city he could invite, he invited *me.*

How is that even possible? People don't fall in love that fast. Do they?

A quick Google search tells me that there's actual science that says all you need is thirty-six personal questions and one hour.

O-kay, so maybe people do fall in love this fast.

I'm literally humming tunes to myself while I head to the kitchen to brew coffee, daydreaming about Jack, who drove me home last night, and then walked me up to my apartment, and kissed me gently at my front door. I wanted to invite him in, but he had an early morning at the bakery today, and besides, I am *trying*—sort of—to keep my #GoSolo pledge.

Because the *Solo February* messages keep pouring in.

> *Help! I got smashed and went home with someone last night. Can I still #GoSolo?*
>
> *My coworker asked me out. Can I go AND #GoSolo?*
>
> *I don't know if I can do this. #GoSolo is just so hard!! Any tips for those of us out here hanging by our fingernails?*

I'm wading through the hundreds of messages feeling like the worst kind of fraud. I'm pretending I have all the answers when clearly, I have none.

I am also about to be on *Let's Talk!* I'll be discussing how I've taken a #GoSolo vow when I'm not at all sure I plan to keep it. Or that I am keeping it, anymore. I feel like I'm living a double life.

Then again, how different is this from the time I ranked concealers for our special cosmetics issue? I work from home. I barely shower, much less wear makeup. Please.

But with every question I answer, every #GoSolo debate I weigh in on, that nagging guilt just gets worse.

And remember how Jack said he's falling for me? Falling for *me*.

I need to tell him I'm going to go on *Let's Talk!* But . . . what am I going to say? "You're falling in love with me, great. I'm going to go on national TV and trash love and relationships. Remember how you spent all of last night trying to convince me to give love another chance? So, I guess the answer is no. By-eeee!"

Larry trots over to me in the kitchen, never wanting to miss the opportunity I might drop food, and tries to come and lean into my leg, but misses it and hits the cabinet door instead. Poor guy. I reach down and scratch him behind the ears, and he looks up at me, his permanent wink on, and lolls his tongue out. Arial calls then.

"Love the 'babysitting on Valentine's' piece? So cute? Yes? But . . . one question? Who is the friend you refer to? 'Friend's niece'?"

Damn it. Why does she have to ask questions like that? Does she think she's my editor or something? "Uh, just a friend."

"Can we identify her?"

"Uh, no. No, my friend doesn't want to be named." Because she is a he, that's why. You can't put a Mann in a Solo piece. I realize I'm skating the line here. But hell. It was a cute piece. Playing Pretty, Pretty Princess sure beats wallowing in self-pity, and shouldn't we all, no matter our age, respect our inner princess?

"Okay?" Arial says, backing down. "Just needed to ask? The copyeditors will be on me about that. Oh, and I've got good news for you. If the *Let's Talk!* segment goes well, my boss says we might have a full-time staff position for you."

"For me?" Full time. Benefits. Being able to see a medical professional outside of a drugstore quick clinic. "Really?"

I glance down at Larry. This could mean all the good kibble. Forever.

"Yes! They are so excited about you? They're talking about you being our singles correspondent?"

My stomach drops. "What does that mean?"

"Just . . . reporting on the single life? Maybe we could call it 'Yas, Single Queen'?"

"Oh. Wow." Being a singles correspondent would mean I'd need to stay single. Maybe forever. I think of Jack. "I'll think about it?"

"Okay. I'll try to be in the studio tomorrow? It's so exciting!" And Arial hangs up.

So, I want to do something good in the world. But what is that? Solo February? Is that even a good thing? Women empowerment, yes, and all those ladies that keep posting comments sure seem fired up. That is a good thing, right? So why do I keep thinking about Jack? Why do I keep thinking that while I can be a great version of myself without him, that I don't want to be without him?

And then there's the morning show. Tomorrow.

I should tell Jack I'll be on. But . . . I don't. There never seems to be the right time to bring up the fact that I'll be on a morning talk show pontificating on why men suck. I fear Jack might take it personally. Or worse, that he'll vow to watch the show, and then I'll feel all self-conscious about talking about the power of being single. So I don't lie to Jack. I just don't tell him. Is this bad? Probably.

All I know is that I've always wanted to write something important, and I don't know that this *is* important, but I do know that I've had more readers for this than anything else I've ever written. And that has to mean something.

I'd rather just neatly compartmentalize my *Solo February* work diary and my personal life, and never the twain shall meet. It's kind of like when I binge on cookie dough ice cream at midnight when I'm trying to diet, handily leaving it off my calorie-counting app. I'm pretty good at putting problematic behaviors in little silos.

Besides, how many people really even watch *Let's Talk!*?

Okay, so it's one million people. One million people watch, give or take a hundred thousand. And the hosts combined have two million followers, so I might be in trouble. I'm staring at "fun facts" on the wall of the greenroom of the local affiliate morning show, the wind howling outside, and the skies filled with snow that threaten a second February blizzard. There's already three inches of the white stuff on the ground, which I slogged through to get inside the building. The slush is currently melting off the heel of my stiletto boot into a puddle on the floor.

The greenroom is lovely, though not technically green. It's charcoal gray, with modern-looking furniture and free bagels and cream cheese and a coffee maker offering vanilla and mocha flavors of joe. I sit nervously twisting my purse strap, wondering why I ever agreed to be on television. And what if Jack finds out? Or someone Jack knows?

I should text him. Now. But what would I say? "Oh, funny thing, I'm on *Let's Talk!* right now! Why didn't I mention it before—oh, huh. Funny. I just forgot!"

Crap.

I glance down at my designer black-and-white dress, courtesy of Arial and the *Slick* closet. It was one of the only samples that wasn't a size double zero, but it fits pretty well, I think. And I'm wearing red-soled stiletto boots that probably cost more than my rent. I feel like I'm looking pretty damn awesome. But that's only because I'm used to wearing worn flannel pajama bottoms and that damn faded Turkey Trot sweatshirt. Plus, what *is* this relentless stabbing across my rib cage? I realize it's been so long since I've worn a bra that I've forgotten what torture devices they are.

"Sora?" asks a perky twenty-something wearing a smock and holding makeup brushes.

"Yes?" My voice comes out as a dry croak.

"I'm Gabrielle. I'll be your makeup artist." She blinks, hopeful. "Want to come to makeup?"

"Do I ever!" I'm so relieved. My makeup is a disaster. When I tried to glue on my fake eyelashes at 5:30 A.M., it became a hot mess real fast. A) I couldn't get them to adhere properly, and B) when I tried to fix the left one, it dropped into the toilet. Ergo, no fake lashes. I might as well just wear a name tag that reads "I'm a mole person."

Gabrielle's a leggy brunette who weighs ninety pounds soaking wet, and as she leads me to a director's chair in front of a giant mirror lit with the kind of big round bulbs that will show me *all* of my clogged pores, I worry that she's going to tell me I need to exfoliate. With a sandblaster. Instead, she surprises me with a warm smile.

"You know, I'm #GoingSolo, too," she tells me, powdering my intensely oily forehead with a brush. "You're, like, my hero."

"I am?"

I can't believe Gabrielle and I have anything in common. She's gorgeous, ten years younger than me, and probably can't go anywhere without literally fighting off the attention of attractive, rich people.

She nods. "Seriously. I've been having so much trouble. My boyfriend . . ." She rolls her eyes. "Ex-boyfriend now. He opened credit cards in my name. Maxed them out. Ruined my credit." Gabrielle gently places one false eyelash on my right eye.

"No! That's terrible."

"The worst part was that I thought he was so generous. Giving me gifts. Taking me on vacations. But he was using my money the whole time. Can you believe that?" She fixes my left eye now. Gabrielle is between me and the mirror, so I can't see myself. She picks up a brush from her small table and swipes a bit of color from her eye shadow palette.

"Well, you deserve better," I say. "I hope you know that. You should just date *you* for a while." I close one eye and then the other, as she gently swipes on eye shadow.

"Oh, I *have*, and I've been loving it so much, and I just wanted to thank you." She backs away for a second to gauge her work, then she dips her brush into more silver shadow and goes back in. "You really helped me out. You . . . you even wrote back to me last week!"

"I did?"

"Yeah, I asked you about tips on staying strong, because I met this super cute guy and was so, so tempted to cheat." She puts down the eye shadow and searches for blush. She swipes some on my cheeks.

"Oh? Really?" I feel a hot flash of guilt at the back of my neck. "What did I say?"

"You gave me this awesome pep talk about staying strong, and it really, really worked. You told me that working on myself was more important than some hookup with a guy who probably would've just ghosted me later."

"Yeah." I smile weakly, vaguely remembering replying to her message, one of probably hundreds I've gone through. What if I'd steered this poor woman away from *her* Jack? And what if Gabrielle ever found out that while I was busy giving her a pep talk, I was *not* living by the same high standards? I felt so torn. Should I tell her the truth? Ugh. No. I can't. But I should. I bite my lip.

"Are you . . . uh, okay?" Gabrielle asks me, because I have no poker face. "You look a little pale."

"I'm fine." I blink. "Just nervous."

"Don't be." Gabrielle moves so that I can see myself in the mirror. I'm a new woman. I barely recognize myself.

"Wow," I say. Turning my face one way and then the other, studying Gabrielle's work in the mirror. "You're . . . amazing."

"It's all you, honey," she says. "And don't worry, people have been talking about you being on *all week*. Everyone's gonna love you. Like, there was a line out the door and around the block for the audience! And that never happens."

I swallow as I meet her gaze in the mirror. "A line, really?"

"Yeah, they got here *early* to see you."

"Oh. Good." Gulp.

"Okay, it's time!" cries the producer, a middle-aged, balding man who pops his head into the makeup room. The butterflies in my stomach jolt awake as if they all landed at the same time in a bug zapper. *Pop, pop, pop!* I don't want to do this. I want to run out of the studio. What am I doing going on television that's in national syndication? I take a deep breath.

"You're gonna do great!" Gabrielle promises me, as she gives my arm a squeeze. The on-air light flicks on near us. The roar of the applause from the studio audience makes talking now impossible. *Thank you,* I mouth to her as she fades back into the dressing room. When the applause dies down, I hear the hosts—Veronica and Eric—introducing me. From behind the small sound stage, I can see the big windows showing Michigan Avenue, which even this early in the morning is somehow already filled with tourists. From my position at the side, I can see Veronica and Eric sitting on the barstools around the glass table. I see the empty one at the edge, and realize I'm going to have to somehow climb up into it. How did I miss this part? I'm wearing a tight-as-hell dress with three layers of spandex beneath at max stretch, so taut its original black is now gray, and knee-high black stiletto boots. How is this going to work? At least I'm wearing clean underwear. Most of the country might be about to see that, too.

My heart pounds in my chest and I close my eyes and wish three times I was back in my condo with Larry when I hear my name called and the audience erupts in manic, almost psychotic, applause. Oh, God. It's time. My feet go before I know what I'm doing, and I'm walking and waving at the audience—which is 99 percent women—and they're on their *feet.* I'm getting a standing O. I've never gotten this much approval from anyone before in my life. Gabrielle wasn't kidding. These women are *here* for it.

I'm temporarily stunned by the warmth of the applause. I get that there are flashing lights and a stage manager with his arms up and hands waggling to get them to cheer, but they don't need much encouragement.

I wobble up to the stage without falling (thank God) and heave myself up on the barstools (are these seven feet tall?). And almost manage to keep my knees together. Veronica Martinez looks flawless beneath the hot studio lights with her perfect long, dark hair, her poreless skin, lashes for miles, and a perfect mauve lip gloss that I suddenly feel I must have in my makeup bag. Eric Littell, a former sports reporter, wears a T-shirt and a checked blazer, his blond, curly hair shorn short, and a big, fat chip on his shoulder I can see from here. Both have teeth so white they look radioactive.

"Welcome," Veronica tells me. "I have to say that I am *so* excited to have you here. And so is our audience, right?" Another high-pitched screech goes up from the crowd. I glance outward to the audience once more, but the hot studio lights make it hard to discern faces. "Of course Eric here isn't so excited."

Eric looks like he wants to punch Veronica full in the face and then high-kick her into a corner, going complete MMA on her perfectly styled self, which means these two have slept together before. The desire for hate sex is burning between them like the first signs of a herpes outbreak.

"Well, I mean, we're talking about *Solo February,* right? I can't help but take that personally. If *all* women decide to go solo or whatever, then what am I going to do with my Friday nights?"

The audience gives Eric some pity *ah*s. Oh, poor Eric. He's somewhere in his late thirties, a local celebrity and an avowed bachelor, and pretty much is a walking advertisement for male toxicity, which probably means his DMs are full of interested women.

"Not everything is about *you,* Eric," snipes Veronica, barely containing her disdain. "Now, Sora, you've become quite the online sensation. Tell us about what inspired you to start *Solo February*."

"Have you met men?" I joke, and the entire audience erupts in tittering laughter. I glance tentatively at them, noticing all their excited faces. Are they really so excited to see *me*? "But, seriously, I'd had a string of terrible relationships . . ." I tell them about Dan, and a little about Marley, and get a lot of sympathetic *ah*s at all the right places. "And then one day I thought, why do I need a valentine? I mean, bacon is my first—and could be my only—love."

Lots of cheers for that one. I also feel a pang of guilt. If Jack saw this . . . would he be offended? Would he think it's funny? Ugh. And what about all these women in the audience? What would *they* think if they knew about Jack? They'd roast me alive. A bead of nervous sweat trickles down the small of my back.

Focus, Sora. Get your head in the game.

"So you're seriously replacing men with bacon?" Eric scoffs.

"Bacon is so much better than men, right, ladies?" I raise my fist and get some hoots and cheers.

"But come on, isn't this just man-hating?" Eric isn't going

to let me get off with all softball questions. He doesn't like anything about this segment. Or me. Well, no problem, Eric. Your cologne smells like eau de pompous ass. And you're wearing enough of it to sanitize half the Chicago sewer system.

"It's not about hating men, it's about loving yourself," I say, trying to keep my voice light. Several ladies applaud. "Solo February is for everyone, so you swear off relationships. It's not just about cis straight women swearing off cis men. Or whomever. It's really about focusing on one's self, getting in a better frame of mind. I mean, I love men. They just don't always love me back." More laughs. And one "Amen!" Eric looks out at the audience and a subtle frown puckers his lips. He's not happy. He glances back at me, and his gaze tells me he's judging everything about me: about how I'm not as slim or as tall or as Nordic as he likes. He's wondering, but not saying, why I would bother with Solo February since *he* isn't interested, and he can't imagine who would be. All of this I glean from his beady little blue eyes.

"Yes, but doesn't it feel a little desperate?"

"How so?" I feel guarded. Like this is a trap.

"Well, I mean, aren't you just playing hard to get?" Eric just shakes his head as if he already knows all the old "tricks" women play when they're trying to seriously tell him no.

"Hard to get?" I echo, astonished. "But, going solo isn't about having people chase after you. It's about really working on oneself."

"Honestly, I think you're just pushing the problem on men. Ever thought if men don't like you, then that's a *you* problem?"

The audience lets out a gasp and a few long *ooooooohs* about the burn. Okay, Eric. Wanna play the toxic masculinity game? I love this game! My turn!

"The problem," I say, "if we're talking about straight men, is that some of them"—I'm talking about you, Eric—"think they have a right to everything they want. They think they can show up and be assholes"—Oops. I swore on live TV—"and we should still fawn all over them. We're supposed to just take what they give us and be grateful. But that's just not good enough anymore. Why are we always tying ourselves into knots for *them*? Why do *they* get to call all the shots? Why do they—with all the privilege they get handed at birth—get to tell us we're fat? Or our boobs aren't big enough? Or that we should like sports more? Or that we should like the beers they drink? Or that we don't make the salaries they make because we don't *negotiate* hard enough, even though when we try to do that, they tell us not to be bossy or pushy?"

Several loud ladies in the audience hoot.

"We can't *win.* We dress too provocatively, then we're asking to get assaulted. We dress too conservatively, and then we're dowdy and don't try hard enough. But when we try too hard, we're high maintenance. We're asked to be *cool,* not be like *the other girls,* but then when we are, we're too manly, too . . . whatever."

Eric's beginning to look a little panicked now and he should.

"The things some of us like—romances and rom-coms and fizzy pink champagne are *stupid and silly,* but the things some guys like, like loud action movies, sports, and beer are *important.* Nobody is paying millions of dollars for a fifteen-second ad for a rom-com Christmas movie on cable. But they should."

Someone in the audience shouts, "Preach!"

"We go on juice cleanses to clear our body of junk food, but what about junk men? Our souls need a cleanse. We need to get all those toxic men out of our lives by fasting. At the end of thirty days, we'll be able to see them for what they are: entitled, privileged jerks who are messing with our lives because we let them." I take a deep breath. "And we're not going to let them anymore."

The audience roars with approval and leaps to their feet in thunderous applause that seems to shake Eric's chair.

Then I glance at Eric. "And, Eric, I'd say, with all due respect, that maybe if you see this as something that's *our* problem and not *your* problem, then maybe, quite frankly, that is the very definition of a *you* problem."

"Oh, she got you. She got you good." Veronica beams triumphantly at Eric. He looks down at his note card, face flushed red. How do you like being called out on live TV, Eric? Did some of that toxicity bounce off of me and stick to you?

I glance up and my gaze falls on the window leading outside. Shoppers on Michigan Avenue have stopped and are watching the segment through the clear glass with a clear picture of the studio. Front and center, I see . . . a familiar figure there. Jack Mann, standing at the window. He's in jeans, a hoodie, and his peacoat, his thick dark hair stuffed beneath a beanie cap, his jawline sharp enough to cut that double-pane glass. He's a walking reminder that there are good guys out there, and it might not be fair for me to paint them all with such an unforgiving brush.

"So, how have you personally been doing with the challenge, Sora?" Veronica asks me right at that moment.

"Me, personally?" Jack waves at me. I swallow. "Fine. Doing fine."

"So, no dates for you until March first?"

"That's right," I say, and nod, even as I remember Jack's ask to the Golden Chef Awards. The last weekend in February. "I'm one hundred percent date-free. Don't want a date. Don't need a date."

I don't even know what I'm saying anymore. I'm just babbling. The audience leaps to their feet with thunderous applause and a few hoots and hollers. It washes, tinny and empty, over me, as I fight back a hot flash of guilt. I feel like an impostor.

Veronica thanks me for coming on the show and sends us to commercial break, and as soon as the cameras are off, Eric curses and leaves the set. Veronica turns to me, beaming.

"You kicked *ass,* girl. Love what you're doing," she tells me, and vigorously shakes my hand. "Galentines forever."

I laugh, the guilt still thudding in my ears. I'm a fraud, I want to tell her. I might have put Eric in his place, but I'm not the crusader everybody thinks I am. But before I can work up the nerve to blurt out the truth, Veronica's back studying her script and a tech guy whisks me away to untangle me from the mic attached to my dress. A few seconds later, I'm standing outside the studio on the icy sidewalk, snowflakes twirling around me. Cabs honk on the street, and a big bus lumbers by, kicking up black smoke into the wintry air. I find myself glancing around . . . and I realize I'm looking for Jack.

What am I going to tell him? How much of the show did he hear or see? My insides churn with indecision.

I hear my name called. Jack Mann is behind me.

"Oh . . . uh . . . Jack. Hi." I feel a blush creeping its way up the back of my neck. God, the man is gorgeous. Pure sex machine.

"Why didn't you tell me you were going to be on TV?" He shakes his head. "I would've been watching from the start! They didn't even have the sound on out here, so I couldn't hear you, but you looked great! Can't believe you were on *Let's Talk!* That's huge."

"I know I should've told you . . . it was kind of last minute." Why am I lying? Let's change the subject. Fast. "What are you doing downtown?"

"Oh, Pierre lives nearby. I was just grabbing coffee with him."

"Solo February!" a random woman on the sidewalk shouts nearby. She makes eye contact and raises her fist. I realize then that the audience from the morning show is filtering out into the street, which is quickly getting blanketed in a fresh coat of snow. I get a high five from a middle-aged woman who then glares at Jack as if he's a maggot wiggling through rotten garbage from a leaky dumpster.

"Thank you for that," she tells me. "You've inspired me."

Another lady shouts, "Men suck!"

Jack looks at her, uneasy.

"So, have you given any thought to the Golden Chef Awards . . ." Ack, here it is. Moment of truth. Am I picking Solo February over Jack? But how can I pick Jack with the sidewalk literally filled to the brim with #GoSolo followers?

He rubs the back of his neck. He's so damn broad and tall that he seems like a man who could chop down pine trees with his bare hands. Just karate-chop those suckers.

"About that . . ."

Jack's face falls just a little. He seems to know already what I'm going to say.

A familiar face parts the crowd then.

"Sora? That was so good?" Arial comes bounding up to us on the sidewalk. Where did she come from? She's wrapped in a geometric scarf and a designer puffy jacket with an asymmetrical collar. "Did you see me? I was in the back corner of the audience? I got in late, so I couldn't come to the greenroom."

"Uh, no, I didn't see you," I say as she wraps me in a tight hug. I feel white-hot panic run down my spine. I try to telegraph a message to Jack: run. Hide. Jack, however, just looks at me, confused.

"We are going to be even more viral? Is that a thing?" Arial laughs at her own joke. Then she sees Jack for the first time, craning her neck up to take in his impressive shoulders, which have begun to take on snowflakes like a mountain range.

"Uh . . . Arial, meet Jack. Jack, this is my boss . . . Arial."

Jack grins. "Oh, nice to meet you," he says, offering a massive paw. Arial takes it cautiously, a gleam of understanding and a sharp look of disapproval in her eye as she looks at him and looks at me.

"My? You are good-looking, aren't you?" she remarks.

"Uh. Only on days I shower?" Jack shrugs a manly shoulder. His self-deprecation makes him sexier.

"How do . . . uh, you two know each other?" Arial asks.

"We went to elementary school together. We're just old friends," I add, quickly, dismissively. Jack shoots me a look. I can't read it.

"Friends?"

"Yeah. Just friends. I mean, come on, we were in kindergarten together." I'm more definitive this time, except that I do read the look on Jack's face. Loud and clear. He's disappointed. Something more. Hurt.

"Oh, good." Arial's relieved. "Come on then, Sora. I thought we could grab coffee? Nice to meet you, Jack!"

Arial pulls me away before I can say a proper goodbye. Jack still looks a little stunned and confused as he turns away from me on the sidewalk and walks away, shoulders slumped in defeat. I want to call after him.

But I don't.

Seventeen

SORA

> I need to date myself, and practice on me, because how else am I ever supposed to get better at dating? And by better, I just mean not being so terrible at it.
>
> —SOLO FEBRUARY CHALLENGE

I spend the next couple of days wishing I'd handled everything differently.

I text and call Jack, feeling rotten, but he doesn't return my texts. Or my calls. It's full-on radio silence. The more he ignores me, the more frantic I get. I can't help feeling in my gut that I've blown it. Just when I'm sure I have, he answers my call.

"Hey, I just want to say sorry about . . ." I begin in a rush. I'm in bed, Larry at my feet. Snow falls outside my window, white against the darkening February sky.

"You don't have to apologize," Jack says, but he still sounds a little . . . off. A little guarded. I've made him this way, too. This is my fault.

"I had to keep up appearances. In front of my boss," I try to explain.

"I know."

"Hey . . . I . . ." I should just tell him I like him. Because I do. Maybe more than like. But there's also the problem of his award show at the end of the month. "I just wanted to talk to you because . . ."

"You can't go with me to the Golden Chef Awards," he finishes, sounding resigned. "I saw the *Let's Talk!* segment. Don't need a date. Don't want one?"

"Jack, I was just . . . it was for the show. It's not that I don't want one with you. It's—"

"I get it." Jack is quick to answer. "Say, how about we just take a little time. I won't bother you anymore until March."

"Jack, you don't have to—"

"I think it'll be best," he says, sounding more definitive. "I just . . . I'd rather see you when you're truly free to be in a relationship. It kind of feels like you're . . . I don't know . . . embarrassed of me."

"I absolutely am not!"

"It just feels like I'm a secret you have to keep, or that I'm someone you're seeing on the side, and it doesn't feel that great," he admits.

Shit. I get what he's saying. I am hiding him. Hiding him from all the *Solo February* fans.

"You're not on the side. Not at all. And I don't want you to feel that way."

"I know. That's why I just . . . think it's best if we wait until

March. Then maybe it won't be weird." Jack sounds sad, but firm. He's thought about this. He's come to a decision. It's now I realize that holding off on seeing each other until March isn't an ask. It's a firm statement. He's drawing the line. Not me.

"Okay," I agree, reluctantly. It's just two weeks, but as I hang up the phone, suddenly, it feels like two lifetimes.

For the next ten days, Jack's as good as his word. There's no texting. No calls. I try texting him a few times, but only get responses like a thumbs-up, or none at all. He's serious about the March deadline. Ugh. What is wrong with me? Why do I let other people in my life constantly set the boundaries? If I think about it a second, that's very likely the root of all my problems. Instead of taking responsibility for my own lack of real self-control or lack of action in key moments, I'd let Dad rein me in with his temper, or Mom with her body issues. I should've been the one to just be honest with Jack. To tell him we did need to wait. But I didn't.

And even as more and more missives from *Solo February* pour in from fans, I just feel emptier and emptier reading them. Can I tell them all that going solo is right? So many of them seem to have found someone they want to date. Who am I to stand in their way? Should I really be telling Gabrielle, or any other Soloist, who to date or not to date? Why did I ever think I was qualified to give anyone else advice in the first place?

As I'm considering this, a new message dings on my phone from Nami. She's been texting me about the bridesmaids' dresses, so I know that's exactly what this is about. And I've been avoiding trying on my bridesmaid's dress like the plague because I've been chowing down on bacon and retaining water like the Hoover Dam. I've not gotten anywhere near a scale for fear I'd step on it and it would scream bloody murder.

Why haven't you come to the shop yet?

I sigh. *I will, okay?*

When?

Soon.

How about today?

Bossy much?

I've got a lot to do today, I text, hoping she'll let it slide. She doesn't.

OMG, Sora! Please! I ask you to do ONE thing!

Okay, bridezilla. Technically, she didn't ask me to do just one thing. She also asked me to bring a date, and not dance with an elderly great-uncle during the couples' dance.

Fine. I'll come today.

I think that will be the end of it. But it's not.

Great. I'll pick you up in an hour.

It's only when I'm in the dressing room and attempting to try on the dress that I realize I might have gone overboard on the bacon this month. I'm starting to sweat bullets inside the tiny gray dressing room in the fancy bridal store downtown. It's the kind of expensive shop where the salesclerk offers you champagne the moment you enter the door, because the markup more than covers the cost, and because you're going to need alcohol when you look at your first price tag.

Currently, I stand inside one of the enormous, cedar-lined dressing rooms, which just might be bigger than my bedroom at my apartment. I am guzzling down all of my free champagne in hopes that somehow, the alcohol will save me. I stare at myself in the mirror, hair a mess, dress only halfway on, just up to my hips. I haven't even *tried* zipping the zipper yet. There's miles of light blue fabric, and why, *oh why*, did Nami pick such a fitted dress? I begged her to go flowy. Begged her. She went suck-to-your-skin fishtail flare because the *other* bridesmaids loved it, the ones who wear a double zero on a bloated day and consider a kale smoothie a "splurge."

I give the dress another hard tug. Nope. No way. I can't get my hips in here. No matter how hard I try. This isn't fitted. It's more like a physical assault. I want to press charges against this dress.

I hear a gentle rap on the door.

"Do you need any assistance?" asks the saleslady, concern in her voice.

I grab the dress firmly and suck in with all my might and yank. Amazingly, it gets over my hips. Now I need to try to get my arms in the tiny little arm holes that seem too small for my wrists.

Wish I had more champagne.

I'm starting to really sweat now, which does not, as I hope, help me slide my arms into the arm holes. But eventually I do it, and now, I must tackle the zipper at the side.

"Uh . . . just give me a minute," I pant, glaring at my bare skin, and the two full inches that damn zipper is going to have to swallow if it's going to make the teeth meet. I might need more than a minute. I start tugging at the zipper and it gives a high-pitched, terrified squeak.

A harder knock comes now. It's Nami.

"Sora." That's her WTF tone. "Let me in."

"No," I cry, tugging at the zipper. Come on, baby. *Come on.* You can do this, zipper. You can. My fingers, slippery with panic sweat, lose their traction on the tiny zipper handle. Damn it. I knew I should've brought pliers.

I get the zipper at *least* up to the bottom of my rib cage, but my girls revolt. There's no way they're going to get sucked into this. They've grown bigger, too, as it seems they like bacon. Quite a lot.

Damn it.

I glance at the white furry stole hanging on the hook of the door. Well, I'll just have to cover up with that and hope Nami—and the seamstress—don't notice.

Nami knocks again, harder this time. "Sora! Come on!" Her voice is high-pitched and clipped. She's pissed.

"Coming!" I say and whip the furry white stole around my arms and open the door. The glare of the lights on the three-way mirror hits me, blinding me for a second. I blink, and when I can focus again, I see Nami glaring at me.

"What took so long?" she asks me, suspicious.

"Nothing," I say.

"Come," says the seamstress—a very tiny, very old Polish woman wearing black slacks and a silk blouse that matches her all-white hair. She motions to the small, carpeted platform in front of the wall of mirrors. I inch-walk, because the dress is so damn tight, and wiggle my way to it, feeling the zipper teeth pressing into my side fat. I manage to get up onto the platform without ripping the seam—a small miracle—and as I look at myself, I realize these dresses look like something Elsa from *Frozen* would wear, except I'm not blond or skinny, and I don't have amazing icy superpowers. Though, the way Nami glares at me, I think she wants to freeze me right here.

"Let's take this off. Yes?" The elderly seamstress grabs hold of the furry white stole, her wizened hands surprisingly agile. But I don't let go.

"We don't need to. It's a great accessory." I hold on to it like it's a door from the *Titanic* floating in the frozen Atlantic.

"Take it off." The seamstress frowns, her wrinkles growing deeper on her face. I hesitate and the seamstress and I lock eyes and I can tell she's confused. I try to communicate silently that all she should do is back away slowly. Let this go. You don't want this heat, lady. Believe me. And I'm not the only one Nami is going to yell at. Because when she gets angry, it's like a nuclear meltdown. She radiates it everywhere. Just like Dad.

"Sora! Don't be like that. Take off the stole." Nami folds her arms across her chest and glares some more. She already knows what's coming. And so do I.

Reluctantly, I shed the stole. Nami gasps audibly and her hand flies to her mouth. The seamstress, who has no doubt seen it all in this dressing room, appears unflappable.

"Sora! What the hell!" Nami cries, as she sees my fatty flesh hanging out of the side of her too-tight Elsa bridesmaid dress. She clasps the zipper and tries to move it up. Good luck, sister.

"Sorry. I *might* have gone overboard on the bacon."

"I *told* you this stupid Solo February was a bad idea. Damn it! I cannot *believe* you!" Her fingers slip off the zipper and she breaks a nail. She stares at her nails in horror. She sticks her finger in her mouth and stares daggers at me. "I can't believe you did this."

"I told you not to go formfitting! I told you we should do flowy." She never listens. I can fluctuate ten pounds in a single day, for goodness' sake. Nami only ever loses or gains maybe an ounce.

The seamstress approaches me and studies the gap in the zipper, taking the measuring tape from around her neck and marking my skin. She studies the zipper.

"Well, I didn't think you'd stuff your face with bacon all month! I mean, are you trying to have a heart attack? Like Dad?"

Her words hit me like a blow. It's a clear, below-the-belt foul. "Hey, that's low."

Nami swallows what she was going to say next. But she's still angry. She blows out a frustrated breath and paces in front of me, panting. "I suppose you don't have a date yet," she says, anger in her voice.

"No, not technically."

"Great!" She throws her hands in the air. "So, the couples' dance is ruined. This is just fantastic."

"Nami—"

"This is so like you. You're always so . . . so . . . careless. I swear to God."

I tell myself Nami is under stress and she's taking it out on me.

"This is just like when you crashed the minivan." Nami is fired up. Eyes flashing.

"Oh no. Not this again."

"Mom was giving me the minivan for my sixteenth birthday, but you were home from college and just *had* to use it, and then you totaled it, *one day* before my birthday!"

"A dog ran out in the road! I swerved to miss it."

"Fine. And what about my iPhone in ninth grade?" Her cheeks flush red with anger. I tell myself I'm the easy target. She knows I'll love her no matter what. She's just venting.

"I didn't *mean* to drop it and crack the screen. It just slipped."

"And my favorite cashmere sweater that Grandma Mitsuye gave me for my tenth birthday?" Her voice gets even louder.

"That's not fair." I might have tried it on and stretched it out horribly. "You always stole my clothes! I could never borrow yours because they never fit me!"

"Here we go!" She throws up her hands, mirroring my frustration. "All I'm saying is that if you were a little more careful, a little more considerate, these things wouldn't happen! It's like you're trying to ruin everything!" In her fury, she snags a heel on the pristine white carpet of the fitting room area. She catches herself, but the stumble makes her angrier, especially because I have to swallow a snicker. "Don't laugh," she warns me.

"Then stop holding grudges."

"Dad held grudges. I can't help it."

We both glare at each other, a lifetime full of resentments bubbling to the surface like a bloated whale. I love my sister to pieces, but sometimes, I just want to kick her hard in the shins like I used to do at age five. A good scuffle and then the argument would be over.

"I'll fix it," the seamstress tells us, moving in Nami's direction. "No problem."

But Nami seems not to hear, or not to care about the seamstress's effort to barter a peace accord.

"I just can't believe you're being so insensitive," Nami snaps at me. "This is my wedding. It's got to be perfect. For Mitch."

"Please," I mutter beneath my breath. Mitch wouldn't care if the wedding happened in a nice hotel, or the back of a courtroom, or, hell, in the bed of a pickup truck. He's the last man to be worried about appearances.

"What did you say?" Nami's laser-focused on me now.

"Nothing," I murmur, not meeting her eye.

"Are you trying to say something about Mitch?"

"Well . . ." I hesitate, thinking about the whatever-you-want-babe, yes-man lump that is her fiancé, Mitch. He's uninterested in politics, books, movies, travel, or anything not related to football, beer, or video games. Hell no, he's not worth the effort, and I've thought so from the beginning. Nami loves Mitch because she can dress him up like a Ken doll, he looks good in couple photographs, and he's safe. But is he worthy of her? No. He's not.

But I can't say all this. Can I?

But then I don't have to. Nami fills in the blanks for me.

"You hesitated too long!" she cries, accusing. "You don't like Mitch!"

"I . . ." I glance at Nami. I could lie. Smooth all this over, but haven't I been telling all the people who are #GoingSolo to be less accommodating and stand up for themselves? Plus, I'm tired of lying. I'm tired of lying to them, and to Jack, and to everybody. The least I can do right now is be honest.

"No," I admit at last. "I don't particularly like Mitch."

Nami looks like I slapped her.

Even the seamstress pauses in her fussing over my zipper and steps back, a worried look on her wrinkled face.

Nami glares at me. "What's wrong with Mitch? Name *one* thing that's wrong with him."

"He . . . doesn't work that hard." I don't know how to say this without *saying* it. I'm trying to be diplomatic about the fact that he has less ambition than your typical eggplant.

"That's not true! He has a job."

"Working for his uncle at a plumbing supply company," I try to gently point out.

"Dad was a plumber, there's no shame in that."

"It's not the job I have issue with. It's that his uncle gave him the job because every other job he ever held, he got fired from. For not showing up on time, or not showing up at all."

"They didn't appreciate Mitch's potential," Nami says. Wow. She's really not seeing the truth.

"He failed out of two colleges."

"He's a creative type. He wants to launch a channel on Twitch, making millions with his gameplay!"

I roll my eyes. Mitch has been bragging about how he'll be making millions one day when he's never lifted a finger to start a channel.

"Yeah, but has he ever even made a single video?"

"He's working on it!" Nami says, defensive.

"He'll never do it because it involves work. And he hates to work." This comes out blunter than I intend, but I'm already angry and the words are out before I can stop them.

"I love him." Nami's eyes blaze fire, promising retribution, but I'm in too deep now. "And he's asked me to take charge of the wedding, because he knows I'll do it right."

"No, he's asked you to be in charge because he's lazy and planning a wedding takes work. Plus, I don't think he really cares about the wedding." I've seen the bored, indifferent look on his face as Nami dragged him to one site after another for potential wedding receptions. "This is all your idea. Not his. He doesn't really care where he gets married. Or how. He likes that you make all the decisions for him but, Nami, that's not a real partner."

"He is a real partner. He's sweet. He's supportive."

"He just never disagrees with you. There's a difference. If he were really supportive, he'd help you with the planning. With anything, really."

"That's not true. You're only saying that because you're jealous." Nami jabs a manicured nail into my chest. It hurts.

"I'm not jealous about Mitch." Far from it.

"You're just jealous because all you could ever get was Marley. And even then, it's only because—"

"Don't say it." I glare at her, daring her to bring up the pregnancy. If she does, I swear to God, her shins won't be the only thing I'll kick. She hesitates. She seems to know she's going too far. So does the seamstress, because she hisses something in Polish, shrugs her shoulders, and backs slowly out of the room. "Look, Nami, I'm sorry I hurt your feelings. I could have lied. But I wanted to be honest with you."

Nami sniffs, indignant, and crosses her arms across her chest and turns away from me. I can see the anger flare across her perfect, poreless face in the three-way mirror.

"Well, as long as we're being honest," she says, and whirls to face me, red-faced. "Have you looked at Marley's social media lately?"

What? Why is she on Marley's social media?

"Why are you following him?" I'd "un"-ed Marley (unfriended, un-followed, un-whatever-ed) on every platform a long time ago.

"I just never stopped."

This feels like a betrayal. "You're following my ex-husband online? What the hell, Nami?" She's scrolling through her phone. I think she's going to show me something I don't want to see.

"I wasn't going to show you this . . . but . . ." She hands me the phone. I know I shouldn't take it. I shouldn't look.

But curiosity gets the better of me. It's a sad fact that if I were a cat, I'd be dead nine times over because curiosity would've run me flat over, stabbed me multiple times, or tossed me off a high-rise balcony.

The first thing I see is a photo of Marley and Lululemon. They're both grinning like morons, looking too damn happy for people who subsist on a diet of kale and kombucha. Plus, Marley has busted out his Pharrell Williams hat, which is a terrible look on him.

Lululemon is grinning, which looks unnatural on her because in the grocery store, all I saw was a puckered face of disapproval. So I dig deeper into the photo, telling myself it's just so I can mercilessly poke fun. They're facing each other, holding a paper cutout of red hearts—three of them between them. I scroll down to the caption, and it reads, *We're so excited to say . . . Our Little Valentine is on the way!*

Our Little Valentine? Then I notice Marley has his scrawny, clammy palm on Lululemon's nonexistent stomach. What the . . . mother-effing . . . what?

I feel suddenly nauseous.

Oh, God. Marley and Lululemon will have a spawn.

I glance at Nami. "How long have you known about this?" I ask.

"Since Valentine's Day. I didn't want to be the one to tell you."

I don't know what makes me angrier: that she still follows Marley or that she refused to be a good spy for me. I feel a whole bunch of feelings rising up in me, none of them good. I'm right back in that place right after college where I peed on a stick and there were two lines instead of one, when Marley accused me of lying to him about being on the pill and then he stomped out of the apartment. It hadn't been an Instagram moment with freakin' rose filters and cutout hearts.

Then I look at the photo again. I know what I'm looking for, and I find it: Marley's grandmother's solitaire on Lululemon's perfectly manicured left ring finger, the one I'd once worn.

Eighteen

SORA

> Who does marriage really benefit anyway? Men. All the studies show that men live longer and healthier if they're married. Women, however, live the same amount of time, with or without a man. So why do we think we need one so badly?
>
> —SOLO FEBRUARY CHALLENGE

I'm not sure what's worse: that Marley and Lululemon will have a baby and get married, or that I care. I should be far, far and away done with Marley—who even cares what he does with his life? But, I realize, I do. I do care. Because he stood up before a hundred strangers at city hall and told me he'd legally be my husband. Never mind that it had been a pregnancy that got him there. I hate, too, that I don't get to call Jack about it, because I'm respecting his desire to steer clear of me until I can get a little bit of my shit together.

My next *Solo February* post is dark and dire.

I got the worst news—my ex-husband is getting remarried. And his fiancée is pregnant. And they look stupidly happy. And, confession time, I had a miscarriage that I've never really gotten over. There, I said it. This has dredged up all kinds of feelings in me, all kinds of bad feelings, when I was trying so hard to be positive. To work on myself. But now, I wonder if, no matter what I do, I'm just always going to end up sad and alone.

Is there any point to anything?

The darkness that came over me after the miscarriage feels as if it's edging closer to me again, that pitch-black nothingness. It feels suffocating.

Then, my laptop pings with the first comment to my new article. And then another. And another.

Hang in there, sister.
We all got dark days.
Just like you told us . . . Keep on doing this for you!

The comments pile up, one after another, the Soloists jumping to my aid. I'm touched, and I tear up. I can barely read the comments, they're coming so fast.

You got this.
It's bad now, but it'll get better.
Been there. Done that. Have the T-shirt. Hang in there.
Don't give up. We believe in you.

This community, this amazing community, makes me feel not alone. And I love it. I love them. All of them.

And don't forget what you told us: take care of yourself. Self-care!

They're right. I have to snap out of it. As much as I want to drown my sorrows in bacon grease, I won't. The specter of Dad is real. He never really took care of himself, always carried extra weight, and scoffed at salads, calling them "rabbit food." He also died of a heart attack at age fifty-nine. Despite what Nami might think, I don't, actually, want to follow him down that road.

Maybe I'll . . . make a salad. For once. Larry sniffs around the kitchen as I cut up greens. I try to feed him a cucumber, but he sniffs at it and looks at me like I've gone crazy. Maybe I have.

"If nobody is ever going to take care of me, I'll have to start," I tell Larry, who whines. Then he heads to the door but hits the foyer table, again. He needs to go out. I drag myself away from my healthy lunch, stuff my feet into my worn Uggs, grab my parka, in dire need of a wash, and lumber out to the frigid, subzero cold snap, the cold wind blasting me so hard I can't breathe for a second or two. That's brisk, baby. Larry whines, heads to his favorite patch of snow-covered grass, and does his business quickly, eager to get back inside to the warmth of our apartment. Overnight, we got a dusting of snow, just enough to wet the toes of my boots.

I trudge inside, Larry on my heels. As I stomp the snow off my boots, I realize it's nearly noon, and I feel how this Saturday is stretching empty and terrible in front of me. Tonight is Jack's big award ceremony. I wish I were going with him. That's the truth of it. I'm wallowing in pity, when I get a text from Mom.

I'm coming over. Be there in five minutes.

What? Mom, I'm

But before I can finish the text, I hear my buzzer sound. I rush to my dining room window and look down, seeing Mom, bundled in her ankle-length, puffy white down coat that makes her look like the Michelin Man. She hits the buzzer again, impatient, and looks up at me, her hood falling back. She points to the door.

Reluctantly, I buzz her up. She clomps upstairs to my apartment and lets herself in. She doesn't even have her coat off before she launches into a tirade.

"What happened with your sister?" she demands, full guns cocked and ready to blaze. So, Nami went and tattled. Figures. She's been doing that since we were toddling around in Pull-Ups.

"Uh, well . . . the bridesmaid dress didn't fit." I brace myself to hear the lecture about how I should be doing FlyFit with her more often, about how we should've been double-dieting, like she'd wanted to do all along.

But she waves off that fault with a dismissive flip of her hand. She doesn't seem to care that I gained weight. Interesting.

"She told me you said something mean about Mitch?" Mom plops down on my couch as she takes off her scarf and hat. Well, just make yourself comfortable. Larry comes over to give her a sniff hello about six inches off from her knee. She gives her grand-dog a perfunctory pat on the head.

I sigh. "Yeah."

"What was it?" She sounds ready to ground me, except she can't anymore, I remind myself. I'm a fully functioning, independent adult.

"I told her she could do so much better than a guy with zero ambition who keeps bragging about a gaming channel that he'll never create because you have to actually do work for it and he's the laziest person I've ever met."

Mom falls silent and pensive, as she laces her fingers together in her lap. I brace myself for the coming lecture about how I need to be a better sister, and think about my sister's feelings, and realize the importance of a wedding day, and make it the special once-in-a-lifetime occasion she deserves, and *blah, blah, blah.* Nami's the favorite anyway and . . .

Instead, Mom lets out a long breath of air. "Oh, thank God," she reveals in a hushed, conspiratorial tone. "I thought I was the only one."

Hold everything.

"Wait . . . what?" I don't understand what's happening. "I thought you loved Mitch."

"Oh, God no. Whenever I visit, he just drinks beer and plays those darn games where he runs around shooting aliens." She rolls her eyes in disdain. "He's not only swimming in the shallow end of the gene pool, it's actually an inflatable toddler pool from Walmart."

"Mom!"

"You think you're the only one who's sassy in the family?

Think again." I have a sudden new and profound respect for my mom. "I've been wondering if dullness can be passed to my grandchildren. He makes couch potatoes look dynamic."

"I can't believe this," I say, sinking down into the couch next to her. "You realize we could've been making fun of Mitch behind his back for years? So much wasted time. How come you didn't say anything before now?"

"Why didn't *you*?" Mom counters.

I send her a sharp glance. "Seriously? You think *I* wanted to be the nail that gets hammered down? No way. I wasn't going to speak up."

"I guess I deserve that." Mom sighs, shaking her head.

"Did you ever think about talking to Nami?"

"To Nami?" Mom looks at me, dark eyes wide in disbelief. "She'd explode. You know she doesn't do well with criticism. That temper . . ."

"Dad's."

"Don't I know it," Mom agrees. "Nobody in this family does well with conflict."

"Tell me about it. Anytime there was a fight, Dad would just start yelling to get everyone else to stop yelling." I remember Dad's explosive bursts of temper at the dinner table. In the car. On family vacations. Everywhere we were, pretty much.

Mom laughs a little at the memory. She sighs again. "That's why I always said 'the nail that sticks out gets hammered down.'" She covers her hand with mine. "I was just trying to protect you. From Dad's temper. He was always overworked and underslept, and he had a short fuse to begin with. I thought if we all just sat still and quiet, then it would pass, and we'd all be okay." Mom glances at me.

"Is *that* why you always warned us about being hammered down?" I blink, astonished. "Because of Dad?"

"Yes. Why else would I say it?"

"I don't know . . ." I rub my neck. "I thought you just didn't want us to take risks in general or share what we really thought about anything. I mean, that's why I never spoke up about Mitch."

Mom blinks, shocked. "Why would you think I didn't care what you thought! *Of course* I wanted to know what you thought!"

This is news to me. "Yeah, but when we'd talk back to Dad, you told us 'don't be the nail.' So I thought it was just bad to speak up."

Mom sighs and pinches her nose. "I was just trying to protect you from Dad. The more you talked back, the angrier he'd get, and I just . . . I just didn't think it was worth it. But maybe I made a mistake there. Maybe we all should've just shouted and screamed and gotten all our anger out. I never meant that you should censor yourself like you do, Sora. I never meant for you to feel like your feelings weren't as important as everybody else's. And for that, I'm sorry."

It hits me then all at once: an epiphany. Nami handled Dad's temper by fueling her own. I handled Dad's temper by staying inert, quiet, and not making any sudden moves. It explains a lot about me. Like how I get stuck. Like how *being stuck* sometimes feels safe and warm and comfortable, even when I know it's not. Like after the miscarriage.

"I am sorry he was so short-tempered," she says, sounding a little sad. "He didn't mean to take it out on you kids. It wasn't your fault, you know."

"Oh, I know," I say, even though right up until this moment, I'm not sure I did.

She puts her head on my shoulder. "I love you, Sora. So very much. You know, you always were the wise one."

"Me? Pffft." Still, I beam at the compliment. "So, *I'm* your favorite. Not Nami?"

"I don't play favorites!" Mom protests, but I know she means me.

I glance at Mom. "Did you hear the news about Marley?"

"Is he moving to Siberia?" Mom asks, hopeful. Mom is no fan of Marley.

"No. He knocked up his girlfriend." Saying this out loud makes this stupidly real. "They're getting married."

"Lord! Has that man ever heard of a condom?" Mom clucks her tongue in disapproval. Then she reaches out to grab my hand.

"When I told Marley that I was pregnant, he yelled and shouted at me that I'd tricked him and then stormed out of our apartment." I hate that memory. "It wasn't an Instagram moment." I show her the photo of Marley and Lululemon. They were considerate enough to make it public so a quick search brings it up every time. She frowns.

"You don't know that this is, either," Mom says, handing my phone back to me. "You don't really know he's changed. Who knows what happened a day before this photo?"

"True." Two months after I peed on that stick, we got married. Nearly three months after that, I lived through that horrible day at the doctor's office. The damn worried look on the ultrasound tech's face. *Something's wrong, isn't it?* I'd asked her.

"You're better off without him. You know that."

"I know. I just want him to be miserable without me."

"Oh, he is. He's always been miserable. Miserable excuse for a man."

This makes me laugh. Ah, Mom. We don't have a perfect

relationship, but when things get really tough, I can always count on her to be in my corner. Always. Mom releases my hand. "You know, I know you're going solo for February or for however long you want. But eventually, I know that you'll find someone meant for you."

I think of Jack and wonder if I already have. "I actually met someone, Mom. I broke my #GoSolo vow." The confession comes out in a torrent. "And he's got this big event tonight, and I should be there, but now I think I've scared him off. And I made a promise to Arial, to my readers . . ."

"Why not just write about it?" Mom asks, simply. "Why not just admit the struggle you're going through? Just admit that you broke your vow. Level with your readers. Once you do that, you can show up for Jack tonight, with a free conscience. Just admit what's going on."

"That'll make me the nail, though."

"We should all be the nail sometimes," she says, with a dismissive wave of her hand. "That's the only way anything ever gets built."

> *I've got a real secret confession to make. . . . I haven't been entirely honest about going solo.* I start typing, the words flying off my keyboard. I feel nervous energy in my fingers as I type. I'm finally coming clean to all the Soloists. I have no idea how they're going to take it, but I at least have to try to level with them.
>
> *I met someone. Actually, I just reconnected with an old friend, a wonderful friend, someone I used to know in kindergarten. I told him I vowed to go solo,*

and he told me he'd wait. But he's got a big-deal awards thing for work tonight, and I don't think it's right for me to leave him alone because I've set an arbitrary time to work on myself. Solo February has been amazing, and I'm so, so glad it's helped so many of you. It's helped me, too. Helped me to take care of myself a little more. To make smarter decisions (about who I date and what I eat), and to just take care of myself a little bit better than I have been.

But the real joy of it was meeting all of you. You've been so wonderful, so supportive.

So, I'm leaving the Solo February challenge a little early. I know a few of you might be upset by this, but hear me out. Sometimes, the universe works in surprising ways. Sometimes, when you stop looking, you just might find the perfect match.

It's not something I ever in a million years imagined would happen. But it did.

And I owe it to myself to see where this will lead.

Wish me the best.

I send the article to Arial before I can change my mind, even though I know she probably won't even read it until Sunday. Then I call Jack.

"Hey, I don't know if it's too late, but I'd love to be your plus-one," I tell his voicemail. "I want to be there for you on this really important night. I think . . . I think . . ."

I want to say: I'm falling in love with you, too. But I pause too long, and the voicemail beeps. "If you're happy with your message, press one . . ."

Crap. I delete my message. I try again.

"Hey, uh, I want to be your plus-one tonight. I've decided—"

Ack, delete that.

"Yo! I wanna go to the Oscars of Baking!"

Delete.

"Hey! Race you to the Oscars of Baking?"

Delete again. Delete all.

Ugh.

Then I write and delete about a dozen texts. I'm running out of time. I need to just decide on one.

> *Hey. I quit the #GoSolo challenge and want to be your plus-one tonight. If you'll have me!*

I get an auto response from Jack's phone: *I'm driving right now and unable to answer my texts. I'll get back to you when it's safe!*

I glance at my watch. He's on his way to the awards already. It's nearly time!

My phone rings, and I perk up, hoping it's Jack. Instead, it's Arial.

"Hey, Sora? I got your article?" Her voice sounds a little tense. A little less upbeat. She doesn't like the article. "And uh, I don't know how this is going to go? Are you really ending Solo February early?"

"Yes. I didn't want to lie anymore."

"Okay, but I'm not sure our readers will like this? They really, really dig the idea of Solo February. And you're kind of like, saying, uh . . . never mind? Like, uh, forget it?"

The old Sora would cave right now. The old Sora would agree and offer to change the article. But the new Sora . . .

"I see why you might feel that way," I begin. "But that's not the point of the article. The point is everyone has to choose the path that's right for them."

"Yes, but the readers have chosen to go solo? And they might hate it if you duck out early? I'm just warning you?"

I have that old familiar fear about sticking my neck out. Then I think about the fact that being quiet hasn't gotten me anywhere, either. If I'd spoken up when Marley hadn't paid his share of household expenses, or when Dan hadn't been around on weekends, maybe I would've ended those bad relationships earlier.

"I know I'm being the nail. But I've just got to do it."

"Uh, the nail?" Arial asks.

"Never mind. Long story, I just mean I've got to stick to my guns on this one."

"Okay, but if the readers revolt, I don't know?" I know she means that if this goes south, she doesn't know if the full-time job offer still stands. I get it.

"I understand it's a risk."

"If you're sure?"

"I'm sure."

Now, all I have to do is get dressed and head to the Golden Chef Awards, which start in less than an hour.

I take Jack's ticket with me in my tiny black clutch bag, as I take a rideshare to the Hancock Tower on the Magnificent Mile. I've glued on my lashes, and poured myself into double Spanx and my old standby, a flattering-for-all A-line black dress. I'm wearing my long dark hair wavy and loose, and I've got Grandma's pearls on. I like to think I look like an Asian Audrey Hepburn, and I try to avoid mirrors to keep reality at bay. I've got red stilettos on my feet because . . . why not? They match my wool coat. Who cares if the weather lady predicts a blizzard later? I need to look good *now* and I refuse to wear snow boots because that would be like admitting defeat to winter. Not this Midwestern girl.

I'm cursing Saturday-night traffic, because I'm even later than I feared I'd be. I rush inside Hancock Tower, past the giant round reflecting pool in the center of the lobby. It's empty. The ceremony is being held at the swanky Signature Room on the ninety-fifth floor, and signs point to roped-off areas near the elevators for Golden Chef Awards ticket holders. That's technically me. I don't see Jack. The ceremony, I realize with a cold sweat, is already underway. I show my ticket to the elevator guard, and he waves me forward, into a super-fast car. My ears instantly pop as I ride the fastest elevator in North America, speeding from the first floor to the ninety-fifth in thirty-eight seconds. Then the doors open to a glittering, gorgeous, golden-hued restaurant with 360 degrees of floor-to-ceiling windows. I suck in a breath as I see the city of Chicago, lights twinkling to one side, and the large, dark expanse of the lake to the other, a big silver half moon reflected in its calm waves.

"Wow," I manage.

Forget the Sears Tower. Or Willis Tower. Or whatever they're calling it these days. This is the best view in Chicago. Very well-dressed people pack the restaurant with the amazingly high ceilings and the golden, flattering low light that washes over the dining room. Beautifully decorated tables dot the huge dining room, all carrying expensive bottles of Signature

Room–label champagne in buckets. The Golden Chef hat logo seems to be everywhere, and it's all gorgeously decorated. It's the perfect spot, I think, for a grand romantic gesture.

Awards are being handed out from a small stage near the windows, and I hope and pray that I haven't missed Jack's event. I glance around the room, looking for Jack. Where is he? The restaurant is low-lit, and there are so many dark-haired men in tuxedos, I can't find him. Utensils clink as people dig into their appetizers from the prix fixe menu, and others sip champagne from crystal flutes. I realize I recognize many of these people. They're famous chefs from all over the country. Actually, the world. Some are reality TV stars. There are a few other celebrities as well, from Chicago-area shows, and a few from Hollywood. It's a big deal to be nominated, clearly, and I'm so proud of Jack.

"Can I take your coat, miss?" a man in a tie asks, and I realize I'm near the coat check.

"Oh, sure. Thank you." He takes my red wool coat and hands me a ticket. I keep scanning the crowd. On the stage, a woman accepts an award for Best Sous Chef, thanking her family.

Where's Jack?

And then, I see him on the other side of the room. He's sitting at a large, round table of ten, the chair next to him empty. He looks fantastic in his tuxedo, his fuller beard looking clipped and coifed, and in short, like the sexiest superspy baker I've ever seen. His eyes widen in surprise as he sees me. *Please* let him not be thinking that I clean up well. Men tend to refer to me like I'm a crab fisherman—shocked when I roll into a restaurant without plastic overalls and galoshes and not smelling like dead fish.

I wave at him, and he waves back, but he still looks stunned. Did he not get my message? I hesitate. Is this big, grand romantic gesture a mistake? Then I see a woman walking to Jack's table, wearing a thin, shimmery gold gown, and carrying a matching clutch. She's wearing her golden hair in finger waves, so she looks like a star from glamorous old Hollywood. I recognize her immediately.

Mal.

Jack's ex-fiancée.

She sits right down next to him. In his plus-one seat. And drapes her arm around his shoulders.

Nineteen

JACK

Love is supposed to solve all our problems, but what if it just creates them?

—SOLO FEBRUARY CHALLENGE

"Why so stiff, Jack?" Mal whispers in my ear as I struggle with the absolute nightmare unfolding before my very eyes.

I can't believe Mal showed up.

But, frankly, I'm more surprised Sora did.

I just . . . didn't think she would. I'm stunned. Mal next to me. Sora a few feet away. Sure, I got Sora's message about wanting to come tonight, but I'll be honest, I didn't get my hopes up. How many times can a guy be relegated to second place before he gets the message? I really thought we were Big-L Love, even though she was telling me and the whole world that she doesn't even believe in Big-L Love.

I'm just this big pathetic puppy trying to make women love me who can't love at all.

But now that I see her standing there, I see she does believe in Big-L Love. And Grand Romantic Gestures, or she wouldn't be here.

But now I'm going to lose her.

Because of Mal.

And my own doubt.

"What the hell are you doing here?" I hiss to Mal, even though I know why. She's been threatening to come for weeks. I didn't take her seriously, but I should have.

"Presenting an award," she says, feigning innocence. "I know someone who knows someone who runs the Golden Chefs. Why? Is this seat taken? Or can't I sit here?"

"No, you can't." But it's all too late, Sora has seen her. And she's clinging to me like a dryer sheet. I watch the blood draining from Sora's face.

"Jack-a-boo," she purrs. "The seat was empty. I just want to keep it warm."

I shrug her off, shooting to my feet, but the damage is done. It's too late. Sora's turned on her heel, already pushing by a waiter, and headed back to the elevators.

"Sora!" I cry, and a few patrons turn and stare at me as I chase after Sora. "Sora, wait."

Sora dashes past the coat check, nearly knocking over the attendant. I catch her right before the elevators.

"Sora, wait."

She whirls. "You could have told me that Mal was your plus-one. That she's the reason you wanted to wait until March. You could have just told me."

"She's not. I promise. There's nothing going on between us."

"So you said." Sora's voice drips with doubt. And I don't blame her.

"I know how this looks, but you have to believe me, I did not invite her here."

"What's she doing here, then?" Sora puts a hand on her hip.

"She's a presenter. She has connections." It sounds like a weak excuse. I dig up more truth. "She's been threatening to be my plus-one for weeks. I told her no, but she doesn't take no for an answer."

Sora stares at me. "Why didn't you just tell me that? Why keep it a secret?"

Because then I'd have to admit that Mal and I slept together a week before I bumped into Sora at my free samples table. That the reason why Mal thinks she can be my plus-one at all is because I made a terrible mistake. But I don't want to tell Sora that. It would just confirm her fears that I'm not over Mal.

"Why didn't you tell me that you were going to be on that morning show? That you'd recommitted to Solo February?" Later, watching her segment online bashing love and all men, calling both a waste of time, hurt more than I'd like to admit.

We both stare at each other, realizing the truth: neither one of us has been totally honest with the other. It shakes the very foundation of everything between us.

"Don't 'what about' me," Sora warns. "This is different."

"Sora, please, I know men have lied to you in the past. But I am not lying. Mal and I are not dating."

"And now, to announce the award for Best Pastry Chef, I give you . . . the heiress to the Starr Hotels, Mal Starr," a voice across the speakers announces.

"This is my category," I admit.

Sora cringes. "Mal's giving out *your* award? That's what she's presenting?"

"I didn't know she was." But I get how ridiculous I sound. Even to myself. And how did I not see this coming? Of course she'd pull strings to present my award category.

"How could you not know?" Pain and accusation flash in her eyes.

Mal's already on stage. I've got one eye on her, and one on Sora, and I've never felt so divided. Sora stalks to the gilded elevator doors and jabs the button.

"Sora, please. Just wait. Five minutes."

"I can't, Jack. I just . . ." Sora's eyes are filling with tears.

"Fine. Then let's go somewhere. Let's talk. I'll come with you." I'd do anything to make her stop crying. Anything.

"As the sole heir to the Starr family fortune," Mal begins, "I've been very fortunate to eat at some of the finest restaurants in the world. My family owns some of them, and it was my late father's favorite pastime to talk to the pastry chefs in our kitchens. He used to say if a hotel couldn't serve good desserts to its guests, then it might as well just be a roadside motel."

A murmur of chuckles ripples politely through the audience.

"Please, Sora."

"Jack, I don't think there's anything to talk about." Sora jabs the elevator button again.

"I'm so very honored to present tonight's award for Best Pastry Chef," Mal continues. She's calling out the nominees. "And the Golden Chef goes to . . ." She cracks open the white envelope. "Jack Mann."

Sora looks at me, eyes sad. "Go on," she tells me. The elevators ding, announcing the arrival of an elevator.

"No, Sora, wait. Just . . ." The spotlight is on me. Everyone is applauding. But I'm not moving. The elevator doors slide open.

"While we wait for the winner to make it to the podium," Mal says, "I just want to take this opportunity to announce Jack's new endeavor. With his prize money, *we* are going to open a bakery *together. Coming next month!*"

The applause kicks up a notch. But Sora's eyes have turned coal black.

"She's backing your bakery?" Her voice is weak and defeated. The elevator doors begin to close, but I stop them with a hand.

"No." I shake my head. "Absolutely not. She's been threatening to get involved, but I told her no."

But Mal is still talking.

"We're so very excited to be announcing the opening of Jack Mann's—the new Golden Chef winner—casual new bakery, complete with the full backing of Starr Incorporated. Starr now owns the property and will be working hand-in-hand to launch Jack's new bakery."

I feel like I've been hit by a Mack truck. The license plate reads "Mal Starr." Everything in my field of vision goes wonky, and I barely hear the applause of the audience.

This cannot be happening.

"Go on and accept your award, Jack." Sora pushes my hand from the elevator, just as Mal appears by my side.

"He's a little shy!" she jokes as she loops her arm through mine and tugs me hard. I'm just . . . shell-shocked. The elevator doors slide shut on Sora, her eyes shining with tears. I recover too late. I jab uselessly at the elevator button, but the car is already gone.

"Come on, Jack-a-boo. Your public awaits," Mal whispers, holding the microphone against her hip. "I told you I'd buy your bakery if you didn't bring me as your plus-one." Her voice is barely an audible hiss.

I take the microphone from her. My ears ring. I suddenly feel nauseous.

"Thank you so much for the award. I'm so grateful." Another elevator slides open. "But I have to go."

The elevator doors open and I step in. In thirty-eight seconds, I'm back on the ground floor. I run out, looking for Sora. Where is she? Not in the lobby. Not near the modern reflecting pool. Nowhere. I run through the revolving glass doors and find myself in the frigid February night, frantically searching one way and then another. I see Sora, sans coat, walking away to the corner.

"Sora!" I call. What is she doing? She's going to freeze. I just have my tuxedo jacket on and the cold already slips straight through the fabric, like ghost hands against my ribs. I run to her—she's working hard to get away from me, though her stilettos and the icy sidewalks slow her down.

Cabs and rideshares rush by on Michigan Avenue. She flings up her arm, trying to signal one. Two cars speed by already carrying passengers in the back seats.

"Sora, wait." I grab her elbow, which feels like ice. "You're going to catch cold." I shrug out of my jacket and throw it over her shoulders, but as she turns, I see the tears streaking down her face.

"You could've just been honest. That Mal is backing your bakery."

"She's not. I promise, she's not."

"I just . . . I can't believe you." Sobs choke her voice. I can barely understand what she's saying. "You . . . lied to me." She flashes her phone in my face. She's found a photo on Mal's social. It's a selfie Mal took of us. On that night. That stupid mistake of a night. She's licking my face. We're both drunk. At the bar. The night I took Mal home. Damn it. I can't deny that.

"See? That look on your face. It's true, isn't it?"

"Sora. Please. Let's talk about this." A cab slides to the curb beside us.

"No." She opens the cab door and slides in. "I can't believe you're just like all the others," she says, damning me. She slams the door before I can say another word. And then the cab leaves me, jacket-less, in subzero wind chill, standing alone on Michigan Avenue.

Twenty

SORA

> If you're looking for someone else to tell you who you are, they are going to get it wrong every time. Only you can define you. No one else can. #GoSolo.
>
> —SOLO FEBRUARY CHALLENGE

Jack calls many times that night. And the next morning. I send them all to voicemail. I just . . . can't. I can't anymore. That's the plain truth of it. But the photo of Mal licking his face . . . the possessive way she'd taken hold of his arm at the awards, the fact that she sat at his table. What am I supposed to think? It's Dan all over again, and me wandering around a banquet hall that is hosting an electricians' union meeting instead of a bar mitzvah. And it's Marley, too, sputtering on about how sexting isn't cheating—technically. And Chris, telling me he was going to Cancún with a buddy from college, but then busting himself when he sent a picture of the view from his balcony, failing to note that the frame included a neon-yellow thong bikini hung out to dry over the railing.

A little voice inside my head whispers, *This is what men do. You knew he was too perfect.* He was going to save Valentine's Day, and now he just reinforced what I thought all along: it's the devil's holiday. How could I be so gullible—again? How could I believe that Jack wouldn't be just like the rest? I should've listened to my gut early on. It had been warning me all this time Jack wasn't over Mal.

I think about Marley. About Dan. About my rotten luck. I'm spiraling down into a pity party even as I'm choking back tears. Why did I ever let Jack in? Why did I believe after a lifetime of evidence that men just *lie, lie, lie,* that I'd finally and at long last found one who would tell me the truth?

My nose is so red and raw that it's peeling, and I'm so incredibly sad that I don't know how I'll drag myself out of this. I've been brokenhearted before, but never sucker punched quite like this.

I can't even imagine considering Jack has an explanation that will make everything okay. It's exhausting me to even try.

I'm so tired. So bone-tired. Of the lies. Of hoping it will be different this time. Being optimistic is freakin' exhausting. Put a fork in me. I'm done. I'm tired of being duped. And the only way to stop being duped is to stop believing what everyone tells you.

In fact, to stop believing anyone. Ever.

Larry wanders over to the couch with his tongue lolling out and I crush him in a bear hug. At least dogs are loyal. From here on out, this will be the only male in my life.

I cry into his fur, acutely aware that I've been here before.

Larry knows the drill. He turns and tenderly licks my face. Miraculously, his depth perception works right then. He doesn't even miss this time. He gets it on the first try.

At least Larry loves me.

Sniffling, I swipe my face with paper towels because I'm out of tissues, and I realize I've been derelict in keeping my condo well-supplied. The fridge stands empty, and Larry's bowl barely has kibble in it. And I'm not even 100 percent sure I have toilet paper.

My phone rings. I fumble for it and see Arial calling.

"Hello?" I answer, my voice sounding like I swallowed a cheese grater. Ugh. The ugly crying jag still lingers, apparently.

"Sora." Arial sounds serious. Zero question marks or upward lilts. Uh-oh.

"Yes?" I sit up on my couch. Larry, who had been zonked out next to the coffee table, raises his head at the sound of my voice.

"Have you seen the reaction. To your piece."

"No?" Now *I* sound like Arial, with all my sentences ending in an upward lilt. What's happening? "Is it bad?"

"It's not good."

I frantically pull up *Slick*'s page and see a billion comments about my "take your own road" post, that I absolutely, positively wish I could take back. How stupid I sound in it. How naïve.

And the comments are brutal.

> *You couldn't even make it the full month for Solo February? Are you that desperate for validation?*

Or . . .

I can't believe I believed you when you talked about empowerment. You were just using it to get with someone. How pathetic.

And . . .

I believed in you. You let me down.
How could you? Seriously! How could you?
You should be canceled. Immediately.
Hate this. Hate you.
Quitter.
Liar.
Fraud.
It's no wonder you can't ever find anyone to love you.
You're pathetic.

The warm community I'd built has turned cold and horrible and mean. All the people who held me up are now tearing me down. I never thought they'd turn this fast. There are hundreds of thousands of dislikes.

"You're going to have to fix this." Arial sounds stoic.

"Let me work on it. I'll get you something in a couple of hours." What, I have no idea.

"Good, because . . . I don't know, Sora. If we can't do damage control now, then no job. No benefits."

I actually don't know that I care. The *Solo February* people hate me. Jack betrayed me. My life is desolate and empty. Who cares about a job that I'm not sure I even wanted in the first place? Larry licks my elbow.

"Don't worry. I'll fix it," I say anyway, even though I'm not sure how.

I hang up with Arial and immediately head to my feeds. It's getting ugly fast.

#GoSoloFraud is trending. Wow, it's brutal out there. Part of me knows I deserve it. But . . . ouch.

A hard knock comes on my door. Larry barks, confused. There was no buzzer, so he's not sure what to make of the knock. A small part of me hopes that, somehow, it's Jack. Another, larger part of me, dreads that possibility.

I head to the door, Larry on my heels, and peer through the peephole. Pam stands on my welcome mat.

I sigh. Really, universe? I crack open the door. Pam literally jumps back when she sees Larry. Maybe she really is afraid of dogs, and it's not just some hate vendetta she's got with me.

"He's really friendly," I try to explain.

"I've got your dog food box." Pam shoves a dented farm-to-table dog food box at me, and I grab it.

"I can't believe you brought me Larry's box," I say, shocked. I would've thought she would've taken this directly to the dumpster out back, given her hatred of dogs and Larry in particular.

"Just trying to be a good neighbor." Those are the words I said to her a few weeks ago. And she's not being sarcastic. Wow.

"Thanks," I say, and mean it.

"Did you really quit Solo February?" she asks me.

"Yeah." I sigh. I wonder if she's going to pile on.

"People are being brutal to you online right now," Pam notes. Now's the time she can gloat. Sure, why not? I deserve it.

"They're not being any more brutal to me than I'm being on

myself, actually," I admit. "It was a stupid mistake. The guy I broke my solo vow for lied to me."

Pam lets out a disgusted-sounding grunt. "Don't they all?" She sighs. "Stupid men. Thom was a liar, too. He spent our mortgage money on a woman he was having an affair with. She was a college sophomore. Can you believe it? *A college kid.* Nineteen years old! Nineteen! He helped pay some of her tuition."

"Seriously?" I had no idea.

"Yeah. It was my fault for trusting him to pay all the bills. We were one missed payment away from foreclosure. But I got everything back on track. Had to dip into my 401(k), though, after I kicked him out."

"Oh, Pam. I am so, so sorry."

"Well, you've been through the wringer, too. With Marley and now . . . this new guy."

"Listen, about Marley . . ." I start.

"It's not your fault." Pam waves a stiff hand at me, to stop whatever I'm going to say next. "He's just one more jerk, just like the rest of them."

"Yeah."

We smile weakly at one another, a Wikipedia of shared disappointments passing between us.

"Hey . . . about Larry," she adds. "I don't have anything against Larry, exactly, I just . . . I got bitten by a dog when I was younger. Never really got over it."

"Oh." Now I kind of feel like an ass. "I'm sorry."

"I know I'm kind of irrational when it comes to dogs." Pam shrugs.

"Larry really is a sweetheart. I promise. He'd never hurt you. Want to pet him?"

Pam glances at Larry's snout through the cracked door, hesitant. "I don't know."

"Only if you want to. You can let him sniff your hand. I mean, you did lug up his fancy kibble."

Pam glances at me and then at Larry. She reluctantly lowers her hand to Larry. He gives it a sniff, followed by a slobbery, full-tongue lick. She jumps back a bit.

"Ew," she says, but she laughs a little as she wipes the back of her hand on her tights.

"He likes you."

"Great." Pam eyes Larry. But do I see . . . a smile tugging at the corner of her mouth? "Okay, well. This will pass. Soon, people will be angry at someone else, and they'll move on, and this new guy, you'll forget him and move on, too. You'll handle it. Because we're the kind of women who just handle our shit."

She nods at me, and I nod back.

This might be the kindest thing Pam has ever said to me. And her encouragement came right at the moment I needed it most.

"Thanks, Pam."

"Well, I've got to get back to my laptop. I've got a meeting. Have a good one."

"You, too—and, uh, thanks," I say, shutting the door as she trots back down the stairs. Well, will wonders never cease? Did Larry and I just call a truce with Pam? Huh. That was a surprise. I think she felt sorry for me, now that all the *Solo February* people want my head on a pike. Still, I'll take the pity. She's been through it and so have I, and maybe we are pretty damn tough.

I kick the door shut with my foot and rip open the box with Larry's gourmet sample bricks, infused with only the freshest and most organic and expensive ingredients, cooked by some celebrity chef for dogs, and packed with only the finest dry ice to keep it cool. At least, at long last, I can finally give Larry the treat he truly deserves. Larry trots over to sniff the box, but misses, again by about six inches. I pull out a vacuum-sealed brick, and wave it under Larry's nose. He smells it, cautiously.

"You're going to love this, Lar. All the influencer dogs are eating it. You're going to be trendy!" I take the brick over to the kitchen, noticing it does seem to have real chunks of meat and peas in it, which I guess is good, but otherwise, it just . . . smells like dog food. Also, it's an unpleasant shade of mud brown. I glance at the brochure inside the box, the one with the adorable little fluffy white dog with one paw raised in anticipation of her owner setting down her fresh lunch. That dog's bowl really looks like it has carrots and chunks of steak in it. Hmmm. Well, we've got it, so why not give it a shot. I open the plastic package and spoon a little into Larry's bowl for a taste, and then place it down in front of him. He sniffs at it, six inches off again, but then sits down and glances up at me, skeptical.

"You don't like it?" I can't believe it.

I take a spoonful and put it right up to his mouth. He licks at it, suspiciously, and then shifts away from it, turning his head to one side, as if I just offered him kale. He flashes me a guilty look with his one good eye.

"You really don't like it." I can't believe it. One truffle-infused lamb brick costs as much as a GrubDash from the local bar and grill. I suspect Larry would rather have the double cheeseburger. What am I going to do with a box full of curated, hand-hewn dog bricks?

Larry lies down in front of his bowl and puts his head on his paws, looking contrite. I guess he just doesn't have fancy tastes. Still, I feel like I can't even do something nice for my dog without it backfiring.

I can't even make Larry happy?

My life is a mess.

Twenty-one

SORA

No one is coming to rescue you. You're going to have to climb on down from that tower by yourself.

—SOLO FEBRUARY CHALLENGE

I hide in my drafty condo and just keep a low profile, avoiding every social media platform ever invented. The last thing on earth I want to do is open my laptop and let all that horrible, horrible stuff claw its way back in front of my eyeballs. Already the criticisms have been circling my brain, like termites eating away at my self-esteem.

You're such a fraud.
I can't believe I even read a single stupid word you ever wrote.
It's women like you who keep other women down.
Shame on you.

This was all a sham. #GoSolo means nothing now. Thanks for nothing.

The worst part is that nothing they could ever say is worse than what I'm telling myself. They think they're hard on me? They have no idea what I'm telling myself. I should've never trusted Jack. I should've seen this coming a mile away. I had something good going with Solo February, and I let a guy distract me—again.

All I can think about is Jack. And seeing Mal hug his shoulders, and the deep, bitter taste of betrayal lingering at the back of my mouth.

I call Stella because I need advice. Preferably from someone with a PhD. in behavioral psychology.

"You should be taking better care of yourself. Have you even eaten today?" Stella asks, taking in my appearance, as she walks into my condo. Which, to be honest, I haven't even bothered to check. She glances at my feet. "Are you wearing only one sock?"

I look down and see I am, indeed, wearing one mint-green sock, and the other foot is bare. I hadn't even noticed.

I hug her tightly to me and don't let go.

"Okay, okay. We're going to get through this," she says, hugging me back a moment before gently peeling me off her. "First thing is, let's find your other sock. Or any other sock. Next thing, let's go wash your face and comb your hair."

I realize I hadn't bothered to do either since coming home from the Golden Chef Awards. One quick glance in the mirror and I see deep black streaks of mascara down my face. I'm a mess. I glance down at the bath rug and see my other mint-green sock there. I tug it on. Okay. One task complete.

"Also, I brought you a nice fresh salad," Stella calls through the door of the bathroom. "And a bottle of tequila."

"The tequila, yes. Not sure if I can eat, though." I walk out of the bathroom feeling slightly better. Also, I found my sock.

"Since when?" Stella stares at me, bug-eyed.

"I'm just as shocked as you."

"But this salad has bacon." She opens the cardboard container to show me. I do a double take. "I mean, it's kosher turkey bacon, but still," she explains.

Normally, I'd be happy to dig in, but the very idea of eating makes me want to throw up. My throat closes up at the mere sight of food. I push the salad away. "I . . . I can't eat."

"I'm sorry. Is it the turkey bacon?"

I shake my head.

"Okay. Tell me. What's wrong?"

I give her the SparkNotes. *Solo February* crashing and burning. Jack. Mal. The disaster that is my life.

"The worst part is Jack had a red flag. The very *day* I met him, Mal was there, and I . . . I . . . ignored it. Just like I said I wouldn't. I ignored this huge red flag, and now here I am, right back in the place where I don't ask the right questions early and then just get rolled." I sigh. "Oh, and everyone online also wants me dead. So there's that, too."

Stella puts her arm around my shoulders and tugs me closer. I go, putting my head on her shoulder. "I think it's time for a liquid lunch." We break apart and she reaches for another, smaller brown bag, and pulls out a bottle of tequila. "Shall we?"

"I think I love you," I say, as she rises, fetches two glasses from my kitchen, and pours a little bit of añejo in each. We clink glasses and then I take a deep swig, the tequila the only thing that can numb the aching pain of my heart, split in two—again. The burn down my throat feels good. "Can I join your team? Give up on men?"

I lean on my breakfast bar. Stella hoists herself up to one of the stools.

"You want to date Terran?" Stella asks, raising a challenging eyebrow. "She's available."

"Right. I forgot. Dating sucks for everyone."

Stella sends me a look of pity. "You're going to have to talk to him," Stella gently tells me. "You don't really know what happened."

"He's just going to deny it all," I say, as I scooch into the seat next to hers. "And the evidence is pretty tough to dispute."

"Yes, but . . ." Stella takes a small sip of her own tequila. "You'll have to talk it out. After you've both calmed down. If you still think he's lying, then dump him. I'm all for it. I just think you need a full discussion about this, and not on a freezing cold sidewalk."

"You really think Jack will tell me the truth? No one tells the truth. I mean, hello, *Terrain*? You know people just suck. They all lie."

"I know. But . . . everything you told me about Jack . . . he seemed like such a mensch. Maybe it was all a lie but I'm just not sure."

"Tell me about it." I sigh.

"Maybe there is an explanation," she tells me gently.

"Aren't *you* always the one telling me that the simplest

answer is usually the right one? What do you say about the zebra?"

"When you hear hoofs, don't think it's a zebra when it's probably a horse?"

"Bingo." I snap my fingers.

"Yeah." Stella nods. "Usually, the simplest answer is the right one."

"Okay, then." I blow my already-red nose. "He lied to me. End of story."

"I think you should talk to him," Stella adds. "Not for his sake. For yours. To be sure. You're right that you didn't ask enough questions early, but you have to still *ask those questions.*"

I know why I'm not asking those questions, because part of me doesn't want it confirmed that Jack is terrible, and I'm a fool.

"Why talk to him? There's no elaborate Mal conspiracy. He wants her as his main and me as his side chick. The story of about every man I ever met. I'm destined to forever and always be the side chick." I think about Dan and his wife. Marley and his endless sexting of every woman he ever met.

"Well, technically, you were Marley's *main* chick."

"That doesn't make me feel better."

Stella's mouth curves into a sympathetic smile. "Yeah, I know."

"And irony of ironies, now all the readers think I ditched Solo February for a guy, and so now they all hate me, too."

"I think it was brave to come clean," Stella says. "I'm glad you did."

"Everyone hates me for it, though."

"I have a question: Even when you were getting all the accolades from *Slick* readers, was that really what you wanted to be writing?"

"No," I say. "I always wanted to write more serious stuff. Not that dating isn't serious, but just more . . . about issues."

"Like?"

I sniff, wiping my nose. "Climate change. Women running for political office. Really, anything that doesn't involve makeup or dating."

"So, what's stopping you?"

"Everything." I sigh.

"Look, you can't be something new and great without saying goodbye to something old and comfortable. You have to make room in your life for the things you want. And if it's not writing for *Slick,* then it's time to move on."

"You think I shouldn't write for *Slick* anymore? I mean, actually, I don't even know if Arial will *let* me write for *Slick*."

"I think you should figure out what you *do* want to write and write that."

I sigh and finish my tequila. It burns on the way down. Just like everything else in my life right now.

She looks at me, worried.

"What's that look?"

"What look?" She frowns.

"That clinical I'm-over-the-deep-end look you're giving me right now?"

Stella takes a deep breath. She always does this when she wants to lay some truth on me, truth I probably don't want to hear.

"I think you need to do some serious self-care."

I roll my eyes. “Oh, geez. Not *this* again. A freakin’ pedicure isn’t going to solve my problems.”

Stella laughs as she crosses her legs at the knee and leans forward, gently taking my glass from my hands and putting it on the breakfast bar. She’s got that squared-shoulders, ultra-focused, counselor stance again. “That’s not what I mean about self-care. Have you been listening to me at all?”

“Yes.” Maybe not. Sometimes when Stella gets too therapy-y I tune out.

“Self-care is about *parenting* yourself. Yes, it’s about being good to yourself with treats like pedicures, but it also means making *tough decisions* for yourself. It means being the adult in your life.”

“I hate adulting.” I pour some more tequila in my glass and then put my elbow on the breakfast bar, resting my chin in my palm. Stella cocks her head to one side.

“Yes, I know,” she says. “But look around you. This is the condo *you and Marley* bought. Why are you still here? I know for a fact that Marley loved this place more than you did. I ran into Pam on the way up here. She sucks all the positive energy from the room. I *know* you want to be away from her.”

“Actually, we did have a nice conversation—”

“Okay, but *one* conversation probably doesn’t change the fact that you’d rather not necessarily live above her, right?”

This is true.

“So why are you still living here? Nobody is making you.”

My old friend inertia is, but I think Stella won’t appreciate that.

“You had a job offer from *Slick,* but you didn’t even want it, and if you want my opinion, I think you self-sabotaged.”

"What does that mean?" I sniff.

"It means you were too afraid to say no outright, so you just worked to make sure you'd mess it up so that *they'd* reject *you*."

"That sounds super cowardly and passive-aggressive." I think about it. "Yep, could be me all right." Stella laughs, ruefully. "Okay, so, you're right about my condo. And my job offer. But, men just . . . I mean, I'm always getting tripped up by them. They are ruining my life."

"No one can ruin your life unless you *let* them ruin your life." Stella takes a deep breath and then takes one of my hands in both of hers. "You keep waiting for a man to rescue you, to make everything better, to take away all these hard decisions but, girl . . . you need to do those things. No man can do them for you. Eat better. Be healthier. Sell this damn condo. Tell Arial you don't really want to freelance anymore and go after the job you really want. You are the one in charge of your own happiness. Not anyone else." She pats my knee for emphasis. "Be the hero in your own life."

Even in my tequila haze, a light bulb goes off. For the first time in a long time, I know what I need to do.

Twenty-two

JACK

Be the hero in your own life.

—SOLO FEBRUARY CHALLENGE

Sora's not returning my calls. Or texts. I should give up, call it quits. She won't let me explain. Not even a little. And I'd be lying if I said it didn't hurt that she's shutting me out so fast. Yes, weeks ago, I got tangled up with Mal, and that was my choice. A drunk choice, sure, but mine. I should've come clean to Sora from the get-go. That's on me, too.

Because, right now, it looks like I've been caught red-handed. Technically, I didn't know *for sure* Mal was coming to the awards ceremony. But I'd also known she'd been threatening to come for weeks. Was there more I could have done to stop her? I think of dozens of ways I could've kept her out of the ceremony. I Monday-morning quarterback myself so hard, I feel like I should try a new career as a commentator on ESPN.

The first day of March dawns dreary and gray with the lingering threat of snow. I sit in my brother's law office, staring out over the high-rise view of Lake Michigan, in some of the most expensive real estate in the Loop, as he reads over my bakery lease. It turns out, Mal did buy the building. And the leasing company, and everything associated with the bakery I thought would be all mine. I'm technically leasing the bakery space from Starr International. Marc takes his time with it, a wrinkle appearing in his brow.

"Why didn't you let me read this before you signed it?" He glances up above his reading glasses at me, his elbows propped on his massive mahogany desk. Seriously, where does a person buy desks this big?

"Because you're busy. And sometimes you're a prick about things like this." I'm teasing, but Marc still doesn't argue. He just goes back to reading. He makes a disapproving sound at the back of his throat.

"Well, it's an ironclad lease. To get out of it, you have to pay a year's worth of rent."

I jump up and snatch the paper out of his hand. "That can't be."

"Page three, paragraph two, line three." He takes his readers off and puts them on his desk. "You're screwed, man."

"What do you mean?"

"The management company is definitely owned by the Starr family," Marc says. "Looks like Mal just signed the paperwork a few days ago."

"I thought she was bluffing." Should've known better. "And this still doesn't rise to the level of bodily harm? A restraining order?"

Marc shrugs one shoulder. "Unfortunately, no. She hasn't physically harmed you, or threatened to do so. Yes, it's a nuisance, but it doesn't rise to a criminal level. Not yet. I mean, if she upped your rent to a ridiculous amount, or hassled you in some definable way . . ." He glances up at me, and I'm struck by how much we look alike. Granted, I'm one inch taller, and have a bit more muscle on me, but we've both got Dad's chin and Mom's dark hair.

"This is a hassle. A huge hassle."

"Yes, but the rent is market value. If she jacked it up, then maybe we could sue her, but the rent is reasonable."

"But she's harming my business. And my sanity. What can I do about this?" I slump into the chair near Marc's desk.

Marc stares at me sternly, looking remarkably like Dad. "Have you talked to her?"

"Of course I've talked to her." Does he think I'm an idiot? "I've told her it's over."

"You're not leading her on."

"No!"

Marc leans back in his chair. "Really? You don't love that she's always begging to be back in your life? Doesn't it feel good to punish her?"

"I'm not trying to punish her."

"Not even a little?" He steeples his fingers and studies me over them, doing his best impression of Dad giving me a lecture.

I hesitate. I told myself I was just ignoring her and hoping she went away, but maybe part of me knew ignoring her would just make her want to be in my life more.

"Maybe a little. Not on purpose."

"Sure, not on purpose." Marc raises a knowing eyebrow. "Maybe, just maybe, Sora was a little bit right in thinking there was something between you, after all."

"No. We're done." I mean it this time.

"Then prove it. Stop letting Mal twist in the wind. Cut the line." Marc leans forward, his big leather chair groaning from the shift of his weight. "*Really* talk to her. Make her see it's over. For good. Punishment time, playtime, it's all over."

Mal needs very little persuasion to meet me at the coffeehouse down the street from my bakery. I tell her we need to talk. She implies she'd rather get naked in my bed. I tell her, "No, talk, with clothes on, in public." The coffeehouse is a small, walk-in joint with a barista in one corner and a line of stools and a small counter across both windows. During work hours it gets pretty tight with all the folks with laptops vying for the four outlets, but now, a half hour before the place closes, it's nearly empty.

The sun sinks below the horizon, turning the sidewalk pink. A mild March day means the snow piles at the corners of intersections have nearly melted, leaving giant lakes of muddy puddles. For the first time since November, I can see patches of dormant grass in the medians at the center of the road. Spring is coming. I take a seat at the counter facing the street, blowing on my too-hot latte. Could it be as easy as Marc says? Is it really about just telling Mal a firm no?

Just then, Mal sweeps into the coffeehouse dressed in form-fitting leggings and a crop top, her Canada Goose jacket open, long blond hair flowing into her coyote-fur-lined hood, her feet clad in furry ankle boots. She's got on a ton of makeup just to make her look fresh-faced. So much expensive highlighting powder and contouring makeup. When she sees me, she bounds up and tries to give me a hug. I stop her with a strong arm.

"Mal. Sit," I say, nodding to the chair.

"What's this?" She glances at the coffee cup sitting at the center of the table. Mine. "Is this my fave? Half-caf, double shot, soy milk, extra hot, super skinny? Like I like it?"

"No." I frown. "It's a latte." My latte, actually.

"Oh. Well, that's okay." She sits down and takes my latte. Not what I'd planned, but oh well. She can have the coffee. Best to get this over with.

"I'm here to ask you to sell the bakery."

"What? Why? Don't you want to be business partners?" She grabs my hands. I pull them back.

"No, I don't. We're done, Mal. For real this time."

She opens her pink lips to argue, but then stops. Something in my voice, maybe my face, I don't know, finally hits a chord with her.

"You didn't think we were done last month."

"That was a mistake. We're over. We're never going to work."

Mal's bottom lip begins to quiver. Tears threaten to spill. I hate it when she cries, and she knows it. But it's not going to work on me. Not this time. I hand her a napkin from the dispenser on the table.

"We're done. For good. You need to sell the bakery."

"No."

"You can sell the bakery. Or . . ." I weigh my options. "I can call your mother."

Mal goes white, and I know why. Her mother, Melody Starr, controls the purse strings. Also, Melody Starr hates me. Never really felt I was good enough for her daughter, but on this, she'd agree. That Mal needs to stay out of the bakery business.

"You wouldn't."

"Try me." I stare at her until she blinks first. "Sell the bakery," I tell her.

She dabs at her eyes. She sniffs, loudly. I don't care if she cries in public. I don't care if people stare. I just want her out of my life. And telling her to go, *really* telling her to go, is the only way to do it.

I pick up my phone and pull up her contact. "I'm blocking you." I show her and hit "block." "We're not going to be friends. We're not going to talk."

She goes pale. "So we're done. For good." She blinks at me.

I meet her gaze. "Yes."

"Is it that woman? Soron? Sara?"

"Sora. And me asking you to sell the bakery doesn't have anything to do with her."

Hurt flickers in her blue eyes. Legitimate hurt.

"I'm done punishing you for your mistakes. It's over. We're done."

Mal stares at the cuff of her coat, playing with the insulated sleeve's edge. She doesn't say anything for a long time. "So, all the time you listened to me about my parents . . . about what they did . . ." Mal's eyes fill with tears. "Did you even ever really care about me? Ever?"

"Of course I did. And I really am sorry that happened to you. No one deserves that kind of neglect." I pause. "But I didn't deserve what you did to me, either."

"So that's why you're going off with Soda." She grabs a napkin this time and blows her nose. Loudly.

"Sora." I sigh. "And she's not taking my calls thanks to the stunt you pulled at the Golden Chef Awards, so I'm not sure where we stand. I'll be honest."

"Sorry." Mal squirms a little, though she doesn't look sorry. "If she's out of the picture, then . . ." Mal looks a tad hopeful for a minute.

"No, Mal. We're not getting back together. Not even if Sora never talks to me again. We're done. For good."

Mal slumps back into her chair, looking resigned.

"You know, no one ever cared about that before you. Everyone just thought, 'oh, poor rich girl.' You really saw me." Mal sniffs. "I really messed all that up, didn't I?"

This might be the first time Mal took responsibility for anything. Ever.

I nod, feeling sad. "You did. Yeah."

"My sister's still not speaking to me either." She balls up the napkin in her fist. I nod. I mean, I wouldn't either if she slept with my spouse. We sit in silence for a bit. An awkward, awful silence, but Mal is really, I think, finally getting it.

"This is why my parents don't love me. I'm unlovable." A small sob escapes her. I grab another napkin and offer it. She swipes it from my hand.

"You're not unlovable." I shake my head. "You just keep making bad choices."

"How do I stop doing that?" She swipes at her nose again.

"How about do the next right thing?" I tell her. "And then the next right thing after that. Then, before you know it, you're not doing bad things anymore. Like start with small things and work your way up."

She considers this. "But what if I do a good thing and then a bad thing?"

"Then you just start over doing good things."

"So, the next good thing I need to do is sell the bakery," she says, swiping at her cheeks.

I nod. "Yeah. That's a good start."

Mal nods. "I'll sell the bakery. Then I need to let you go, for good." Her eyes meet mine. They're full of real pain. I hate that, but this has to be done. "So you can go be with Sora."

I can't believe she got her name right. Makes me think she really knew her name all along.

"If she talks to me again." I'm not at all sure of that yet.

"She will," Mal promises.

Twenty-three

SORA

They say time heals all wounds. But why does it have to take so much time?

—SOLO FEBRUARY CHALLENGE

I'm still brokenhearted and sad, but I am starting to clean up my own messes. As Larry snores at my feet, on my "office" duvet, I grab my shiny silver laptop from my bedside table and open it up. I flinch, as if worried a bomb of hateful insults will lob themselves out of the bright screen like criticism grenades, but they don't.

I stare at the blinking cursor of my laptop.

Slick readers deserve an explanation. That much I can give them.

I pull up my last *Solo February* entry and want to punch myself. Look at these words I'm throwing around. I sound ridiculous. No wonder *Slick* readers hate me.

I begin typing.

To everyone pissed at me, I get it. And you are right to be pissed at me. I'm pissed at myself. I told you all I was #GoingSolo and then I bailed, hoping I'd get my happily ever after, but you know what? I didn't.

I pause, hands above the keyboard. Am I going to out Jack to the hundreds of thousands of readers of *Slick*? I should. He'd deserve it. Yet . . . something stops me. Blame-shifting doesn't solve my problem here. I can't blame Jack for my decisions. *I* decided to end Solo February early and brought the wrath of basically everyone down on my head. That's on me.

And you all called me fake and a fraud, and in some ways, I was. I pitched this story to my editor, but I'm not sure I ever really truly believed in it.

Sure, I was bitter.

I was angry at men I'd dated.

But I started the Solo February challenge for the wrong reasons. Because I wanted to get paid for more articles, and because I was angry at my exes and sick of the dating game. I never really believed in it. I never really intended for Solo February to become so big.

But it became big because of YOU, not me.

You made this real. Not me.

And, yes, I blew it. But blowing it actually helped me see Solo February not as a gimmick, or a joke, but as something truly meaningful and important. And that's all because of you, readers. You all helped me see that putting our mental health first is important, that getting to know ourselves IS important.

I know you're angry at me and I get it, but just know that I'm cheering you on, if you decide to go solo forever, or if you decide to get married tomorrow. I trust that you can make the best choices for you. You actually don't need a Slick *confessional to get you where you want to go. You don't need me telling you what to do. You've been doing a pretty good job of making decisions for yourselves all along.*

You can be mad at me. I can take it. But the real secret is you didn't need these columns. You didn't need me. You were making yourself better, all by yourselves. You made this happen, not me.

Keep on doing it. Even if you fail.

Especially if you fail.

My mom used to always tell me not to stick my neck out. Not to take risks, and I always thought that not taking a risk was better than taking one and failing. But now I realize how wrong that thinking is. If you don't risk some, you'll never win some. Sure, you'll fail sometimes. Life will hammer you down.

But Mom also told me taking a risk is the only way to build anything meaningful in your life. So, go on. Take the risk. Whether you win or lose, you'll be on the path to being better, and being your best self is worth the risk.

I send off the article to Arial.

During the coming week, the article turns the tide of the pitchfork-carrying online mob.

A majority of supporters forgive me.

> *Thanks for your brutal honesty.*
>
> *That took courage.*
>
> *You made me realize it's okay to blow it. All I need to do is pick myself up and try again. Thanks for letting us know you're human.*

Sure, there are still those angry at me. Those who don't forgive me and who let me know it all the time.

But in the end, I let it go. I said my piece.

I'm focused mostly on applying for new freelance gigs, reaching out to women's health magazines and feminist non-profits, looking for more meaningful articles to write. Then I throw myself into massive spring cleaning. I'm putting my condo on the market. I am finally doing it. Goodbye, Pam (even though Pam is nicer than I gave her credit for). Goodbye, memories of Marley. Time for me to move on.

Because Stella—and her behavioral psychology degree—is right. I've been a passive observer in my own life, and it's high time I get into the damn game. Even better, the real estate agent I talked to thought I could get a pretty penny for my place, and if I move three blocks west, a little bit away from the train (and why is being near transportation such a big deal again when I work from home?), maybe even upgrade to a newer condo. One with . . . drumroll . . . central AC and a washer and dryer in the unit, a little piece of luxury I haven't had since I was eighteen and living full-time with my parents. So, I'm cleaning out the whole place. Time for a spark-joy or get-the-hell-out super clean.

Plus, keeping busy helps me not think about Jack. Okay, I still think about Jack. Pretty much every morning when I wake up. Logically, it doesn't even really make sense. We'd only been together a short time, but man, he'd wormed his way deep inside my heart. No matter how I tried to temper my expectations, part of me, my inner thirteen-year-old girl, had already planned our future years together, skipping through the aisles of IKEA and picking out our new furniture.

A hard knock comes at my door. No buzzer. Larry lifts his head and gives a cautious bark. I pull myself up from the pile of clothes I've been sorting into different stacks: keep, donate, hope-to-fit-into-one-day, and no-chance-of-fitting-into-any-day-but-I'm-keeping-it-to-show-I once-did piles. I swing open the door. Pam stands there, holding some of my junk mail.

"The mailman put it in my box by accident," she says. Then her eyes grow wide as she sees the massive mess behind me. "What happened in there?" she interrupts me. "Did you get burgled?"

Of course Pam would use the term "burgled," like she's ninety. Then I remember we made up. We're not enemies anymore.

"No, I'm doing some cleaning. I'm putting the condo up for sale."

This stops Pam cold. "You are?"

"Yes. Long overdue, actually. My real estate agent says she hopes it sells fast. And then, I mean, look at the bright side, you won't have to worry about Larry anymore. He's the last dog grandfathered in, so the condo building will be dog-free."

Pam perks up for a moment. But only a moment. "Yeah, but it's still kind of a bummer. I was actually going to ask if you wanted to come over to my place for one of my girls' nights? I have them the first Thursday of every month."

"I know." They get a little bit loud down there after the third bottle of rosé.

"Oh, right, well. I mean, you're welcome to come by. Even after you move."

"Really?" Pam nods. Well, will wonders never cease. "Thanks, Pam. I'll come by one month. That would be great."

We smile at each other, genuine smiles.

"Uh, and let me know if you need any help. With packing or whatever."

"I will, Pam." Wow, it's nice having a neighbor who doesn't hate you. She trots downstairs again. "And, uh . . . thanks!" I call after her.

"No problem," she calls back up, throwing up an arm. I head back to my bedroom, taking a break from the deep clean to check email on my laptop. Larry trails after me, taking up his post curled up at the foot of my bed. I lean against my pillows, just as my laptop chimes, announcing my upcoming video meeting with Arial, which I had temporarily forgotten about. I take a deep breath and click the "accept" button for the meet. I don't bother heading to the "conference room" of my kitchen. I think we're both beyond pretending that I don't work full-time in bed.

"Hey?" Arial says, sounding guarded but optimistic. She looks perfect as always, cinnamon hair in perfect waves to her shoulders, as she sits in front of the stunning view of Lake Michigan in her expensive high-rise office.

"Hey?" I answer. We both stare at each other.

"You did do a nice job of cleaning up?" Arial says. "And I talked to my bosses, one more time?" she offers. "But they've decided maybe not to hire another full-time writer. I mean, you did a nice job recovering that last series? But they're just not ready to offer you full-time?"

"I get it." I do a gut check. I'm actually relieved. I didn't want a full-time position after all. Why? Larry only wants the cheap kibble, anyway.

"Well, maybe we could do a new series? Can't guarantee I can get my boss on board, but maybe I can. We could call it 'It's Raining Men March' or 'March Men Madness'?" Uh-oh. I don't think I'm going to like this very much. "Maybe go on tons of dates? Splurge on men after taking a break?"

My heart aches at the thought. I'm not ready. I'm still . . . not over Jack.

"Actually, I don't think I'm the right person for that," I admit. "But . . ." I glance around my disaster area of a condo, clothes, shoes, and boxes strewn everywhere. "What about a different lifestyle story? For April. I want to call it 'Spring Cleaning.'"

"Cleaning?" Arial wrinkles her nose in disgust. "That's not very glamourous? Or fun?"

"I don't mean *cleaning* cleaning, like cleaning your apartment. I mean, decluttering your life. I mean, unpacking all that emotional baggage in your life. Doing the hard work of self-care."

"Pedicures?" Arial echoes.

"No, I mean, sure, get a pedicure, but I mean self-care like being the parent in your own life. Doing the hard things, making the tough decisions, and in the end, taking better care of yourself."

This has been my mantra since my breakthrough with Stella. I'm selling the condo. I'm eating better. Okay, not perfectly, because, I mean, it's me we're talking about.

Silence greets me as Arial struggles to come up with a diplomatic answer.

"What do you think?" I prod.

"Well? I just think that 'March Men Madness' has so much more of a ring to it?" Arial manages, taking a sip of her coffee and not looking me in the eye.

I'm tempted. I hate to admit it, but I'm tempted. I tell myself I can just walk down this path I've always taken, even though I know where it ends: with me not being true to myself. Really, hasn't all this writing I've been doing for *Slick* been a lie, anyway? I wanted to make a living writing, but I never wanted to make a living writing *this*. I realize I let the idea of easy money, and working from home, get in the way of what I truly want to do with my life. In fact, I've always taken the easy path, the obvious path, without really considering whether it was the path I really wanted at all.

I realize, with perfect clarity, that if I'm busy writing March Men Madness, then I might miss out on writing the story that really means something to me. I remember Stella telling me I have to make room in my life for the things I do want.

"No, Arial. I'm sorry. I can't do that story."

"Oh?" Arial sounds shocked. She sets down her coffee. "Really?" I know why she's shocked. *Slick* pays well. It's high profile. Whatever she wants, she usually gets. But not this time. This time, it's just . . . too personal.

"You know what? I think I'm going to step back from *Slick* for a while."

"You are?" Arial can't believe it. And, really, neither can I.

"Yes." Even though I only have a small bit of savings, and going without income is terrifying. I glance at Larry, who is curled up on the couch, sleeping. I know I'll take care of him and me, somehow. Time to take a risk. For once.

"You're sure?"

But doing something I believe in is more important right now than piling up credit card debt. And I feel an inner confidence: I know I'll land on my feet. Because while I may not be able to count on men, I absolutely know I can count on myself.

"I'm sure."

I end the video call with Arial feeling . . . upbeat. Saying no isn't as hard as I thought it'd be. Energized, I send out emails to *Politics Today* and *Women International* and a dozen more positive e-zines. I apply for different freelance gigs. I'm hopeful that maybe, at long last, I can write stories that mean something.

My door buzzes, announcing I have a visitor trying to get in downstairs. Larry barks on cue and jumps off the couch, padding over to the door and sniffing it, except he's about six inches away from my actual door and he's sniffing the wall.

Part of me worries (hopes?) it's Jack, as I pull myself off the couch, amble over to the front door, and hit the intercom button. But why would it be Jack? I've made it clear I don't want to talk to him.

"Sora?" Nami croaks, sounding . . . upset. Immediately, my big-sister radar is on high alert. Something is wrong. It's nine on a Friday morning and she should be at work. "Can I come up?"

"Of course." We haven't talked since the blowup in the fitting room, and each of us has been waiting for the other to extend the olive branch, so for her to show up here means something terrible has happened.

I buzz her up and unlock my front door, even as I try to tidy up a little (the stacks of clothes make this impossible). Then Nami bursts through my door, tears streaking down her face. She runs over to me and throws herself in my arms.

"What's wrong?" I manage, panic in my gut, as my mind moves through all possible tragedies: cancer, car accidents, death in the family.

"M-M-Mitch," she stammers. I've never seen her this undone, and so it can't be a simple fight about the music for the wedding processional. I grab my mostly empty box of tissues and hand her one. She whips one to her face and blows her nose like a B flat on a trumpet.

"The wedding's off."

"The wedding is off?" I still don't compute what my sister is saying. She grabs another tissue and blows her nose again, sniffing, as she swipes it across her nose. She spies the tequila bottle on my kitchen counter near the sink, grabs it, and takes a big swig straight from the bottle. Then starts hacking uncontrollably.

"Ugh! That's so . . . so bad." She swipes at her mouth.

"Whoa," I caution, because Nami is a lightweight. She gets tipsy after half a glass of wine. "Sit down. Tell me what happened."

Nami doesn't sit; she paces, hugging herself as she sobs, then sucks back tears, and then sobs again. For a second, I think she's going to have to tell me via sign language, because she can't actually control her voice.

"Okay, maybe you do need this." I hand her the tequila bottle and she takes another swig to calm herself.

She makes a sour face and glares at the bottle. "How can you drink this straight? Ugh. Don't you have anything else? Maybe a hard seltzer?"

"I have red wine?"

She wrinkles her nose. "Ew. I don't like red. I only drink rosé—and only if it's got bubbles. You seriously do not have hard seltzer? I'll even take a gross flavor."

I want to make fun of her for her sorority-girl taste in booze, but I refrain. Now's not the time to tease her.

"Sit. Tell me what happened." I pat the couch next to me. Nami sinks into it, sniffing.

"Mitch had his bachelor party last night. They rented a party bus."

Oh, Lord. Mitch and his cavemen buddies out on the town inside a neon party bus spells trouble.

She sucks in a breath. "He . . . he cheated on me." Nami holds up her phone. She's got video, somehow, that one of Mitch's friends sent to him. While part of it is blurred, it's pretty obvious Mitch is getting a blow job in boomerang style in the back of a party bus. Ew. That is so much more of Mitch than I ever wanted to see in my whole life.

"How did you get this?"

"I hacked his phone," Nami says, unashamed. "All his passwords are some combination of 'Ditka' and '1986,' in honor of the Bears' Super Bowl victory."

"Of course they are."

"How could he do this to me? How could he?" Her raised voice is thick with anger and betrayal and shock. She covers her face with her hands and sinks into my couch. I gently take the seat next to her, and wrap my arm around her shoulders. They shudder with her sobs.

"I'm so, so sorry, Nami." Now would probably not be the time to mention that I always thought Mitch was a dud, and that his friends were only half a gene sequence above Neanderthals, so it's no surprise he did this. He'd probably been thinking about it all along, as he quietly said, "Yes, babe" to everything Nami said.

"You were right. About everything. About Mitch not deserving all this effort. About him being lazy." She sniffs, loudly. "When I asked him why he did it, why he cheated, he said, 'Babe, what was I supposed to do? Say no?' He couldn't even say *no* to a blow job from a random stranger. Because that would take *effort*."

I sigh. "I'm sorry, Nami. I'm so sorry."

"You were even right about going solo. All this time, I thought you were . . . I don't know . . . selfish for doing it, but you were right, Sora. I should've listened to you."

I feel like the clouds might part and a divine light might shine down on me, because there's no way Nami just admitted *I* was right about anything.

"You're saying I'm *always* right? That you should *always* listen to me?"

"Don't push it," she growls. Nami leans into me, though. "Oh! And I haven't even told Mom, yet. She'll be heartbroken!"

"Do you . . . really think so?" I ask, skeptical, remembering just how much Mom doesn't like Mitch.

Nami blinks and pushes away from me. "What do you mean? Mom *loves* Mitch."

"Does she?" I stare at Nami. Nami stares back at me.

"Are you serious? She doesn't like Mitch either? Why didn't you two tell me? Why are you always ganging up on me?"

"Us ganging up on you?" I ask, shocked. "It's you and Mom who are always ganging up on me! With the diet stuff and the exercise classes and my personal life choices."

"Not true," Nami sputters. "You always gang up on me about the guys I date. Remember John?"

"In college? He was always jealous of everything you did." I snort my disapproval.

"See? You two are always talking about me. Judging me."

Huh. That's exactly what I think Nami and Mom are always doing. Maybe I'm not the third wheel I always thought I was in this family.

"Ugh. I miss Dad. At least he'd just yell at us and then we couldn't argue anymore," Nami says.

"Yeah. He did that." We stare at each other a beat, both realizing that's probably not the healthiest way to communicate as a family. "His temper was—"

"Awful? Do you remember how any little thing could set him off?"

"Of course! He'd step on a Lego and start cursing up a storm," I say, remembering.

"Or if we left the cereal box open."

"Or if we were too loud."

"Or if we were too quiet!"

We both laugh at this. Dad was so hard to please. "But remember when he'd go down to the school, though? Like when my eighth-grade teacher thought I cheated."

We look at each other. "Yeah. Or when my soccer coach

benched me for the district final game." Nami whistles. "Dad gave them all a piece of his mind. He did try to protect us. In his way."

"Still, he could've used therapy."

"I think Dad is why I picked Mitch," Nami says, biting her fingernail as she hitches up one knee and loops her free hand around her leg. "He never raised his voice. He always agreed with me. Never was short-tempered."

"That's true." He's a blob devoid of all personality and emotion, and that includes anger.

Nami glances at me. "Hey, I'm sorry. About the other day. Saying you were trying to have a heart attack like Dad." She swipes at her wet eyes. "I just . . . I don't want to lose you, too."

I see fear in her eyes. We both lost Dad without any warning. I pull her in for a tight hug. "You're not going to lose me," I promise. "I'm going to be here to annoy you—and ruin couples' dances or whatever you need ruined—for years."

"Good. You better be." Nami sniffs into my shoulder. She draws back, wiping her nose. "And you're not really careless," she adds, somber again. "I'm sorry I said that."

"It's okay. I did crash the car. That's legit."

Nami chuckles.

I think about all the ways our parents shape us—Mom and her endless dieting, Dad's short fuse. And Dad's sudden exit from our lives. "You know, Mom and Dad, they just did the best they could. They're flawed, and we're flawed, and we just all have to live with it."

Larry trots over and sniffs to the side of Nami's knee. She gives her dog nephew a scratch behind the ears.

Nami stares at me. "Since when are you so . . . zen?"

"Self-care," I say.

"Pedicures?" she asks, clear skepticism in her voice. "That's all it took?"

"It's more than that."

"Okay." Nami shrugs. "Hey. I'm sorry if I was a bitch during wedding planning."

"I was pretty bad, too." I sigh. "Let's just blame Mitch. I think it's all his fault."

Nami laughs, rueful. "Damn straight it is." She sniffs. "Can I stay with you for a while? Sleep on your couch? I just . . . don't want to go home."

I guess she doesn't want to go back to the condo she and Mitch shared. I don't really blame her.

"Of course," I say. "Stay as long as you need to. But I am putting the condo on the market."

"You are?" Nami sits up ramrod straight on my couch. Larry lifts his head, and Nami gives him a pat. "It's about damn time! Mom says you should've sold this place years ago."

"Uh-huh. What were you saying about *not* ganging up on me behind my back?"

"Oh, please," Nami says, but she snuggles into my arm. She leans her head into me. "I need more tequila." She holds up the bottle and takes a swig. "God, I just . . . I feel so broken."

"Give me a turn," I say, and she hands me the bottle. I take a hard sip, too, feeling the liquid burn down my esophagus. "Yeah. I know. Life plays rough sometimes." I glance at a box sitting near my coffee table. Grandma Mitsuye's Japanese dolls poke their heads out. Near them sits Grandma Mitsuye's bowl. It's been in the family for generations, an old gray and blue ceramic rice bowl from Japan.

"Is that Grandma's bowl?" Nami asks, pointing.

"Yeah. She gave it to me after . . ." The miscarriage. "After I lost the baby."

"Oh," Nami says, and she leans over and picks up the bowl. "It's cracked," she says, pointing to the gold-lined cracks along the side of the bowl.

"Do you remember what Grandma Mitsuye always said?" I ask Nami.

"She says we hold our chopsticks like peasants," Nami says. "She reminded me of that when I took her out for sushi last week."

I laugh. That's Grandma Mitsuye. "No, no. Remember what she said about the bowl. The gold?"

Nami squints, trying to remember. "Oh, yeah. That broken ceramics in Japan are repaired with liquid gold. What did she call that? Ken-something?"

"Kintsugi," I say, remembering.

"Right. Wait. What was that again?"

And for the first time, all the things Grandma told me after the miscarriage start to make sense. Maybe I was too much in the moment at the time to understand what she was telling me. But now, years later, I finally *get* it.

"Japanese see the flaw as a unique piece of the object's history," I say. "So instead of hiding it or covering it up, they outline it with gold paint. The crack adds to the beauty of the piece. It makes the piece unique and beautiful." I glance at my sister, who's running her finger along a golden crack. "And the metal paint makes the ceramic even stronger. You see, those scars are beautiful, and they're even stronger than the rest of the bowl. Scar tissue is strong. And so that's gold."

Nami studies the bowl, holding it up to the light.

"So, you see? You're not broken," I tell Nami. "You've just made a beautiful new scar. Let's fix it with liquid gold."

Nami puts the bowl down. Then she grabs the bottle on my coffee table and takes a swig. "Or with tequila?"

"Sure. Your choice."

Nami holds up the bottle of tequila. "To beautiful scars," she says.

"To beautiful scars," I echo, and we both share a weak grin.

Twenty-four

SORA

> Ask yourself: Who do you want your soul mate to be? Then be that person. Because the soul mate you're looking for all along is you.
>
> —SOLO FEBRUARY CHALLENGE

Nami moving in actually works out nicely. She helps me clean, tackling the mold in my bathroom grout like she's scrubbing off Mitch's face. Turns out, spring cleaning helps both of us. I'm still sad about Jack. More than sad about Jack, but I also realize that I'd been hoping he'd save me when I have to save myself. That's the true spirit of Solo February, I realize, learned a month late and a Jack short. But there it is. Live, learn, repeat. When cracks appear: apply liquid gold and move on.

Of course everything reminds me of Jack. That's the problem. He just won't go lightly into the "loved and lost" file. Every time I see a torte or any damned dessert, I think of Jack. Some guy with *any* facial hair: Jack. Valentine's candy that's 75 percent off: Jack. I stand in the aisle at Margo's once dedicated to Valentine's Day and mourn the loss. Now, it's a single shelf, filled with the *worst* candy: white chocolate filled with *nougat*? Really? Then there's the one or two stuffed animals left, and one is missing an eye. I take it, figuring Larry might enjoy having a stuffed animal handi-capable, just like him. The rest of the aisle is stocked with St. Paddy's Day green. "Kiss me, I'm Chi-rish" and "Beer Makes Everything Better" shirts, and I feel a real pang of loss. I can't believe it. I *miss* the freakin' Valentine's aisle. I remember Jack, bringing me chocolate and wine. Remember spending the best Valentine's Day of my damn life eating heart-shaped pizza and babysitting Jack's firecracker of a niece.

The loss hits me hard. I'm not just heartbroken, I'm grieving what could have been. I realize that neither Marley nor Dan ever touched this level of heartbreak, because deep down, I never really believed Marley or Dan had what it took to go the distance. But Jack . . . Jack was different. No matter how briefly we dated. Or didn't date. Jack held promise.

I wheel my cart toward the bakery, but I know Jack isn't there. He's replaced by a purple-haired woman with shorn hair and lots of tattoos, and I know that she's not going to give me any free tortes. Jack's off to open his new bakery, I assume. We haven't spoken. He last texted about a week ago. *If and when you're ready to talk, I'm here. But I also respect your decision not to. Know that I care about you. So much.*

That was a hard one to ignore. But I just . . . I just can't. Anytime I'm tempted to reach out to Jack, I remember Mal in her gold, clingy dress, hanging on his shoulder, and I feel the betrayal and the hurt all over again. How can I trust him? I wheel my cart to the checkout line. Now, I've actually got greens in my cart. Spinach. Cucumbers. Grapes. Oat cereal to lower cholesterol. And a smaller, mini pack of bacon instead of the family size, because I'm cutting back a bit. I'm taking better care of myself. Being the adult in my own life. It kind of . . . feels good, actually. I mean, don't get me wrong. I'm not loading up with kale and kombucha, but . . . eating right isn't all bad.

I buy my groceries and take my reusable bags, heavy now with mostly healthy food, down the sidewalk, free of ice for the first time in weeks. A couple walks by, holding hands and eating ice cream. I realize that for the first time in months, the weather is actually nice. The sun shines above me, and the temperature hovers near fifty-five. Green sprouts poke out of nearby tree limbs. Spring is about to spring. Not a cloud dots the bright blue sky above my head as another couple pushes a stroller down the sidewalks. The toddler inside meets my gaze and gives me a bright, joyful smile. I smile back at him, and he giggles.

I round the bend, seeing my old meatpacking baron's castle standing tall, the "For Sale" sign a beacon in the small grassy patch of yard. I'm adulting. It feels fine. I trudge up to the small black wrought-iron gate that fences in the bit of green, and I'm swinging the door open when I hear a voice behind me.

"Sora? Sora Reid?" I turn to see a woman in a fur-trimmed coat and black, pointy stiletto boots emerging from the back seat of an expensive-looking Mercedes. Her driver clicks on the parking flashers.

"Mal?" The last person on earth I ever expected to see.

She gives me a disdainful once-over, judging my old parka, my sweatpants, and my old Uggs.

"Good. You do live here. I was about to fire the PI I used to find your address."

"You hired a private investigator to find me?" What the hell is going on?

"Yeah, yeah." She waves a leather-gloved hand dismissively. "It's because I need to talk to you."

"You do?" I put down my bags, suddenly worried. "Is Jack okay?"

She frowns. "Jack's fine. I think. I don't know, really. We haven't spoken lately." They haven't? A tiny spark of hope lights in my chest. And then I snuff it out. "I take it you haven't spoken to him either?"

I shake my head.

"Okay, good. Then I'm glad I'm here." She taps her foot impatiently on the sidewalk as she clutches her oversized Louis Vuitton. "Anyway, Jack never invited me to the Golden Chef Awards. I surprised him there."

I blink, uncertain.

"But what about the bakery?"

"I bought it without him knowing. He'd already signed the lease when I bought the building." She reaches into her designer tote and pulls out a manila file. "But I don't own the building anymore. Here's a copy of the papers showing I just sold it this morning. I just came from the closing."

I take the papers, still stunned. I look at them. Could this all be true?

"What about that picture on your social . . ."

"Me licking his face?" Mal rolls her eyes. "One hookup. After being broken up for a year. And I plied him with drinks. And kind of begged him. And it didn't mean anything, and, anyway, I think it was before you and he . . . whatever. So don't get hung up on that." She flicks her wrist dismissively.

I'm stunned. I glance at the papers and then at Mal. "Why are you telling me all this?"

Mal lets out an exasperated sigh. "I'm trying to do good things or whatever. Well, I'm trying to do the *next* good thing, anyway. God, it's exhausting." She fans her face with a gloved hand. "*Way* harder than I expected. Anyway, you were on my list. Next good thing to do. Whatever. So. Go on. Call Jack." She shoos me off, even though this is my stoop.

I hesitate.

"Go on," she shoos me some more. Then she shakes her head, pursing her lips in disdain. "*Jack didn't do anything wrong.* It was me. All me. It was all my fault." Mal makes a face like she's eating something rotten. "Oh, geez. That left a terrible taste in my mouth." She sticks out her tongue. "Ack. Gross." She makes a gagging face. Then she looks at me again. "What are you waiting for?" She shakes her head in disgust. "Talk to Jack."

I stare at her. "Did Jack send you?"

"Ugh? Seriously with that? No. He didn't." Mal sighs, exasperated, flicking her fingers at me. "Just go talk to him. Don't make this a wasted trip for me."

"Uh, okay."

"Seriously. Go on. Shoo."

"But this is my building." I nod backward to my home.

"Ugh. *Fine.* I'll go then." Mal looks to the sky as if asking the universe for patience. She turns in a huff, heading back to her chauffeured Mercedes. "No good deed goes unpunished," she moans, ducking into the back seat of her shiny black car.

I trudge up my stairs, open my door, head reeling. I turn her words over in my mind. Jack never lied to me. I'd been blaming him all this time for something he *never* did. He never invited Mal to be his date. Never agreed to have her buy the bakery. Never was seeing her behind my back.

Oh, God. If that's true, then I've completely and totally been an ass to Jack. I never let him explain. I just cut him out, like a cancerous tumor. I never let him even try to tell me his side.

Maybe I'm the asshole.

I open my condo door and find Nami vacuuming. She's getting the place ready for its first open house tomorrow. It's pristine, and smells like lemon-tinged cleaner. She shuts off the vacuum.

"Did you get more glass cleaner? We're out."

I sink into my couch. "Nami, I was wrong about Jack."

Nami snorts, loudly. She's still in man-hating mode. "You weren't wrong about Jack."

"I was," I insist. I hand her the manila folder. "Mal gave me these just now. She bought the bakery behind Jack's back. But she's sold it. At least, I think she did. That's what she said."

Nami grabs the papers and gives them a once-over. As a corporate attorney, she's all about the fine print.

"Uh-huh." Nami nods. "Yep, that's what this is. She sold it this morning." Nami scans the document. "And she sold it at a loss, so she really wanted to be done with it." Nami bites her lip. "Also, she originally purchased the bakery by a blind proxy, anyway," Nami says, tapping the papers.

"What does that mean?"

"It means that not even the management company knew the Starr family was buying the property," Nami continues, as she thumbs through the documents. "So, you're right. Jack didn't know she bought the building. He was only the tenant the whole time. And his paperwork never had the Starr name on it, according to this."

"Who's the new owner?"

"Some guy named Pierre Benoit." She hands the papers back to me.

"Wait. That's his old boss." The wheels in my head turn. Jack said Pierre Benoit was helping him. "So he didn't lie to me."

Nami sighs. "Well, I hate to admit that there might be a man who's not terrible out there . . . given I think all of them are terrible right now, but . . ." Nami glances at me. "You might want to go talk to Jack. I think he really, seriously didn't know about Mal's plans. Not the way this is written."

"You really think so?" I feel hope flare in my chest.

"I really think so. Go find him. He might even be at the bakery. The address is in those papers."

A quick ride to Logan Square brings me to a quaint street crowded with local flavor: the musicians, artists, and other twenty- and thirtysomethings that largely make up the neighborhood out enjoying the March sunshine. I see Jack's bakery straightaway, adorable modern signage hanging above the big glass windows: MANN BAKES.

"That's cute," I say. The place couldn't be better positioned: homey, cozy, and a prime location for passersby headed for the L and their blue-line train commute to downtown. Jack and his sexy beardstache will be all the rage. He'll be fighting off suitors every day. I feel my stomach lurch a bit at the prospect.

The bakery isn't quite open to the public yet. The sign is up, but brown paper covers the big paned windows. I jump out of my rideshare and head to the glass door, knocking on it, tentatively at first. Then harder.

Crap. Why didn't I text first? Because I've got too much to say to fit into a text, that's why. And because I'm half afraid he'd ignore me, or tell me it's too late.

Then I hear a voice call from inside, "Just a minute!"

Jack's?

Then, I hear a bolt slide open and the door swings wide, as an adorable little bell attached to the top of the door dings. Jack stands before me, wiping his hands on a tea towel. He's so tall. So broad. I forgot. His beard is perfectly trimmed, his brown eyes surprised to see me.

"Sora?"

"Jack. I owe you an apology." The words tumble out. "Mal came by . . ." A worried look crosses his face. "No, it was good. She told me the truth. She told me everything. About the bakery."

I hold up the manila folder I brought with me. "And I just want to say how sorry I am, how . . ." For the first time, I get a glimpse behind Jack. Of the bakery itself. Jack moves aside, letting me in.

Empty glass cases line one wall, and there are a few small wooden tables and chairs. A huge chalkboard covering one wall lists the specials. Raspberry tortes. Lemon tortes. Cakes. Pies. Cookies. It's an impressive menu. And then . . . a big heart in the middle. Around it is written: "Bacon Is My Valentine." Inside are special bacon desserts: bacon scones, bacon-maple cupcakes, bacon macarons.

"What is all this?" I say, shocked.

"It's for you," he says, coming up close behind me, so close I can feel his body heat. "I thought you'd like it." He takes a deep breath. And I turn to face him. Those damn puppy-dog eyes are so warm. So soft. So gorgeous. How could I ever believe he's anything but amazing?

"You did this for me?" I can't quite believe it.

"Sora, you're beautiful. You're smart. You're amazing. You're funny as hell."

I have no idea how to respond to this many compliments, which contain zero sarcasm. He's the beautiful one, in truth. He's kind and generous. I remember him saving me that day from Marley and Lululemon, and then how patient he was with me all through the Solo February debacle.

"You're kind, and generous, and so, so thoughtful. You're the beautiful one," I say. "I am so, so sorry about thinking the worst of you. For not giving you the benefit of the doubt." Then I'm stuck in his gaze, soaking up the warmth in it, the heat. I don't know if he's moving closer to me, or I'm moving closer to him, but it feels natural, as if it were meant to be.

"No, I should've been more honest with you," Jack says. "I should've told you that I'd hooked up with Mal. That she thought it was an invitation back into my life. If I'd just been honest with you, then there wouldn't have been the misunderstanding at the Golden Chef Awards. But I was afraid of what you might think of me."

"And I should've been honest with you, too. About how big *Solo February* was getting. About how I had my doubts about Mal. And I should've given you a chance to explain."

"Yeah. You should've. But we'd both been burned. I guess we were both a little gun-shy."

"Maybe a little."

Jack grins at me. I grin back at him.

"I should've trusted what we had earlier," I admit.

Jack shakes his head. "No. You took the time you needed to be sure. I can't blame you for that."

"You were always so sure, though!"

"That's because I've been a little in love with you since kindergarten." He laughs and rubs his neck sheepishly.

"Yes, but . . ." I take a step closer to him. "I love you right now, Jack Mann."

He looks shocked. "You do?"

I nod fast because my throat feels thick with tears. Of relief, and love, and *all the feels.* Love pours through my heart, like a tsunami, and tears rush to my eyes. I cannot speak. But I will.

"Yes, I love you."

"Well, it's about time, Sora Reid." He flashes a grin. "I love you, too."

Then I throw my arms around him and kiss him.

Epilogue

SORA

VALENTINE'S DAY, THE FOLLOWING YEAR

The snow just begins to fall on the windshield as Jack kicks the windshield wipers on and keeps driving down Ridge Avenue, headed north from the city. Traffic on the narrow road feels light, but it is a Sunday afternoon, and all the meteorologists forecast snow beginning now and continuing through the night.

"Are you sure you're not telling me where we're going?" I ask him, a smidgen worried. I love surprises, usually—just not on Valentine's Day. Jack grabs my hand and squeezes it. Instantly, I feel my blood pressure go down. Those lovey-dovey endorphins begin flowing again through my veins. That's Jack's effect on me.

"Trust me," he says, and I find that I do.

The last year has been amazing. More than amazing. Better than I'd ever imagined life could be. I kicked the *Slick* gig, and started writing for a few nonprofit websites. Now I spend my time encouraging women to run for political office or to dream big, and, well, now I can say, without any irony at all, that I am doing my part for feminism.

"Not even a little bit of a hint?" We've been driving north . . . awhile. Then I start recognizing the quaint suburb just north of Chicago. The leafy-lined streets with vintage condos and old farmhouses, right near a lively downtown of boutiques and restaurants. "Wait. We're in Evanston. What are we doing here?"

Before I can question further, Jack pulls up to *our* neighborhood grade school, Dewey Elementary.

He parks on the street in front of the familiar blue and white sign. It's changed a bit since the nineties. Are those new swings? Still, I'd recognize that one-story, redbrick building anywhere. He parks the car against the curb by the playground and grins at me.

"Jack Mann. What are we *doing* here?"

It's a Sunday, so there's no school, and we've had little snow so far this winter, so very small clumps of white stick on the ground. He gets out of the car, and heads around to my side, opening my door and offering his hand.

"My lady," he says, and tilts his head downward. I laugh a little and take his hand, and he helps me out of the car. I zip up my parka and shiver a bit in the cold. Snowflakes swirl in the air, and my breath comes out in white clouds. Jack reaches behind my seat and produces a brown paper grocery sack.

"What's that?" I ask.

"You'll see," he tells me, and his brown eyes sparkle with mischief.

I tug on my gloves. He offers one of his hands and I take it.

"Should we race to the swings?" I ask.

"I'll let you win, like always." He grins.

"Excuse me, you'll *let* me? I'm just fast." Then again, I do have an old memory that floats to the surface. The little boy with the dark hair, little bit heavy, who might have pulled up at the last minute, shyly smiling at me from behind the anchor pole as I took the last free seat.

Now, Jack leads me to the swings. He dusts off one, sweeping the thin layer of snow that's already beginning to form on the black rubber seat, and then cleans one off for himself. We sit together, on this playground I knew so well from kindergarten all the way to fifth grade. I kick out and swing just a little bit. He watches me, a smile growing on his face.

Jack holds the mystery bag with the paper handles with one hand, and the chain of the swing with the other. "So, I brought you here, because I know *this* school. This is where Valentine's Day all went wrong for you. So . . ." I dig my toes into the snow-covered woodchips, slowing my swing. He reaches into his big brown bag with the paper handles and pulls out a shoebox covered in red construction paper and painted with all manner of pink glitter, all shades: from pearl pink to hot fuchsia. It's covered in puffy hearts, and stickers of Cupid, and has big blocky sticker letters that read "Happy Valentine's Day."

"Allie helped me with it," Jack admits.

"I can tell," I say, and laugh, thinking about Allie, and her new pink and silver light-up sneakers and the fact that *she's* a kindergartner now.

I'm still not sure what all this means, but then Jack puts the box on my lap, and I open the lid. Inside, there are stacks of tiny little envelopes. And boxes of message hearts and red heart-shaped lollipops and Valentine's chocolate.

"What the . . ." And then, glancing at the names written on the tiny little envelopes, it hits me: kindergarten. Valentine's Day.

"Someone—*not* me—stole all your valentines, and now, I'm returning them."

I paw through the envelopes, and sure enough, everyone's represented: Casey, my best friend at the time, Maya, Miya, and Myra (the names that sometimes drove the teacher crazy).

I tear open the first one. It's Tiny Toon Adventures. Then the next . . . Rugrats. And the Magic School Bus . . . and Powerpuff Girls?

"How did you . . . ?"

"Found them on eBay," he says, and grins. "Vintage valentines."

"I can't believe you did this." I rip into all of them, laughing at each new familiar cartoon face.

"Now they're not actually *signed* by our classmates, since . . . it's nearly impossible to track them all down."

"You tried?"

"I might have. The only one I had any success with was Casey."

"My old best friend!" I cry. I grab her envelope. It says, "Piggy Jack is damn fine now. When did this happen?" I have to laugh at that. Then I flip over the card and see she's written a postscript. "Also: This one is a keeper. Seriously. You don't need a cootie catcher to tell you that."

She's right.

I open one more. From Stella.

"She wasn't in our class!"

"Yes, but when I told her what I was doing, she insisted."

I read her card. "This is just another part of self-care. Choosing a partner right for you. Now, go on and be happy. You deserve this."

I glance up at Jack. I do, I think. I do deserve this.

Jack reaches back into the grocery bag. "I have our yearbook, too." He pulls the small, paperback photo book out of the grocery bag. I grab it from his lap. I flip to my page. I'm smiling too big, my eyes like tiny, thin slits. In grade school, I never quite figured out how to smile without looking like the sunlight wasn't blinding me.

"I look like such a dork! I've got *pigtails*."

"You're adorable," he says, and then I flip to his page. He's cute, even though a little chubby. He doesn't deserve the nickname "Piggy Jack." Not at all. He looks a little pensive as he stares at the camera.

"I hated having my picture taken," he explains. "I hated everything about grade school." He looks at me. "Except you."

My heart is going to burst. I lean across the swing set and kiss him. I want to kiss all that hurt away, now and forever. "I love you," I say.

"Oh . . . you're all right," Jack teases.

I punch his arm.

"Ow! I'm kidding. I love you, too." I turn my attention back to the box. I dig into my box and open the last valentine, but soon realize there's one missing.

"Jack?" I dig around in the candy hearts, chocolate kisses, and the lollipops, worried that I'd missed it. "Where's the one from you?"

That's when Jack reaches into his jacket pocket and pulls out a small white envelope. He hands it to me, a smile on his face.

"Go on, then. Open it."

I peel back the small flap and pull out a beautiful, glittery, homemade valentine, with Jack's mangled bee, only it's decked out in glitter. I burst out laughing.

"No!"

"Yes." Jack nods.

Then I open the glitter bee card.

Inside, it says, "I love you so much. Please, *bee* my . . . wife?" But inside the question mark, there's a single solitaire diamond ring taped there.

My heart stops.

For a full second. I can't breathe. Can't do anything but stare.

A ring . . . ?

But Jack plucks the ring off the valentine and kneels before me.

"Sora Reid, you've changed my life in ways I never imagined possible. This last year has shown me how amazing it is to share my life with someone who really gets me, who's a wonderful partner in all ways, and my best friend."

Tears spring to my eyes. Also, I might faint. Seriously, I might. Jack is proposing.

Jack.

Is.

Proposing.

Holy.

Mother.

Of.

Everything.

"In kindergarten, you had a bad Valentine's Day, and you've had a few more since. We're here now because I think you need a do-over," he says. I notice he, too, is starting to get emotional, his puppy-dog eyes wet with emotion. "In fact, Sora Reid, if you'll let me, I'd like to make this Valentine's Day, and every other Valentine's Day in your life, the very best it can be. Will you be mine? Today and every day?"

He offers up the impressive diamond, and it sparkles like fire beneath the snowflakes falling gently around us. I suck in a breath, my brain buzzing with a million thoughts: Is this what I want? I thought I'd never get married again. Thought I'd never even consider going through all this. Not after Marley. Not after having my heart broken so often.

Do I have the courage to take this ring? To risk heartache one more time?

I look into Jack's eyes, and I see sincerity. I see honesty. I see trust. He's putting himself out there. He's risking it all. To gain it all. He's brave. I can be brave, too.

And I'm filled with a serenity, a certainty, I've never felt before.

Jack is my person. And I am his.

And who knows what life has in store for us, but whatever it is, we should face it together.

"Yes!" I cry, when I can finally find my voice. "Yes! Oh, yes, yes, yes!"

I tug off my glove, and he slips the ring on my finger, and it fits. Perfectly. And then I pull him to me, and kiss his beautiful lips, sealing that promise. I'll be his. And he'll be mine. I break this kiss, staring into his dark brown eyes.

"Does this mean I have to give up bacon as my valentine?" I tease.

"Hell no," he says, a chuckle low in his throat. "After all, you're marrying *Piggy* Jack."

I laugh. There's absolutely nothing "piggy" about the kindest, most loving, most amazing man I've ever met. "I think you're more like Hot As Hell Ham-hock Jack."

"I think that has a nicer ring to it," he agrees.

And this, I have to say, is the best damn Valentine's Day I've ever had.

Take that, commercial love machine.

Acknowledgments

Thank you to Deidre Knight, longtime friend, mentor, and the best agent, and the best person, you could meet in this business, and much gratitude to everyone at the Knight Agency. Thank you, thank you to my razor-sharp, insightful, brilliant editor, Alexandra Sehulster, and everyone at St. Martin's Press. You deserve all the expensive chocolates. ALL the chocolates!

To my husband, PJ, the real-life Jack in all ways, who single-handedly convinced this skeptic to give Valentine's Day another try (and I'm so very glad he did). Thank you for always believing in me, for brainstorming scenes with me, and for being the best partner anyone could ever ask for. No hero I write will ever come close to you.

Thank you to all my amazing kids, both biological and by marriage (Hana, Miya, Pete, Sarina, and Sophia), for being their incredible selves and for giving me the most privileged seat in the house in the front row of their lives. Keep on writing your own stories!

Thanks to the entire Tanamachi clan, and especially Mom, Dad, Matt, Jill, and Patty, who gave me the courage to be the nail. To all my truly wonderful and supportive friends, with special shout-outs to Craig and Shannon Gatta, Hillary Leisten, Gretchen Hartke, Elizabeth Kinsella, and Carroll Jordan for helping me weather the very worst Valentine's Days. Thanks also to the ever on-call North Shore Support Group: Julie Friend, Dani Houchin, Annie Laures, and Beth Zadik. A very special thank-you to Christina Swartz for being such a thoughtful sounding board for this book. And heartfelt thanks to Victoria Baum, relationship guru, whose wonderful wisdom you'll find in these pages.

And last but not least, thank you, readers! Without you, I'm just muttering stories to myself. Thank you, thank you, thank you!

About the Author

Meagan Shuptar

CARA TANAMACHI lives near Chicago with her husband and five children (two by biology and three by marriage), and their eighty-five-pound Goldendoodle, Theodore. Raised near Dallas, Texas, by her Japanese American dad and her English-Scottish American mom, she was the oldest of two children (the debate still rages whether she or her brother is currently the family favorite). The University of Pennsylvania (Go Quakers!) grad worked as a newspaper reporter and then published many novels under the name Cara Lockwood. A former single mom, she spent eight years dating (hilariously and awkwardly) before finding the love of her life on Bumble (yes, Bumble!). She believes we all could use a little more happily ever after.